Explore the Erotic Side

During the sex act, your atten ... ..ser beam" of concentration for a moment. All great systems of magic teach the power of concentrated thought—sex magic is no exception. Sex magic's "secret" is that it is a tremendously potent way to direct consciously controlled sexual energy to accomplish material and personal goals.

Secrets of Western Sex Magic describes the erotic secrets of sex magic—one of the oldest magical disciplines—in a frank, explicit, and nonjudgmental style. Unlike other published sex magic manuals that have a traditionally male orientation, this book equally addresses your unique magical needs and wants whether you are a male or female magician.

Frater U∴D∴ openly explores all aspects of sexual practice and preference—from the fundamentals of sex magic training to auto-erotic, heteroerotic, homoerotic, group, and so-called "deviant" practices—with a system of specific techniques to build your magis and broaden your magical and sexual horizons. You need not belong to any lodge or occult group to apply these esoteric secrets—you reap astounding benefits no matter what your level of magical experience.

About the Author

Born in Heliopolis, Egypt, Frater U∴D∴ has been working within the magical tradition for decades. He lived in Africa and Asia and trained with Yoga and Tantra masters, as well as studying languages and literature at the univerisities of Bonn and Lisbon. He is recognized as the founder of Pragmatic Magic, and has written articles for many magazines, including *Unicorn, Thelema: Magazine for Magic and Tantra, Anubis* (Germany), *The Lamp of Thoth,* and *Chaos International* (Great Britain). His published works include *Practical Sigil Magic.* Among his translations are the books of Peter Carroll and Ramsey Dukes and Aleistar Crowley's *Book of Lies.* At present, he lives in Belgium, working as a freelance writer, workshop speaker, and software developer.

To Write to the Author

If you wish to contact the author or would like more information about this book, please write to the author in care of Llewellyn Worldwide and we will forward your request. Both the author and publisher appreciate hearing from you and learning of your enjoyment of this book and how it has helped you. Llewellyn Worldwide cannot guarantee that every letter written to the author can be answered, but all will be forwarded. Please write to:

Frater U∴D∴
℅ Llewellyn Worldwide
P.O. Box 64383, 1-56718-706-4
St. Paul, MN 55164-0383, U.S.A.

Please enclose a self-addressed stamped envelope for reply,
or $1.00 to cover costs. If outside U.S.A., enclose
international postal reply coupon.

Many of Llewellyn's authors have websites with additional information and resources. For more information, please visit our website at http://www.llewellyn.com

Magical Energy and Gnostic Trance

Secrets of WESTERN SEX MAGIC

FRATER U∴D∴

2001
Llewellyn Publications
St. Paul, Minnesota 55164-0383, U.S.A.

Third Edition
First Printing, 2001
(Previously titled *Secrets of Sex Magic*)

Cover art "Aurora and Kephal" c. 1811 by P. Garain © Pushkin Museum of Fine Arts, Moscow / Superstock

Cover design by Lisa Novak

Library of Congress Cataloging-in-Publication Data
(Pending)
1-57618-706-4

Llewellyn Publications
A Division of Llewellyn Worldwide, Ltd.
P.O. Box 64383, Dept. 1-56718-706-4
St. Paul, MN 55164-0383, U.S.A.
www.llewellyn.com

Printed in the United States of America

Other Books by Frater U∴D∴

Kursus der praktischen Magie
(A Course of Practical Magic)

Practical Sigil Magic

acknowledgements

The author wishes to express his thanks to all people involved in writing, reading and publishing this book, especially to Ramsey Dukes for co-reading it. Thanks, too, to the people at Llewellyn Publications, who made this edition possible.

dedication

This book is dedicated to all those hardliners on the magical path with whom I have spent so many years of toil and fun developing a modern and more efficient approach to the Black Arts, tasting the heavens and the hells of magical power—and never giving up, the whole bunch of us!

table of contents

introduction

Until today no other discipline of secret lore has remained shrouded in so much mystery as sex magic; none makes feelings run so high at both extremes of the esoteric spectrum; none is more powerful—and none so misunderstood! Nevertheless, general interest in this important branch of magic is still increasing. Not least has been the popularization of the Hindu Tantra and the so-called "Inner Alchemy" of Taoism in recent years, and hardly any bookfair passes without titles appearing on this topic. It is therefore amazing that sound, *practical* introductions to sex magic are still so scarce.

Before getting down to the actual practice, we will first have to explain some basics, sort out some possible misunderstandings and make clear which path we will be following in this book.

Above all, this is a *practical* book. It does not withhold or conceal, nor does it exaggerate or glamorize. Previous authors have too often tempted their readers with mouth-watering hints and promises, only to leave them frustrated for lack of any definite techniques. This probably reflects their ignorance: these writers try to tackle a subject about which they know little only because it sells well. There is also a vein of arrogance which looks down on the readers and believes that they are not yet "mature" enough for "real" knowledge. Such an attitude is all too common in the occult field. True, one of the basic rules of all secret lore is: "To Know, To Will, To Dare and To Be Silent," but in our opinion the "To Be Silent" aspect of this principle is being overstressed at the expense of other parts. Secrecy has its place during learning and practicing, but not among authors who claim a desire to convey knowledge out of an inner commitment.

This leads us to another aspect of the principle: "To Dare." Nobody can do the practice for you, and there is nothing to be gained from "armchair sex magic." As a pure fantasy it may indeed become dangerous: releasing psychic drives which afterwards have to be once more suppressed by the timid "everyday Ego," with catastrophic consequences. More about this later.

Let us not forget that everybody has to make their own choice about the "To Will" and the "To Dare" aspects and will be ultimately responsible for the consequences. "Do what thou wilt shall be the whole of the Law" was Aleister Crowley's motto, and we do not intend to lay down the Law by telling you precisely what you have and have not to do.

There is another way in which this book differs from others on the same subject. Whereas sex magic used to be considered as a male prerogative with women playing merely a supporting role, we now regard men and women as holding equal rights and having the same value. Admittedly, male and female energies are often entirely different and it would be silly to deny this; but experience shows that female magicians can be particularly successful in using and developing sex magic. Consequently, this book is aimed at both male and female readers.

There is also the question of taboo, which has in past centuries suppressed sexuality in general, and sex magic in particular. Until recently it was impossible to discuss subjects such as homosexuality in public. In those days a book like this would have been banned outright. Even relatively "liberal" works with a sex magical content do not usually step beyond the bounds of heterosexuality. There may be a passing reference to autoeroticism, which is particularly important for sex magic, but such other practices as homosexuality or fetishism are never mentioned, let alone any further "deviations" like intercourse with succubi and incubi. There is little point in getting sidetracked into further examination as to which inhibitions, fears or authoritarian philosophies we owe these failures. Sufficeth to say that the variety of human sexuality is as great and splendid as human thinking and feeling itself. The true sex magician will not allow outmoded taboos and bans to restrict his practical work. Instead, sex magic is seen as a welcomed discipline and an optimum route to the attainment of magical aims. Without making needless distinctions, traditional attachments and moral codes are set aside in favor of "Do what thou wilt." For the sex mystic, sexuality is a holy expression of one's highest destiny anyway.

Not least, sex magic is about breaking limits, a recurring theme in this book. Sex magic has nothing to do with ignorant and fearful sexuality. The sex magician strives to expand the limits of expression further and further, to reach that liberty known as "optimum contingency of choice and decision." We will therefore talk freely about practices and forms of sex magic which cannot be found anywhere else in the literature. It is up to the individual reader to decide how much of these ideas to utilize and translate into action.

There is one more misunderstanding that we must deal with, namely the relationship between Tantra and sex magic. It has already been mentioned that Hindu Tantra and the Inner Alchemy of Taoism has attracted more and more attention recently. After the much-praised "sexual revolution" of the '60s had fizzled out, the literature about Tantra and Tao has done precious pioneering work by sharpening and developing our consciousness of the transcendent possibilities of sexuality, not only among occultists but also within a wider context. In the currently developing conception of the world, sexuality is given a more constructive status than it had in the post-pagan, life-hostile culture of the Occident, dominated as it was by Christianity and church dogma. Looking for a new "art of love" (the ancients called it *ars amatoria)* we search beyond the borders of our civilization which is so entangled in materialism and science, and we are once more discovering the wisdom of Eastern cultures. They have been developing the art of loving for thousands of years: we find such splendid examples as the *Kama Sutra* in India or the *Perfumed Garden of the Sheikh Nefzaui* in Islamic culture, to name but two. It would be silly to claim that Western sex magic owes nothing to these cultures. Quite the opposite: like most Occidental secret disciplines, sex magic has gained much from its encounter with those teachings, and every sex magician is seriously advised to study them in depth.

Nevertheless, it would be wrong to confuse sex magic with Tantra, for they follow different aims. Tantra is always oriented sacrally, towards "worship" and sex mysticism, and aims to combine the polar powers of the Male and the Female (Shiva and Shakti or, in the Inner Alchemy of China, Yang and Yin) in order to transcend them. Sex magic however, is oriented more towards the earth element. For the sex magician the sexual power is first of all a neutral energy, to be directed magically for whatever purpose. Experience shows that it is very suitable for "success magic": for example charging talismans, amulets and sigils; for binding, harm and defence sorcery; for the achievement of professional, material and psychological advantages, etc. Such aims are not totally unknown to the Tantrist or Ching Chi master, but they can hardly be found in the literature because they are meant to be the "highest secret" of those innermost circles and fraternities which gather around a few "illuminated" masters of the art.

Maybe it is in precisely this point that Western materialism and the scientific outlook have an advantage. Here, at least recently, we have been prepared to "call a spade a spade" and have become increasingly open to the practical, material basics of the high art of sex magic. Let us never forget that the cultures of the East, despite popular misconceptions, far surpass our culture in prudishness and taboo thinking—with just a few exceptions. Tantra and Inner Alchemy were reserved for a chosen few, mostly rulers and their courtiers, and even nowadays they are not really open knowledge. It has always been the establishment's aim, and not only in Christian cultures, to keep the "stupid" masses stupid when it comes to the knowledge of sex magic. To this extent, we think that western sex magic is actually more honest about its materialist aims.

The borders between sex magic and sex mysticism are, however, far from clear. One should not therefore fall to the opposite extreme and completely deny the mystical, transcendental aspects. This is precisely what is so great about sex magic: namely that it represents a system which knows how to balance its material and transcendental aspects. It is a common and erroneous dualism to consider spirit and matter as opposite, antagonistic poles. Mysticism does not strive one-sidedly to heighten spirit at the expense of matter. This would be hatred of the body, and the Inquisition has shown us all too well where that leads, as have other fanatical political ideologies and religions which cold-bloodedly slaughter humanity on the altar of some "higher" ideal. On the contrary, mysticism, and sex mysticism in particular, strives to transcend the opposites and seeks to lead us into the realms of the transcendental, of the divine beyond Good and Evil. With this in mind, a special chapter is included on the "Mystical Hierogamy"; in it, some practical tips on sex mysticism will be given. If sex mysticism seems otherwise in this book to have been pushed into second place in favor of more materialistic and "earthy" considerations, it was mainly because the subject evades simple analysis. What could really be said about the Unnameable? "The Tao which can be described is not the true Tao." Thus Lao Tse begins his *Tao Teh King*, and in these few words gives the sum total of what can be said about mystical experience.

The exercises in this book are mostly structured hierarchically, so they build up in sequence. This is done partly to save space: it would have been easy to double the book's length by repeating instructions with small changes in each context, as is often done in Eastern Tantra literature. It will, of course, be made obvious when a section refers to former exercises. However, we do not insist that all practices must be performed in the exact order given: the reader is free to arrange a personal program of exercises. Nevertheless, it is most important to read the book as a whole to get a thorough overview before this is done. In general we would recommend following the preparatory exercises with autoerotic practice because it helps to become familiar with the basics of sex magic on one's own body without external pressure from partners. How far to take it, how much to "dare," is left to one's own discretion. As said before, nobody can dictate to you!

We will end this introduction with a few words about the charge "To Be Silent." Despite today's apparent sexual liberation, it is far from advisable to air your sex magic experiences in public. There are several reasons for this, and the two most important will now be considered.

First, a *practical* reason. Most people fear sexuality, whether they admit it or not, and they fear magic. In every modern man, however liberal, lurks the primal fear of "sensual unconsciousness" which sexuality offers us. Although magic is widely scoffed at in public, magicians, witches and sorcerers are enjoying a boom — as is the fear of them! If you tell your friends about your sex magic, they may suddenly behave strange and distant. You might just as well publicly declare an interest in sadism or sodomy. You will be asked — in a manner half shocked and half fascinated — for details about "Black Magic"; and in no time you will find yourself labelled a "Satanist" or "Devil Worshipper," and the spectrum of defamation may even extend to "pervert," "sex fiend" and "child abuser." Anyone who thinks this is an enlightened world shaped by cosmopolitan, worldly tolerance should take a look at the reports in the gutter press. Turn a deaf ear to this advice and you will find out the hard way!

Now, one may righteously object that a magician striving for personal liberty should be above caring what the neighbors think. But even the most experienced magician needs certain working conditions, especially for sex magic, and these include quietness and lack of distraction. Medieval books of spells often state that the magician should be in harmony with his religion: Aleister Crowley pointed out that this means avoiding unnecessary estrangement from one's surroundings. This is so because such alienation demands a lot of psychic strength as well as magical energy. The magician is a reality-dancer and an artist, able to jump from one reality to the other, but the physical body does need to be protected during astral travels. Accordingly, the sex magician needs a certain outer peace to avoid constant conflict between the personal reality and that of the environment demanding endless awkward attempts to defend and justify oneself.

This leads us to the second, magical, reason for the rule of discretion. By being silent, the magician learns how to strengthen the personal magical reality and let it germinate and flourish undisturbed like a seed. This grows into a major source of magical power and security. Those who have learned to be silent, will no longer worry about the doubts and scepticisms of their environment, even if directly confronted by them. They'll pass like "water off a duck's back."

Of course, these reservations do not negate the value of serious exchange of ideas among like-minded people. As with all things, there is a time and a place for silence.

—Frater U∴D∴

A SHORT OUTLINE OF THE HISTORY OF SEX MAGIC AND SEX MYSTICISM

It has become trendy to begin any exposition on secret lore with the words: "The history of theory X is as old as mankind itself." Not that such statements are always wrong, but there is little value in suggesting the long continuity of any tradition if it cannot be proved.

The history of sex magic is no exception. It is certain that sex magical cults and practices existed in ancient times, but little definite is known about them. Most probably these cults were similar to those still found today in the shamanic societies of the Amazon basin, Papua New Guinea and some parts of the Arctic and Inner Asia. Prehistoric shamanic cults used strong sexual symbolism: *vide* the Stone Age female figurines with their supple breasts and hips, or their sacral portrayals of vagina and penis. In ancient Sumeria, sex cults existed around the moon goddess Ishtar or Astarte, and the Chaldeans had a highly developed form of temple prostitution which may have had purely sacral and magical characteristics, at least at the outset. In Egypt there were, for example, the cults of Isis and the worship of the phallus, while India and Tibet developed Tantrism and Kundalini Yoga. In ancient China the Inner Alchemy of Taoism (also called "Taoist Tantra") was cultivated mainly in court circles. In Plato's Greece Eros was sacred, chiefly in its masculine aspect, but the Demeter mysteries balanced this with their emphasis on the feminine. In some branches of the esoteric Kabbalah,

Judaism developed its own sex magical and mystical principles, and there were also sects like the Sabbatarians, which practiced those teachings.

The late-Hellenistic Gnostics, who were concerned mainly with Judaism and Christianity, included scattered sects and sex cults like the Ophites, the Simonites and the "Barbelo"- or "Spermal Gnostics." These also employed sex magic as we understand it today.

World religions like Christianity and Islam also have their sex mystical and magical aspects: consider the medieval *Minne* cult of courtly love or certain esoteric sects within Sufism. For the most part independent of these world religions, but sometimes in collaboration with them, followers of pagan religions performed fertility rites and conjurations at least until the late Middle Ages. This latter-day "neo-shamanism" was revived after the Second World War by the Wicca cult which, at least in its highest form of ritual working (the so-called "Great Rite"), rests upon sex magic and sex mysticism.

The infamous order of the Knights Templar was accused by its destroyers of sex magical practices in the course of its persecution, but it was not alone in this: other sects within medieval Christianity like the "Brothers of the Free Spirit," the Beghards and Ortlibians, were well acquainted with these practices. In general, however, sex magic and sex mysticism in Christianity were sublimated and neutralized: *vide* the already mentioned High *Minne,* the general mysticism, later pietism and alchemy. There are interesting parallels to this development in India, Tibet and China and also in Hassidic Judaism.

It is hardly surprising that the primal power of sexuality has attracted mankind's interest throughout the ages. It has been openly or secretly feared and adored, worshipped and condemned, tended and suppressed. Our current attitudes towards it are basically no different from those of our prehistoric ancestors. Despite of all the relevant research, sexuality remains a mystery to us, a book with seven seals, both fascinating and frightening.

Despite all these historical precedents, it would nevertheless be wrong to speak of a continuous centuries-old tradition of sex magic. Although tempting to believe, it cannot be proved. We must rather recognize the way in which great reservoirs of human knowledge are forever falling into oblivion only to be rediscovered anew later. There is a consistent tradition which can be proved, but it goes back no further than the end of the 19th century. It is this proven tradition that we want to concentrate on here because it is the undeniable forerunner of today's sex magic.

Apart from isolated groups around figures such as Edward Sellon in England and Paschal Beverley Randolph in America and France, relatively unknown even in their own days, the beginning of modern sex magic may be clearly dated from the foundation of the O.T.O. by Karl Kellner at the turn of the century. There were indeed some forerunners leading up to this event. Already by 1870 Hargrave Jennings had tried to propose a sex magical-mystical interpretation of Rosicrucian and Masonic symbolism in *The Rosicrucians, Their Rites and Mysteries.* The Ordo Templi Orientis (O.T.O.) documents a clear, unequivocal endorsement of sex magic and its practice in the higher grades (from VIII° to X°). It derived originally from Czech and Austrian occultists involved in the sex magical practices of the black American magician, Paschal Beverley Randolph. Randolph shot himself in Chicago in 1875, the year that Madam Blavatsky founded the Theosophical Society, Eliphas Levi died and Aleister Crowley and Theodor Reuss were born. Randolph's own order, the Brotherhood of Luxor, gained a certain following and notoriety, and his work was continued by Marie de Naglowska, who translated his book *Magia Sexualis* into French. A group working on theses lines is purported to have still been active in the Paris of the '30s. It is interesting to note that contrary to common assumptions the O.T.O. was basically not so much a "German" (or, rather, Austrian) order as regards its original influences, but instead drew rather heavily on American sources! This was pointed out to me by Josef Dvorak of Vienna, who is currently working on a biography of Kellner and who has full access to Kellner's papers and library.

Another less well known fact is that Rudolf Steiner, the founder of Anthroposophy, was leader of the German branch of the O.T.O. for nine years before the First World War (although he is said to have quickly dissociated himself from its sex magical practices). While Anthroposophists prefer to hush this up, I do know from a reliable source that, after his death, Steiner was laid on the bier in the full regalia of a Rex Summus X° O.T.O. There are even photographs to prove this. I consider this to be an important point because it does something to bolster the all-too-often-underestimated significance of the O.T.O. Today's sex magic owes much to this order, not least because of its later leader, Aleister Crowley (1875-1947). In fact it was Crowley, the most misunderstood magician of all times, and certainly the one with the worst reputation, who has made the most significant contribution to modern sex magic—and not alone through his introduction of an additional grade (the XI°) based upon homoerotic practices. Whatever else one may think about the Master Therion, his tremendous contribution to modern, pragmatic sex magic is undisputed.

It is amazing that Crowley never in his lifetime exposed the innermost secrets of his order to the public, however much he thirsted after glory and scandal. It was only through the posthumous publication of his diaries and the subsequent decipherment of his published works that we have seen such development taken up long after his death by writers such as Kenneth Grant, Francis King, Louis Culling, Israel Regardie, Michael Bertiaux and Peter J. Carroll. *The Forbidden Book of Knowledge,* by the American magician Charles Fairfax Thompson, a book known only to a few cognoscenti, borrows heavily from this tradition, as do so many recent writers, especially in the Anglo-American realm. Most of these, however, simply copy the old master Crowley without making any attempt to develop his ideas any further.

Lesser known in this connection is the Englishman Austin Osman Spare (1886-1956). Spare did indeed enrich sex magic, especially with his sigil magic and his concept of "atavistic resurgence," which we will deal with later in more depth. Spare was also a member of Crowley's order of the A∴ A∴ for a short while. This order merged with the O.T.O. under the aegis of the Master Therion. But Spare soon went his own way. His influence can mainly be seen in the modern Chaos Magic of Peter J. Carroll and Ray Sherwin, who revived his Zos Kia Cultus within their own order, the I.O.T. (Illuminates of Thanateros). Today this order is better known as The Magical Pact of the Illuminates of Thanateros, and Spare's system has been rejuvenated with recent concepts of quantum physics, existentialism and structuralism.

Another influence on sex magic not to be forgotten is that of the Fraternitas Saturni, which split away from the German Pansophic Movement under Gregor A. Gregorius (Eugen Grosche) and which, in its 18th grade (the "Gradus Pentalphae"), employed sex magic— at least in theory. This order will also be occasionally mentioned in the pages to come. Gregorius maintained a friendly relationship with Aleister Crowley until Crowley's death, and it may be true that the Fraternitas Saturni continued to foster the sex magical knowledge of the O.T.O. after the latter had divided into splinter groups upon Crowley's death. This same fate eventually befell the Fraternitas Saturni itself until its restabilization and consolidation in the early '80s. Nevertheless, the "special papers" of this order as well as some editions of its internal organ, *Saturn-Gnosis,* give many an interesting insight into the earlier practices of sex magic.

This brief outline of the history of sex magic should suffice for our purpose, and we need not go into the numerous minor orders which also employed sex magic—from the Adonists' Bond of Ra-Omir-Quintscher to the lesser known, usually quite tiny groups of magicians of pseudo-masonic and/or Rosicrucian extraction. This overview has been written merely to provide some background material. There is, however, a comprehensive bibliography provided for those readers who wish to follow this up. The works of Evola, Hemberger and Frick are the main sources of information about the historical connections of organized sex magic before the Second World War.

While we are aware of our debt to these predecessors and wish to give them every credit, let us reiterate once more the point that there is no such thing as a consistent, continuous history of sex magic. In fact the story of sex magic appears to be as much of a muddle as the story of sexuality itself!

Detailed examination of its history is of use to historians and theorists, but to the practitioner it has little value beyond what is outlined in the next paragraph. Reading the early pioneers of this subject often proves a bitter disappointment. These writers rarely call a spade a spade, and the reader usually has to fight through a tangled web of allusions, obfuscations and moral admonitions. In this book we intend to remedy the situation.

The historical context does help us to recognize our own stage of development better. The sex magician too is a child of the times, depending on his or her culture as well as profiting from it, and it would be dishonest to forget this. It would moreover be unwise because through this very realization we may gain magical power: one who understands the strengths and weaknesses of the epoch and its historical context may use this knowledge more effectively than the historically rootless and unaware, who are forced to expend so much energy constantly redefining their point of view. They forever repeat their old mistakes. A knowledge of one's roots is particularly necessary when dealing with atavistic sex magic, so we would for that reason advise every prospective sex magician to have some awareness of the history of sex-magical thoughts and culture. Yesterday determines today, and only those who know yesterday and today may hope to master, form and mold tomorrow. Although mysticism knows only the Eternal Now, it is itself far from rootless nor does it deny the future, which is the now of tomorrow, both fulfilment and aim. Only when this attitude is internalized may one stretch the Now so that it includes and embraces yesterday and tomorrow, transcending the need for distinction. Orgasm is timeless, but it still has its history and its effects—it is both temporal and eternal.

Do not imagine that one should only practice sex magic after long and intense study of its history. In the long run it is personal practice that counts, but this must be seen in the context of the past as well as the future. If you think there is nothing to be learned from history, then do without it: but you will probably miss many a valuable clue and find yourself forever "re-inventing the wheel." Nor is it sensible to go to the opposite extreme and stare at history in awe without forming any links to today's practice. Sex magic takes place today in the here and now, in the physical as well as in psychic practice. Between these extreme attitudes there is the golden middle way of learning and planning, of receiving and creating. This is the path we want to follow here.

The Premises of Sex Magic

Old sex-magical writings frequently tended to present sex magic as a discipline reserved for the "highest initiates" only, a lore of unspeakable danger to body and soul. These writings, therefore, present little actual practice; warnings and moral strictures predominate instead. The raised forefinger is the most prominent characteristic of the earlier magical literature in general and the sex magical in particular. When we look at sexological literature up to the late 1960s, we find that the same applies: sexuality was largely hushed up, minimized or elevated with idealistic moral standards and made "untouchable." Thus we can see that the disciplines of sex magicians were historically embedded in the societal structure of the day. Sexuality was suppressed by church, state and society, and the same applied to sex magic. This secretiveness is therefore partly understandable; after all, even in the '50s, such authors still risked being denounced as "corrupters of youth and morals," so one cannot blame them for a certain caution.

Another characteristic of these works about sex magic is their exclusively male orientation; even Crowley was no exception. This may be explained historically. Female sexuality in Occidental culture was rediscovered only very recently after thousands of years of suppression, so little wonder that sex magical scripts before our time show women as, at most, mere assistants and magical lust objects. At the end of the '50s, writers of the older generation still formulated such advice as, "the magician should get hold of a female medium and enthrall her"—which of course meant sexual dependence and exploitation, a precise reflection of contemporary society. We do not want to indulge in self-adulation nor do we want to state that everything is perfect nowadays, because no epoch recognizes its own mistakes as clearly as it recognizes the faults of its predecessors. Let us simply acknowledge that the general attitude toward human sexuality, toward the part of women and toward the relationship between the sexes has greatly changed. Today we can talk more openly and bluntly about many things (although not about everything!) than we could do 20 years ago. Consider male or female homosexuality, so-called "pornography," etc.

Furthermore, the knowledge of secret lore and the "black arts" has become more accessible. Never before has it been possible for the amateur to find out so much about this subject through books, courses and seminars. Even shortly after the First and Second World Wars when occultism was also very popular, those interested could not get hold of as much material, especially practical material, as they can today. The time is therefore right for a work like this. Even more so because many former prejudices—"all magic is the devil's work," "sexuality is evil," etc.—appear to have lost at least some of their force. The current harangues of some extreme groups of Christian fundamentalists, however, have led to excesses of physical assault and cold-blooded gasoline-bomb assassinations and murders of occultists in England and the United States and would seem to denote yet another unwholesome change of trend.

Of all secret lore, sex magic has been reputed through the centuries to be the most dangerous. Today we know that this attitude was largely a reflection of the hostility towards the flesh held by omnipotent Christianity, but this is not the whole answer. It cannot be denied that sex magic has its dangerous aspects, but they are not at all the perils you would expect. To illustrate this we give an analogy which we will reconsider from time to time: sex magic, like magic in general, is no more nor less dangerous than driving a car. It demands training and practice, has its own rules and laws, and to perform it one has to be both fit and attentive. One should surely not minimize the perils of sex magic, but neither should one overstress them because nobody benefits if you do. Incidentally, it is a deplorable but undeniable fact that the people who shout the loudest about the perils of sex magic are the most inhibited types who have the least practical experience of the subject.

If one attends a driving school, one does not expect to be frightened off by tales of accidents and dangers in traffic. Sensible driving instruction will point out the real perils and risks during the lessons but will not break the beginner's nerve. In a similar fashion, we do not want to point out the perils of sex magic too early, but we will tackle them as they occur in the recommended practices, and at the end of the book briefly summarize and comment on them once again.

Sex magic is equally for men and women. We will, of course, go into the differences which exist between male and female sexuality where appropriate, but at least we will not confuse the matter with value judgments; to do so would contradict the entire philosophy of sex magic. This is because sex magic is not exclusively for man or woman, Asian or European, initiate or neophyte, etc., but for humanity itself without consideration of racial, denominational, social or sexual differences.

Nevertheless, sex magic never has been a subject for the masses and probably never will be. Let us not forget that humanity's experience of sexuality has the emotionally explosive power of a hand grenade! No drive controls us so completely, so irrationally and so exclusively as sexuality. No other instinct has had to bear the weight of so many primal existential fears and insecurities. But sex magic is more than the ritual channelling of sexuality; it seeks to overcome the boundaries by which our sexuality is shaped on the one hand and those which it builds up itself on the other hand. Hence, without exaggeration, we really do "grasp the nettle" when we practice sex magic.

It takes courage to practice sex magic. Courage to jump over one's own sexual shadow, to confront and overcome one's sexual fears without merely suppressing them. This readiness, which during the course of practice will be frequently put to trial, is indispensable. Without it sex magic could become an emotional hell, comparable to the fate of a learner driver who refuses to adapt to the average speed of the traffic and who stops arbitrarily and unpredictably only to accelerate the very next moment. To extend the metaphor, this does not mean that everybody has to develop racing ambitions! Sex magic has nothing to do with competitive sport, and, when somebody feels that they have had enough, it would be stupid to force the pace. On the other hand, you cannot learn to swim without jumping into water; thus everybody has to find their own balance between hardness and softness. To demand too little from oneself in sex magic is as bad as to demand too much. Finding one's own golden mean, one's own middle course, is the door to success.

Secondly, sex magic demands determination. It is, at least to start with, not performed simply for its own sake. A clear, straightforward desire must succeed, unless one wants to practice a somewhat bizarre form of sexuality without applying any actual magic. Why should anybody decide to do sex magic? There are many possible reasons, some of which we shall list here: general interest in the possibility of enlarging sexuality by magical dealings with the powers of the soul and the universe; interest in a particularly efficient magical technique; the spirit of exploration; the desire to extend one's limits; interest in conscious work on fears and emotions; the desire to complete and round off one's magical development; pleasure in magical sexuality; an intuitive insight that this is one's true path, and so on. Before you start practicing sex magic, you should ask why you want to do so, both for psychological and technical reasons. First, you will sort out your own feelings about sexuality and magic if you look deeply enough into yourself; and, second, you will probably work better and more intensely when you know which fields of sex magic are most relevant to your requirements.

Please note that we are not laying down the law as to what are "noble, right, base or false" motives for practicing sex magic! Nevertheless, I want to point out certain motives which experience has shown to be a possible source of trouble: if you use sex magic as compensation or as a substitute for frustrated sexuality, you will experience difficulty. Although sex magic does not demand perfected magicians beyond good and evil and free from human needs, it is no substitute for an unrealized sexuality! I hope it will become clear that sex magic is not the same as sexuality—an important point which cannot be overstressed. We hardly need to point out that you should leave sex magic alone if all you are looking for is kinky excitement, or just some excuse to try out everything which you would not otherwise dare—for example group sex, partner-swapping, homosexuality, etc. It is possible that such motives could eventually lead to true sex magic, but it would require a particularly thorough application of the preparatory exercises. Without this you would soon find sex magic adding some more (particularly "ugly") experiences to your collection of sexual disappointments! Although sex magic works with the libido energy, it is not always pure pleasure; it can be very hard work.

Contrary to the principles of Eastern Tantra, Western sex magic emphasizes the importance of actual orgasm, both male and female. An ability to achieve orgasm is therefore a necessary prerequisite of this art. This assumes physically healthy people who are organically capable of having an orgasm. Purely psychosomatic blocks to orgasm do not necessarily exclude one from practising sex magic. It would just require preliminary work to release these blocks in order to advance to the so-called "higher" levels, using the principles explained in this book. Practices which avoid orgasm such as Tantra, Taoist Yoga, Carezza, etc. do play a supplementary role, but many sex magical operations indeed demand actual orgasm of the male or female magician. This does not necessarily mean pure genital orgasm (the so-called "peak orgasm"), the whole-body or "valley" orgasm, in which the male does not usually ejaculate, may also be used and can be preferable to the peak orgasm. More about this later.

One last requirement: the magician must be in a stable psychological condition. This rather delicate point needs to be looked at more closely. First, the term "stable" is somewhat vague. Suffice it to say that anyone on the brink of nervous breakdown, or permanently in danger of slipping from one psychotic or schizophrenic state into another, should keep well clear of any form of magic—this cannot be overstressed.

The second difficulty is that, in a sense, almost the direct opposite holds true: often a certain inner psychic tension proves a necessary prerequisite to practical magic! Gregorius once clarified this point using astrological symbolism. No astrologer of the old school likes to see too many squares (that is to say, 90° aspects) in a birth chart. They are traditionally seen as problematical and stressful aspects, although modern psychological astrology has qualified this view considerably. Gregorius, however, suggests that a magician cannot have too many squares! He explains that they are "cosmic stress lines" opening one up to transpersonal—and so magical— powers. In the psychological model of magic, this means that these tensions open us up to magical powers which extend beyond us and allow us to access them more easily. In other words, if the magician is so stable as to be in absolutely no danger of slipping into "insanity," then the power is not available to do the job! In this sense, magic can be seen as a sort of therapy for mental-psychic disturbances, a form of directed schizophrenia. This is especially true of so-called "theurgic" obsession magic.

This leads us to raise the question, "what is magic really about?" Study the literature and you will encounter endless definitions, but we will confine ourselves to an extension of a well-known definition by Aleister Crowley and state that, "Magic is the Science and Art of causing Change, on a material as well as a spiritual level, to occur in conformity with Will by altered states of consciousness."

"By altered states of consciousness"—remember this principle, because the words of *Liber Null* are exactly to the point: "Altered states of consciousness are the key to magical powers." The states of consciousness employed in magic we will call, again following *Liber Null*, "gnostic trances" or, in short, "gnosis."

Gnosis is a late-Hellenistic term and means something like "intuitive, revealed knowledge." The term is used here in this modern context, because it underlines the intuitive and subjective part of magical action and because the "gnostic trance" is a sort of "hyper-lucidity" or "trans-knowledge," an increased clarity of vision for which we have no proper term in our language. This state could perhaps be best described as a mixture of "revelation" and "clairvoyance."

Sex magic draws a great deal of its power from the fact that sexuality in general and orgasm in particular provide us with an ideal "natural" gnostic trance for magical workings. Crowley used the term "eroto-comatose lucidity" for a form of clairvoyance similar to a coma or unconsciousness and achieved by erotic methods. This means that we can largely bypass the need for extensive meditative and mystical trance training, because we begin with this natural trance which we call orgasm or sexual excitement. It should be obvious that the term "trance" used here does not mean a full hypnotic trance, where the patient loses all control of his actions and can be manipulated in any way the hypnotist desires. The gnostic trance has some superficial similarities to the hypnotic one, but the free will of the magician is in no way impaired, even when in a different — and sometimes quite bizarre— reality!

The three pillars of Western magic, as we understand it today, are will, imagination and gnostic trance. We chose to describe the last one first with good reason: will and imagination are completely useless without it! On the other hand, knowledge of it has only recently been introduced into magical literature—since the 1970s in fact, although the old masters even in the Middle Ages showed signs of understanding its principles. Up until recently, will and imagination have been considered sufficient for magical practice. The result is a form of magic hardly different from "positive thinking" and other, less effective, psycho-techniques. It is especially through our relatively recent encounter with shamanism, and through the development of "freestyle-shamanism" based on the modern Chaos Magic of Pete Carroll, Ray Sherwin and others, that we have become fully aware of the key role of gnostic trance in magic.

Will and imagination correspond respectively to purposefulness and power of visualization. They were much employed in the Western tradition, reaching their zenith in the works of Franz Bardon. It will not be necessary to expand on them here, instead suitable references will be given in the appropriate places.

It may be worth reiterating the point that sex magic and sex mysticism differ, that sex magic is mainly aimed at a purposeful outcome whereas sex mysticism is geared rather toward experience and ecstasy, which is itself a form of gnosis. At the end of this book we describe a ritual of sex mysticism to round things off. Beyond a certain point, the distinction between magic and mysticism becomes increasingly ridiculous. In the end both magician and mystic become one, because both become God. As God they can exert their right of creation, even if only to abandon its practice!

HANDLING SEXUALITY INTELLIGENTLY

Past attitudes towards sexuality have always tended to swing between two extremes. Sexuality was either condemned as "the demon lust," a dangerous urge which threatened the order and salvation of one's soul, or it was placed on a pedestal and elevated into something extraordinarily holy and sacrosanct. In both cases the effect was the same: sexuality was considered inviolable, either because it defiled us or else because we impure human beings might risk soiling this heavenly gift. The results have been the neuroses, repressions, taboos and inhibitions which still haunt us, even though perhaps only at the deeper subconscious levels. Although in the West the surface attitudes towards sexuality have become more liberal and the hold on the reins has slackened somewhat, we still have not adjusted inwardly to this outer liberty. Jealous scenes, alienation, feelings of emptiness and impotence are still the order of the day; the number of sexual offences is increasing steadily, and much modern sexuality takes the form of a spectator sport, via pornographic books and videos stimulating the imagination, instead of including and embracing the entire body. The resulting sexual frustration seems to give the lie to the supposed benefits of sexual liberation and its promise of individual self-realization, and the eventual result is a return to revulsion and scepticism. This backlash is not just a Western phenomenon; the traditional champions of the Oriental "Art of Love," such as India, China and Islam, darlings of Western romantics, now have the strictest taboos and the most severe punishments for those who break them. Prudishness is international and does not just apply to the Catholic Church and its puritanical offsprings.

Humanity, as usual, is the loser. This "crown of creation" has a source of the highest form of energy at its disposal, a force which forms, inspires and makes possible the entirety of life as we know it, but what do we do with it? Humanity fears it, suppresses it and at best allows it carefully restricted expression in the coy confines of the matrimonial (or extramarital) chamber or the mindless anti-eroticism of the peepshow booth. Even recent promiscuity and the flourishing of sex clubs and brothels has not changed very much; they smack more of frenetic compensation than of any real appreciation of the flesh. The hounding of sex is undiminished, despite the Kinsey report, love manuals, sex therapy and other signs of sexual emancipation—a problem exacerbated by hysterical fear of herpes, AIDS and other such self-punishing mechanisms often interpreted as "the wrath of God."

When Charles Darwin proposed his theory of evolution, with its suggestion of a common origin for man and ape, a cry of outrage swept through European civilization. When Sigmund Freud, almost half a century later, announced the sexual drive as the primal factor in the psyche and suggested that most psychic disorders are caused by incorrectly handling this drive, all hell once more broke loose. Church and reactionary forces joined to oppose such a conception of humanity, and with the same motive in both cases: a refusal to acknowledge our animal nature, whether genetic (Darwin) or sexual (Freud). In Freud's case, the suppressive mechanisms were especially obvious, because the (pagan!) classical Greek philosophers' sexuality had always been branded as an "animal" drive which had to be overcome. Such reactions are perhaps understandable, reflecting as they do our primordial fear that the entire arduous evolutionary process could be endangered. (Interestingly enough, this fear was even expressed by Darwin's critics, to the extent of humanity's cultural and moral development in the history of salvation.) After tens of thousands of years of development, does nothing else remain but the fact that man is basically only an animal, and one not necessarily much better than the others? We will return to this animal nature when we deal with atavistic magic; for now it is sufficient to state that these evolutionary theories are necessary to clarify our contemporary position and to remind us *that we not only bear the genetic but also the philosophical inheritance of our ancestors within us!*

Despite all changes, one constant remains: the fear of sexuality! Now, modern psychology has analyzed this "fear nature" of humanity in many ways. If one hears modern psychologists talking, it is clear that they are inspired by a human ideal more or less familiar to all of us: namely *the utopia of humanity without fear.* Freud and Adler had already striven to liberate humanity from its complexes and neuroses; Groddek tried the same with his psychosomatics; and magazines nowadays are full of terms like "pedagogy, freed of fears and repressions," "liberation from sexual fears," "partnership, freed of compulsion," etc. Just look at yourself: do you not also think that we should endeavor to become as "free" as possible—free from fears and compulsions, from repressions and inhibitions, from complexes and neuroses—in short, free from any compulsive behavior?

This attitude has led to many an excess, some of which have already been forgotten. Just think of the communes of the student revolt in the '60s or "Antiauthoritarian Education" following the Summerhill thesis. What remained from the stormy late '60s (to put it in a somewhat exaggerated way) is a sort of psychological version of the pedestrian, middle-class "spic 'n span kitchen" ideal. Most psychologists seem to consider the entire psyche as little else but a challenge to "clean up." Everything not completely "sterile" and still exuding even the slightest whiff of fears and complexes is supposed to be eradicated root and branch. This applies particularly to sexuality, which must also be made as "free from repressions" as possible. Fear is regarded as "evil," as much as the demonized "devil's work" debauchery and promiscuity used to be.

Now, psychology's attempts to liberate mankind shall certainly not be belittled here. After all, magic, sexual or otherwise, follows very similar goals. However, magic chooses a different path, one in our opinion more sensible, more effective and more realistic, taking into account the fact that a mankind completely free of fears does not and cannot exist. We must never forget that fear is an essential principle for biological survival. The will to survive and the fear of death are nothing but two sides of the same coin. If it were not for the fear of freezing to death, of famine and dying of thirst, there would be neither clothing nor architecture, neither agriculture nor irrigation, neither food silos nor drinking water fountains. In short, there would be neither civilization nor culture.

But that is not all. Fear sometimes plays a decisive part in magic because it provides immense power, if handled correctly. The magic of the Middle Ages knew the principle of "initiation through terror." The candidate had to perform gruesome conjurations in a tomb or graveyard at new moon or at midnight, the ominous, eerie "hour of ghosts." It was often necessary to perform a blood sacrifice or to face the "forces of hell." Shamanism and Kaula Tantra, by the way, share similar practices. Without fear and terror, demons cannot usually be evoked to visibility; they seem to be able to nourish themselves from this emotion in the magician.

We will not expand on the highly complex subject of demonic magic, since I have already dealt with it elsewhere.[1] One aspect only shall be mentioned, because it is important for our dealings with sexuality and sex magic. Instead of banishing fears and neuroses, instead of suppressing them or even eradicating them, the magician comes to terms with them. They are projected in the form of demons in order that one can conclude the infamous "devil's pact" with them. This is a sort of horse trading with one's fears: keeping them alive personified as demons, in return for the necessary power (*magis*) crucial for special magical operations.

This is very important. If we see fear as an immense driving power which we can utilize, it is no longer necessary to employ an equally huge amount of energy to exterminate it. In other words, it is not necessary to become a perfected, fear-free being to practice sex magic. It is only necessary to face up to one's own fears and inhibitions with brutal frankness. If magic shall actually lead to freedom, then it must be a transpersonal freedom, optimum in breadth of choice, and not some predefined norm which once more degrades humanity and wants to impose some new straitjacket. One simply has to consider the "spontaneity obligation" in certain forms of group therapy, which in the end creates nothing but a new, slightly different form of inhibition. Such "joy-creating ideologies" are legion, and we magicians have to be especially aware of setting such traps for ourselves...

Once we have recognized our fears and compulsions, we can decide whether to exterminate them or utilize them. It is certainly not necessary to explain that such dealings with one's "demons" need maturity and strength of will. On the other hand, such practice leads to the point where fears lose their prominence in one's life and become just another part of the psyche.

The same applies to sexuality. If you already hold the opinion that this primordial force is "bad," evil and degenerate, you probably would not bother to read this book. But what is your attitude towards "deification," and oversacralization of sexuality? This can often be seen in conventional esoterica, and it does suggest a deep subconscious problem. Because one does not dare to admit sexuality as something completely normal, natural and ordinary, one makes something holy and supernatural out of it and so restores it to abnormality again! But we do ourselves no favor, because this once again forces us into patterns of suppression by making something entirely unnatural out of sexuality. Often enough the seeming spiritualization takes the place of corporeality, and the "seamy" sides of sexuality are generously overlooked as if they were nothing but an accident of creation.

Such an attitude is of little help in serious sex magic. Sex magic does have its sacral aspects, its mysticism of the flesh which leads eventually to a transcendence of all carnal limitations, but this again forms only part of a greater whole.

We propose a more pragmatic approach: let us examine sexuality in a more sober and unprejudiced way than is usually the case. Let us not trivialize it—it is too important for that—but neither let us attribute more significance to it than it deserves. Only when this is done can we really reap the full benefits of sex magic.

Taboos are another problem when dealing with sexuality, but even they have their value. Tantra systematically exploits them. For example, with *Pancha makara,* where the conscious breaking of taboos around food and sexuality serve as a source of energy for advanced meditation and the heightening of awareness. Like the common tests of bravery in shamanic cultures, still perpetuated in our culture by children and teen-age gangs, the facing up to one's Jungian "shadow" represents an important step on the path to self-assurance. Not everybody will want to go so far as the chaos magician who seeks trance for magical ends through sexual loathing, but the basic principle remains: by employing bizarre, unusual practices, we access those altered states of awareness which provide the key to magical power. Do not be tempted to make excuses such as "I don't need this, because I can get into a gnostic trance anyway," or "such methods are unnatural and dangerous." First, such excuses betray exactly those weak points that need attention if one is serious about magical development. Secondly, not all trances are the same, gnostic trance included. With some experience you will realize that the *magis* (which, by the way, is similar to *chi* or *prana*) may have different qualities depending on the means by which it is released. The beginner tends only to differentiate between "weaker" and "stronger" magical energy, as in such prejudical utterances as "black magic is more powerful than white magic," "Voodoo is stronger than Western magic" etc. The experienced magician makes more careful distinctions, recognizing, if he or she is pragmatic, that each magical operation needs a different form of *magis*. This is an individual matter, and no rigid guidelines can be drawn up. One magician might consider that the planetary energies of Jupiter and Mercury were the only suitable medium for money magic, whereas another will equally insist on sigil magic, while a third relies entirely on sex magic. Magic is not just the art of mastering energies, but also the art of doing so in the most appropriate manner. This can only be learned by intuition and experience, and so every magician should experiment with as many techniques and methods as possible in order to gain this experience. In magic, as in any other discipline, we find the precisionist, the artist and the pioneer, those who prefer hard fact and those who delight in fantasy. Each to his or her own talent and temperament. The difference between the magician and the layman is that the former does not strive to create a watertight, catastrophe-free prison of a reality. Instead, the magician aims for variety and the colorful life—this too distinguishes magician from mystic. Certainly this demands courage, not only to break others' taboos, but all the more to break one's own.

If you find certain sexual practices revolting, you can be sure that strong inner energies are involved at these points. Force yourself to examine these practices consciously and you will invariably discover that they liberate a kind of power and *magis* completely different from that generated by less "repugnant" techniques. Not that the power is particularly pleasant; far from it. "Initiation through terror" is never a pleasant or comfortable experience. No doubt that is why it leads one so much more thoroughly, quickly and effectively to the next stage than squeamishness ever could. Consider this point before refusing any sex-magical experiences. Refuse if you must, but make sure it is through strength of knowledge and not just fear.

There is no point in breaking taboos without the right attitude and aims to guide you. Pure fear does not make an initiation, nor does the sheer relief of having survived your fears. This is why it is so important that each magician finds his or her own will, to have a clear aim and know exactly why any taboo needs to be broken. It can be very difficult to do this on your own, and so many a prospective adept seeks a "guru," or teacher. The guru-disciple relationship has its perils, however (for example, see pages 205-206). Even if the student manages to avoid false teachers who have no real knowledge and are either deluded or seeking selfish advantage (monetary and/or sexual), the guru may force disciples to do certain things against their wishes (although, if the guru is authentic, not against their true wills). The feelings evoked will all too often be directed against the teacher as anger, hate and rebellion, instead of being directed to the actual task set. In return, the guru has to use a great deal of energy redirecting the disciple onto a real inner rebellion—to a rebellion which leads to true independence.

Aleister Crowley, whose contribution to magic was not least that he instilled the principle of self-initiation, pointed out that beginners tend to prefer those practices which suit them best and which they can most easily perform. Crowley explained that thereby any pre-existing imbalance will only be magnified, whereas the purposeful breaking of a taboo has both a pedagogical and a balancing function, aiming towards a more harmonious magical personality. In hardly any other area will this become so apparent as in sex magic. I dare to assert that sex magic draws most of its power from the following fact: working as it does with sexual fears and taboos, it initially releases a tremendous amount of success-energy, such that beginners are surprised at its effects. If a taboo has been broken once or even several times, it begins to lose its "suppressive power," like opening the valve on a boiler repeatedly to reduce the steam pressure. But do not think this is all there is to sex magic. Once the steam has been let off, one can use the energy of the boiling water itself. This image should clarify the fact that sex magic means more than merely breaking taboos. Breaking taboos is a valuable supportive technique and should be respected as such, but it is not the only power-principle, let alone sex magic's main-purpose!

A serious problem in sex magic is the problem of love. The reasons why we do not want to delve into this topic are briefly as follows: It has not always been recognized that love and sexuality are so strongly linked as is thought today. Especially in times of sexual suppression, "pure" love, "undefiled" by sexuality, was extolled above all. But nowadays most people, apart from a few religious fanatics, agree that sexuality forms part of love. Regardless of whether we insist on institutionalized marriage or whether we allow so-called "free love," or "common-law marriage," the fundamental philosophy remains the same.

But is the reverse equally true? Does sexuality need love? If this were so, prostitution and pornography could hardly exist. Often the objection is made that this commercialized sexuality, also known as "venal love," wherein love and sex are completely equated, is a typical manifestation of male-patriarchal societies and therefore reflects mostly male rather than female sexuality. But not everyone agrees on this point, and we are in no position to expand further on this debate; it would lead us away from our original subject. Let us simply recognize that this matter is highly controversial.

It is of course a completely different problem whether love has anything to do with sex magic. Much depends on the precise way in which "love" is defined, but once again this is not our task. I can only give you my personal opinion and leave you to decide for or against.

If you see love as a projection of your own acquisitive drive, your fear of loss, your vicarious satisfactions as well as a stronghold of jealousy, envy and "well-meaning resentment" fixed on one partner, then there is certainly no room for love within sex magic. The same applies if your lover disapproves of anything magical, let alone sex magical, for whatever reason. An exclusive fixation on monogamy can also be a barrier to practical sex magic, as can other sexual taboos which frequently get muddled up with love. In general, magic tends to liberate and not to enslave—and even more so does magic in the field of sexuality.

But, if you understand love as respect for another and his or her unique individual right to personal development ("Every man and every woman is a star," as Crowley says in *The Book of the Law*), and if your conception of love includes having trust and confidence in others to make their own sexual decisions, even if you do not always approve of them, then your love is mature enough for sex magic and can only further it.

After all, the practice of sex magic does not usually start with partner-workings but rather with autoerotic techniques. One reason for this is to avoid possible conflict in these areas. Many sex magicians work exclusively on an autoerotic level or, at most, have intercourse only with succubi and incubi. Nothing can be said against this as long as it does not strengthen a pre-existing lack of balance or inability and so excludes other practices. Let us again take the example of driving a car: A driver only prepared to drive at 60 mph and only capable of driving around right-hand bends has a very limited field of action and will very likely endanger others because of these rigid reactions. But more about the importance of autoerotic sex magic will follow in chapter 4. As already mentioned, the real sex magician should be familiar with as many aspects of sex magic as possible until he or she is ready to start developing a personal, completely individual system.

And now for the first practical preparatory exercise. This exercise, which we call "the mirror of the soul," should be repeated occasionally so that one becomes able more accurately to follow one's own development in strength as well as in weakness.

The Magical Diary

Before we start, we need what may turn out to be the most important tool of every magician: the magical diary. An accurate and detailed record of one's own magical workings is indispensable, because successes and magical effects frequently look like coincidences and because magic often leads to experiences which seem as superficial as dreams. Furthermore, this document provides us after several years with an interesting insight into trends which otherwise even the most perfect memory would overlook.

People who already keep a regular diary do not have to bother with a new, separate one for sex magic. People who do not yet keep one are advised to observe the following:

• The magical diary should be large enough for your entries, but not so large as to become an unwieldy and conspicuous piece of luggage on your travels. Furthermore, there will be times when you wish to lay the magical diary on your altar where space is usually quite limited.

• The following must always be entered: date, time, place and subject of the magical working performed. If no work has been done, then this too should be noted.

• Leave enough room for a postscript; this is particularly important for monitoring successes and later on for evaluation. Possible mistakes may be recorded here as well.

• Whatever else you enter is up to you. In the beginning, for example, you could write down your impressions of rituals, observations of coincidences, sudden inspirations, etc. You should also comment on the development of a magical operation; brief notes should suffice. After the 15th Mercury ritual, for example, it is enough to state: "Mercury ritual from 7:30 to 8:45 p.m.," instead of having to spell out every single candle used. Once again, routine helps save a lot of time and work.

• Always keep your magical diary locked away and do not show it to anybody, with the possible exception of your magical teacher. If necessary, you may also write in code or metaphor, or even use a secret script.

• When evaluating your earlier workings, be very self-critical and do not pull the wool over your own eyes. After all the magical diary is meant to help you avoid such self-deception!

The Mirror of the Soul

This "mirror of the soul" consists of a questionnaire. Unlike most questionnaires, this one does not require you to answer all the questions at once, and the order in which you answer them is entirely up to you. Consider the questions rather as suggestions for meditation, contemplation and self-exploration. Allow yourself time to consider the answers, and above all be completely honest. Enter all your answers into your magical diary and leave room for later comments.

1) What does sexuality mean to me? What do I expect from it?

2) How satisfied/dissatisfied am I with my existing sexuality?

3) What are my sexual weaknesses?

4) What are my sexual strengths?

5) What are my sexual taboos? What forms of sex do I consider impossible?

6) What are my sexual insecurities?

7) Mentally reviewing my earliest, say, 15 sexual experiences—autoerotic as well as hetero- or homoerotic, how far have these first sexual encounters shaped my current sexuality?

8) Am I sexually active or passive?

9) How do I react to sexual disappointments and frustrations?

10) Why do I deal with magic? What do I expect from it?

11) Why do I deal with sex magic? What do I expect from it?

12) _____

13) _____

14) _____

Add at least three individual questions which you consider personally relevant and important. This exercise will help you to build up further, ongoing mirrors of the soul. Please note that no answers are suggested here and no pointers are given! There are no wrong answers—only dishonest or incomplete ones. Just as you alone are responsible as a male or female magician for everything you do or do not do, so is it with this; only you yourself can gain from it!

If you are a complete beginner to magic, do not start with sex magic before you have completed your mirror of the soul. If you already have sex-magical experience, you should nevertheless draw up the mirror of the soul to provide deeper insights and enrich your practice.

In the course of this book, you will be confronted again and again with such questions because we believe in backing up our sex magic on every level: physical, mental-psychological and magical. That is how the following chapters are structured.

Note

[1]Compare Fra V∴D∴, "Wie schächte ich mein Alter Ego? Anmerkungen zur Dämonenmagie," *Unicorn* 13 (1985), pp. 64–69 and 119.

SEX MAGICAL TRAINING

For purposes of flexibility, and to keep the instruction "open ended," philosophical and theoretical background material will be inserted to introduce the practical exercises as a sort of "secondary comment." These interjections are presented in a deliberately unsystematic way to balance the purely technical and hierarchically structured format of the exercises. These comments may seem like digressions but, after having read the entire book, you will realize that they are not only closely connected to one another but also intended to stimulate receptivity of the knowledge presented on the affective, intuitive level.

Secondary Comment

Old magical books love to lay down the law on timing. The reader is advised to perform exercise X for at least three years, and for 30 minutes every day, before he dares try exercise Y. In my opinion, the only value of such recommendations is that they put off those people who might think that magic works in a fairy tale manner; that is, at the snap of the fingers or the wave of a wand merely provided that one has the right "knowledge." Paradoxically, this *is* true for the ultimate stages of magic; it is just that the required "knowledge" is not simply intellectual knowledge but rather a "gnosis." Gnosis means knowledge that includes and penetrates all levels—body, soul and spirit—or, according to our division, *physis*, *psyche* and *magis*.

Austin Osman Spare said concerning sigils (magical will-glyphs) that they "become flesh," and this has to be taken in a literal sense. If, as psychological magic assumes, the primordial magical powers slumber deep in the subconscious, then this subconscious has to be understood not just as a "back room of the brain" but as a totality which penetrates and includes every cell of the body. In other words, our instincts are grounded so deeply in the physical that perception of and reaction to the body are practically one. We are talking about "reflexes," but also, in older texts, about "knowledge of the flesh."

This genetic, primordial knowledge, which is preprogrammed in our chromosomes, is said by numerous critics (magicians and shamans included) to have largely atrophied in modern humanity. However, I do not share this view despite certain powerful arguments in favor of it—for example, that we are the only animal (apart from our domesticated species) which no longer nourishes itself naturally and we have accordingly lost many of our instincts; only in the most extreme cases do we instinctively "recognize" harmful food. We disregard the cycles of nature, turn night into day and offend against fundamental rules by poisoning ourselves with alcohol and nicotine, interfering with our hormone balance and destroying our environment.

But it would be very one-sided to consider the problem only from this viewpoint. There is also the opposite view that we are the only creatures which have gained absolute supremacy on this planet; the only animals that are not at the mercy of the weather; the only creatures which have been for centuries increasing average life expectancy, which can transcend the environment and populate the universe. This view merely confronts the previous pessimism with the optimistic belief in progress, without being able to disprove it—perhaps the truth lies *between* the extremes?

In my opinion, neither party correctly evaluates our capabilities. We should not constantly underestimate ourselves against the dubious myth of the noble savage who supposedly lives in perfect harmony with his environment. Two remarks on this: first, you cannot utterly rely upon the instincts of even a child of nature; second, primitive people live in bondage to taboos and tribal rules—a heavy price to pay for their allegedly superior instincts! It is high time we realized just how tremendous our reserves of *magis* really are. Consider again the driving analogy: It is almost incredible what an experienced driver can do. The driver not only guides the car through dense traffic, passing within inches of death at every moment, but he or she can also react to road signs, change gear and deal with a host of outer stimuli, while at the same time chatting with a passenger and adjusting the car radio! Compare this "traffic jungle" with that of the primitive hunter reading tracks and scenting deer for hunting. Although his magical skills might seem more obvious, it is surely because we take our own skills so much for granted—not to mention the fact that, among shamans and medicine men, there exists professional mystique and in-group secrecy. The shaman may seem "eerie" to his fellow tribesmen because he handles knowledge which is not accessible to everyone, but they certainly do not think of him as unnatural.

Our much lamented "loss of naturalness"—which, by the way, was already being bewailed by the ancient Greeks, and again during the Renaissance, the Baroque and the Romantic periods—well, actually it goes back to the story of Adam and Eve and their expulsion from paradise—seems to be no more than a sort of very doubtful selective perception. Selective perception is, *per se*, vitally necessary because it saves us from being overloaded by a host of outer stimuli. Recognizing magical events and omens is, strictly speaking, also a form of selective perception. It only becomes doubtful if one is no longer aware of one's selectivity, if one muddles the personal, segmental perception of reality with the whole. Do this and the crusader mentality soon develops. One really obscene aspect to Western history is the way that a religion which has raped nature at every opportunity, with its hatred for the flesh and its exploitive mentality, could have the impunity to accuse magic of being *unnatural!* It is moreover a fact that a misunderstanding of the essence of Greek thought as well as a misunderstanding of Christianity have combined to prevent our perception of the natural *magis* of humanity but not the perception of the *magis* itself.

If we want to be magicians, particularly sex magicians, we must liberate ourselves from the realities indoctrinated by the establishment and find our own center. Pete Carroll once said in a conversation that humanity, in relation to its stature, is capable of astonishing achievements. This introduces the other kind of danger: whereas religion and science tend to belittle humanity, reducing us to God's slaves or to biological mechanisms, respectively, and so sceptics will deny the magical abilities of *Homo sapiens*, magic can encourage megalomania, so that we absurdly overestimate our capabilities. Such inflation betrays just as much narrow-mindedness and ignorance as the former viewpoints. The fact is that, if you remove our veneer of civilization, you soon uncover the primeval being with all its animal drives and instinctive skills, to be sure, but also with its shortcomings and fears. Each war proves this anew, although in general our instincts may not surface as blatantly as in former times and may be largely sublimated in such skills as driving. It is therefore advisable to look out for magic in everyday life and to recognize it as such when it occurs. This not only encourages better access to the source of our own magical powers *(magis)*, it also makes magic more familiar, easier to handle and therefore ultimately more effective.

Is magic therefore nothing but instinctive wisdom? Yes and no. Yes, because in magic we deal with gnosis which works largely on the subconscious and etheric level. No, because it not only includes the instincts, but also eventually goes beyond them. Western magic has been called "applied mythology," a term which hits the nail on the head—even if it does not allow sufficiently for the more technically oriented branches of magic. Mythos is not "head" so much as "gut" feeling. The exact difference between instinct and intuition is not easily defined, even in magic. Those instinctual messages which do not lead to immediate reflex actions—such as fleeing from fire in a public building—are called "intuitions" or "inspirations." Because our society does not train us to handle intuitions in a matter-of-fact way, we become wildly excited when our intuitions prove to be accurate—but we react with equally exaggerated disappointment if our intuition misleads us or foretells something evil. This is not natural! Whereas we are realistic about intellect and recognize that it can go wrong, the whole world breaks down for us if some nice "hunch," on which we pinned our hopes, proves to have been groundless. This superstitious overestimation of magic is actually the reverse side of the coin of our unacknowledged fear of it. If we clutch at magic as the last straw which will keep us above water in a hostile life; if you, the magician, behave as a sort of astral Zorro, the avenger of the disinherited and karmically displaced, then this may very well be your idea of what is "mythical"—but it is wrong! Magic is flesh; it exists in the midst of flourishing life; it is nothing without life, just as the lives of many magicians without magic would be nothing but illusion. It is not a substitute for life; it is part of life. It *is* life. In this sense, and in this sense alone, can one say that "everything is magic."

The concept of carnality has to be taken literally. Most effective magic uses the actual, physical human body, just as a radiaesthesist needs the human body as a sensor so that the rod or pendulum can do its job. If we learn one thing from shamanic cultures, it is the strong emphasis upon the role of the body in magic. Shamanism uses dancing, techniques of exhaustion, stress, drugs, fever etc. to bring the organism to the limits of its capacity *before magic takes place at all!*

Once when I was with a group of German magicians working with an African fetish priest, after an introductory ritual which was in itself pretty strenuous, he made me spin on my axis for about three-quarters of an hour! In those days, I was prone to dizziness at even the slightest rotation, and several times I would have collapsed had it not been for three colleagues who had been directed to stand in a circle around me in case I fell. After a while, the dizziness changed into exhaustion, and I came close to a full trance that nearly caused me to forget what we were doing. I "talked in tongues" and was almost delirious.

Eventually the medicine man ended the action and I, in a state of total exhaustion, was allowed to recuperate and pull myself together. The greatest shock, however, was his final comment: "With us in Africa," he said in his somewhat broken German, "medicine man does this for about three hours; then somebody goes to chieftain and says: medicine man is in power."

The mere thought of having to endure this spinning for *three whole hours* made me shudder. His remark also gave me an idea of the criteria by which "primitive" peoples judge their magical achievement. Most Western magicians I know, however, work quite successfully with far less drastic techniques thanks largely to the previously described gnostic-trance concept. The important thing is not the fierceness of the exercise, but rather the final achievement of a gnostic or magical trance; the main thing is "that medicine man is in power"! This does not alter the fact that gnostic trance nearly always works via the body. Such trances go hand-in-hand with physical symptoms such as panting, coughing, slight dizziness, trembling—even vomiting and heavy muscle spasms may sometimes occur. Still, the gnostic trance is usually far less spectacular than the beginner might expect. Often unexplainable abnormal behavior is the only sign that one is in a trance at all, just as most hypnotized people are not aware of being hypnotized—because of the fact that their mind seems to be completely normal even when their behavior is uncharacteristic.

Our sex magic *training* is structured in three parts because magic works on several levels. Therefore, the following sections have the respective headings "Physical Practice," "Psychological Practice" and "Practice of the *Magis*." Although these fields will be separately covered, in actual sex-magic practice such separation would be an impediment; in reality, the magician acts on all levels *at once*. This is why further hints of how to deal physically, psychologically and magically with *magis* and magic will also be found in later chapters. But the advantage of the present breakdown is that you will get a more systematic overview of what to expect from sex magic, while most of the separately listed exercises may in fact be linked together and performed in parallel, often even at the same time. Anyway, when you begin reading, you should examine your own shortcomings self-critically with a view to compiling your own individual exercise program. Do not start your own program, however, until you have *actually* mastered the other techniques which you might be tempted to skip over! Practice these occasionally too, to stop yourself from "rusting up" magically. Do not worry that certain exercises overlap and that some hints will be repeated later. This is done deliberately to stress the really important points and also to spare you from having to turn back the pages too much.

Physical Practice

Relaxation

A basic condition for all body work is the *ability to relax*. Already we encounter an overlap with psychological practice, because physical relaxation is only possible with mental relaxation. Nevertheless, there are distinct physical and mental aspects, and we will first direct our attention towards the former. Many of the tips given here are equally relevant to psychological relaxation and will be repeated later only briefly.

If you have not yet had any experience of Hatha Yoga or autogenic training, you are strongly advised to take a look at those disciplines. Both offer valuable tips and techniques which can im-

prove your ability to relax. The same applies to "psychological practice" insofar as these disciplines help with thought control,
concentration and meditation.

In this chapter, you will be introduced to a form of deep relaxation which you may already have met elsewhere. Our technique is
geared to the specific requirements of sex magic, but it uses techniques common to Taoist Yoga and Tantra. I therefore recommend
that you experiment with our technique even if you already have
experience with other approaches.

Why do we rate relaxation so highly? Isn't sex magic supposed
to work with sexual *excitement?* With movement rather than with
stillness? There are several answers. First, the majority of sexual
problems can be traced to an inability to relax. Fear makes one tense,
and conversely tensions can anchor fear in the subconscious and in
the body's own memory circuits. Forms of therapy which empha-
size the body, like bioenergetics, rebirthing, Rolfing and postural
integration, demonstrate how traumas fix themselves in the actual
physical system and may be neutralized by proper physical
exercise.

Second, the sexual *magis* is dealt with in a similar way to the handling of *chi* or *prana* in the Budo and Wu-Shu (martial) arts of Asia; it
is also similar to acupuncture and Tai Chi in that the energy is first
concentrated in a state of calm relaxation before being directed ex-
plosively towards its target.

Third, relaxation is the prerequisite to mastering one's body. In
sex magic this mastery includes having a strengthened pelvis, an
ability to delay or hasten orgasm, the use of breathing techniques
and much more. Do not forget that in sex magic we usually work
with an orgasm-trance which could all too easily overwhelm us.
This will probably happen a few times to start with and it won't
harm the beginner; however, the long-term aim should be to get as
much control over the sexual *magis* as possible. This is the aim of the
following exercises.

Depth Relaxation—Level 1

This exercise is best performed skyclad (i.e., naked), but this of
course requires a comfortable room temperature. If necessary, a
light blanket should be enough to prevent catching a chill. Furthermore, make sure that you remain undisturbed for half to three quar-
ters of an hour when you perform this exercise.

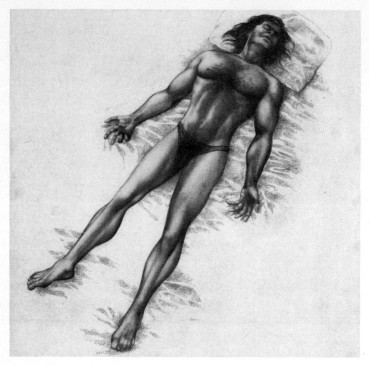

Death Posture

The starting position is the so-called "death posture": lying on your back, with your arms at your side and slightly distanced from your body (about 6 inches), your palms are facing upwards with the fingers loose and relaxed; your legs are slightly open and your eyes are closed. The lighting of the room should be subdued; the use of music, even so-called "meditation music," should be avoided for the time being.

Now relax. Imagine, say, that you are a cat that enjoys resting. During the first few minutes you might as well wriggle about until you feel really comfortable before assuming the final death posture. From then on you should remain motionless.

At first, breathing is calm and deep, but with increased relaxation it becomes shallower, though even more calm. Do not concentrate too much on your breathing at this stage; that comes later. Your mouth should be closed so you breath through your nose. Your teeth may be gently in contact or may be fractionally apart, but the most important thing is that the tip of your tongue should lightly touch the roof of your mouth (don't press!) without moving in order to reduce salivation.

Now for the depth relaxation. Focus your attention on your right or left foot. Whichever side you start with is up to you, but it should always be the same side. So, if you start by relaxing your left foot followed by the right one, you will then proceed to your left lower leg before doing the same with the right one; then you continue with your left arm and so on. Direct your attention to your little toe and say mentally (not aloud!), "My left (or right) little toe is relaxed and calm and warm." Repeat this suggestion until you actually feel it. The result is a pleasant warmth in the relevant part of the body together with a certain feeling of relaxed heaviness. You then repeat the process with each individual toe of your foot in turn. When all five toes are relaxed, you mentally repeat twice, "All toes of my left (or right) foot are relaxed and calm and warm."

Then you do exactly the same with the other foot. When these toes are completely relaxed too, you go back to the first foot and relax the instep and the sole of that foot, then the heel, then the ankle, until you can eventually say, "My entire left (or right) foot is relaxed and calm and warm." Then switch to the other foot. When that is completed say, "Both my feet are relaxed and calm and warm."

Proceed in this way with your entire body and in the following order:

- calf
- knee
- thigh
- complete leg
- each finger
- palm and ball of the thumb
- wrist
- whole hand
- forearm
- elbow
- upper arm
- whole arm
- genitals
- abdomen
- abdominal wall
- chest
- shoulder

- neck (cervical) muscles
- entire torso
- lower jaw
- mouth
- nose
- eyelids
- brow
- back of the head
- entire head
- entire body

This list may seem a bit pedantic and overdefined, but it is a sad fact that beginners tend particularly to neglect those parts of the body that most need relaxation. The knees, genitals, abdomen, lower jaw, brow and back of the head are especially neglected. Later on you should also include the inner organs (heart, lungs, stomach, liver, kidneys, spleen, gall) and several of the meridians particularly pertinent to sex magic. More about the relevant meridians later.

Some people need nearly an hour to complete their first depth relaxation; others have immediate success. Others may demand several weeks of practice before they get the feeling of how to do it properly. This exercise has to be performed at least once a day, and the best time is either first thing in the morning or last thing before falling asleep. Feel free to practice depth relaxation more than once a day if you like. It is important that you practice *regularly*. I advise you to persevere about four weeks on the first level before starting with the second level. If possible, avoid falling asleep during the exercise. With practice you will be able to maintain a semiconscious state, quite near to the magical trance in which you remain *fully conscious*.

Magical Protection

During depth relaxation it is wise to protect oneself magically. People already familiar with magical protection may project it before they start the actual relaxation; those new to it should should follow the instructions below, at their third depth relaxation at the latest. If you are satisfied with the quality of energy, you may practice building up magical protection during the day—in your office, while waiting at traffic lights, when shopping, or whenever you like. Once you have a feeling that you may have mastered this practice (when you really have succeeded, your heightened sensibility will tell you so), then you should surround yourself with magical protection before you start the depth relaxation. Before this technique is described, there are a few initial comments.

What is the purpose of magical protection? Here we must clear up a misunderstanding which is unfortunately most common among amateurs. They ask, "Why do magicians have to protect themselves all the time? Is everybody really out to get them? Or are they just paranoid?" Now, there is some truth in such accusations, thanks partly to numerous "well-meaning" esoteric authors, who feel obliged to warn the whole universe of the seeming perils of magic—without themselves having any real knowledge of the subject. All too often fear and ignorance are the parents of those admonitions, and the same authors would be horrified to learn that most of their techniques and basic principles are themselves derived from magic.

In reality, you very rarely encounter magical attack. First of all, few people are capable of practicing combat magic effectively without proper training. Second, magical attack is very costly and time-consuming, and serious magicians seldom do it without grave provocation. In other words, there has to be a really good reason for any serious magician to attack you and start a long, persistent "war." On the other hand, it certainly tickles one's vanity to believe that one is important enough to be attacked magically! In my experience, 90 percent of all supposed magical attacks are nothing but glamorous projections by people with overactive imaginations.

Magical protection is primarily meant *to keep away undesirable energies;* it is all about concentration. The term "concentration" means literally to lead something towards its center, but it also implies selecting and excluding the superfluous. This is the exact basis of magical protection. It is mostly done by drawing a circle, placing the magician symbolically in the center, so that nothing can interfere except that which has expressly been invited. Thus the circle keeps out disturbing influences while at the same time holding in the energies summoned. Just as the scientist in the laboratory needs to exclude extraneous effects such as rays, dust, humidity and temperature fluctuations, as well as distracting noise and light emissions which might interfere with sensitive experiments, so too the magician will create optimum working conditions. These conditions are: concentration, control of mind and body, and a precise awareness of subtle energy—and all of them can only be achieved with concentration. It would be wrong to imagine legions of evil demons and astral larvae lurking outside the circle and waiting to get you. As with magical warfare, these energies do exist, but they are very exceptional. Because these energies are so unpredictable, sensible precautions should always be observed, but this is not the same as paranoia. Like the champion rock climber who instinctively shows greater caution than the less skilled amateur, it is simply the mark of the professional. The real dangers in the form of "demonic energies" and "astral vampires" will be dealt with later.

That is how magical protection should be understood if it is to be truly effective, whereas excessive fear of danger weakens your protection and makes it apt to break down at the slightest challenge. In other words, *when building up* your magical castle, you should concentrate on the positive energies within the circle rather than dwelling on the dangers and enemies without, for "along with the weapon cometh the foe." The more one becomes fixated on forestalling enemies, the more one's energy becomes bound to the opponent, until all initiative is lost. It is much more sensible and strategically effective to focus on developing one's own abilities in the optimum way, to remedy mistakes and to build up a feeling of true security. This is much more a question of attitude than of technique.

Magical protection therefore helps concentration and only secondarily does it serve as protection from enemies and perils in the traditional sense. More correctly, magical protection could be called an "energy-filter" or "polarizer" which also works as a "power-accumulator." This realization gives the lie to a frequently uttered objection; namely, that it is foolish to block everything from outside by magical protection because this would reduce the fullness of the experience and lead to paranoid egocentricity. Magical protection does not block *everything*, only those influences which do not serve the moment.

From this point of view it is clear that a general magical protection maintained all the time has a different quality from the protection one specifically creates for, say, a sex-magic ritual. The general protection may in a sense be "coarser," but it is also more stable, while the special protection with its high-toned sophistication is more open to disturbance because it needs a more precise aim and greater accuracy. Note that these descriptions are only an attempt to put into words feelings which cannot really be conveyed but need rather to be experienced. You will find exercises in this book that will help you to cultivate this more general sense of genuine security.

These detailed remarks on the side issue of protection are necessary because the subject is fundamental to all that follows. Mark them well to avoid misunderstanding and error. Now, let us proceed with the actual exercise.

Magical Protection 1

The most common form of magical protection is a circle, the so-called "magic circle." Like all other protective symbols, it has to be imagined or visualized. One should aim toward projecting the symbol in such an intense manner that one is able to perceive it as a conscious hallucination. It is not important whether this perception is visual as long as it is intense; one may "smell" or "taste" the protective symbol or "feel" it physically with one's hands. As a matter of fact, these words are just an approach to a reality not recognized in our vocabulary; namely, those imaginative perceptions received by a seemingly non-material organ which uses the sense organs as its channels without really occupying them or granting them independence.

Ideally, anyone else who is present and sufficiently sensitive or trained should be able to perceive the protection symbol without having their attention drawn to it—but the development of such skill takes many years. Luckily, we can start to do magic long before we work up to this level of expertise. Nevertheless, this should always be the eventual aim of magical projection. Achieving it is to attain that mastership which ensures working without mistakes.

There are several reasons for the circle's popularity for magical protection. First of all, it is infinite, with neither beginning nor end, so it serves as a symbol of infinity for the magician who seeks to become God. On the other hand, the circle represents the horizon of humanity's vision and so "perception and maintenance of truth." Furthermore, the sphere and the circle have always been symbols of the Absolute, not least because of their geometric properties, which inspired the mathematicians of antiquity—one need only consider the discovery of *pi*. The circle has numerous archetypal associations—of protection, safety, clarity and perfection. People talk about "rounding something off." The famous words which Archimedes uttered shortly before his death are often quoted: "Do not disturb my circles." Other expressions used include "higher circles," "inner circles," "round about here," "one's personal sphere," "to go round in circles" and "cycle," as in "life cycle." Magicians also talk about colleagues with whom they have "stood in the circle"; i.e., with whom they have once shared a common universe.

In fact, the circle symbolizes the cosmos of the magician, his or her outer world and reality. To do magic means to jump from one universe into another, to live one moment in one reality and in the next moment in another one, but to do this purposefully and with mastery.

Although the circle is a suitable symbol, it is not the only protective glyph. Indeed it is better if each magician chooses his or her own symbol for the general, permanent protection we mentioned. Rituals, on the other hand, are better performed in accordance with tradition, especially when working with other people. The following exercise helps to find out one's own optimum symbol of protection.

The exercise can be performed alone or with others. If there are several participants, one has to be the leader. If the ritual is performed alone, all functions will be performed by yourself.

Each magician is seated, adopting a relaxed state of mind with eyes closed. After a while, the leader (or the solitary magician) sounds a bell or cymbal and says, "You are seated in a circle of burning fire which surrounds your hips, twenty inches out from your body and two inches thick." (If working alone, say "I" instead of "you.") Once the image is clear, pay attention to how you feel inside the symbol and study its energy quality for 10 to 20 minutes. Then again, the bell or cymbal is sounded and the next suggestion can begin.

This time you repeat the suggestion using a different symbol in place of a circle of fire. Traditional symbols such as "silver sphere," "golden pyramid," "blue egg," "crystal wall," "black cube" or "transparent cone" may be employed, but personal forms can also be developed. In each case, the magicians must picture themselves located inside the symbol. Some people may prefer to make each exercise shorter and perform it more often. In either case you will, little by little, discover which symbol makes you feel most secure, so safe that you would even go to sleep inside it. From now on, you should use this symbol for your own personal protection, carrying it day and night with a sort of "second attention," further reinforcing the

Protection Symbol

image before falling asleep or starting deep relaxation and most especially in times of threat or insecurity.

Sometimes this personal protection symbol has to be changed, but this is rare. The most important thing is to be entirely sure which is "your" symbol and which is not. Do not make this decision merely on logical grounds; do it with gut-feeling—this is the only sure way. Try to give your protective symbol more and more substance, and dig it more and more deeply into your soul.

If you have difficulty with visualizing or imagining, the following additional exercise will help:

Seat yourself two feet away from a blank wall, a white sheet or similar screen, and stare at it with wide-open eyes without blinking. Eyeglasses and contact lenses must first be removed. As your vision starts to flicker, or if the eyes start to water (this is normal and completely harmless), try to "see" your symbol of protection on the outer "screen" or try to perceive it by whichever sense you prefer. Once you have succeeded—even a vague outline will do to start with—you close your eyes and "suck" the symbol into your inner eye. If you do not succeed, open your eyes again and start from the beginning. Once you can hold the symbol clearly before you, let it expand until it completely surrounds your body. Now continue as described above. Sometimes it needs a bit of patience to get the desired result, but if you follow this advice it will probably not take as long as you expect.

Strengthening the Pelvis 1

(For male and female sex magicians alike)

I hardly need explain why the pelvis is so important in sex magic. According to the traditions of Taoist Yoga, Tantra and Kundalini Yoga, we assume that the sexual *magis* slumbers in the coccyx area or "root chakra." When it comes to knowledge of bodily exercises, we have to admit that the Eastern cultures were way ahead of our ancestors, and we are quite happy to call on this knowledge.

Start the exercise in a seated position, the back straight but not tense. Like any "asana" or Yoga posture, this one should be "firm and comfortable," in the words of Patanjali. Later, once you have mastered this exercise, you can and should perform it in any position, even when walking or climbing the stairs.

Breathe in deeply and calmly, taking care to fill the lower lungs.

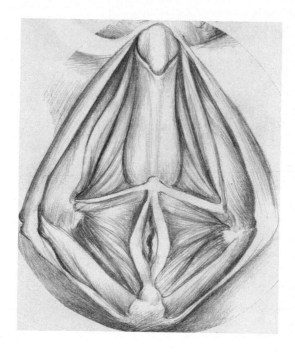

Perineum

Women tend to neglect stomach breathing, whereas men are more inclined to neglect chest breathing. A detailed description of correct breathing technique will be given later. In the beginning it is enough to breathe deeply and slowly without strain, following your own natural rhythm.

After about ten cycles, draw in your perineum every time you *breathe in*. The perineum is the point located between your excretory organs. You may support this process by imagining that the skin of the perineum presses against the base of the spinal cord. When *breathing out* you relax the perineum again. Repeat this about six times and then return to deep breathing *without* contracting the perineum. After about ten breaths repeat the whole exercise again. Ten breaths without contracting the perineum, six breaths with contraction of the perineum, ten breaths without contracting the perineum; this is one complete cycle. Repeat this cycle three times.

The number of breaths and muscle contractions in the perineum are only suggested as an average. Be careful not to overstrain yourself, especially in the beginning. Should you, for example, find that the muscles of your perineum weaken after the fourth contraction or even that they become painful, just relax by breathing without contracting the perineum and then discontinue the exercise. With older people this can frequently happen. In this case it is advisable to perform a shorter version of the exercise six to eight times a day and then increase the length gradually over the weeks and months. Otherwise it is enough to practice three times a day.

Warning: Do not use force in this or other such exercise. Do not struggle and strain—this has nothing to do with competitive sport! It is better to halve the duration of certain exercises and perform them twice as often than to force yourself.

Once you have mastered this exercise, you can perform it inconspicuously in everyday life. You will no longer need to include the longer phase of calm breathing; just contract the perineum slowly when breathing in and loosen it again when breathing out. However, the exercise "Strengthening of the Pelvis 2," given later, is much better suited to inconspicuous use in everyday life.

You may well discover that this exercise improves your entire bearing if practiced regularly. You will acquire a much straighter way of walking; bad posture is eliminated or at least relieved; the muscles of the pelvis and abdomen are strengthened; men may find problems with the prostate gland remedied; women may note a strengthening of the uterus; and the etheric energies will be flowing more freely in the body. Your sexual vigour will also be considerably increased. And this is only the beginning of our exercise program!

Breathing 1

Breathing is particularly important in sex magic, as it is in Yoga. If you have already mastered "pranayama," or Yogic breathing, you may skip this exercise. Unfortunately, we cannot treat the whole complicated area of pranayama here. It should be enough to point out that, on one hand, our breathing reflects our emotional state, while on the other hand our emotions can be influenced by breathing. Most importantly, by means of breathing we channel and direct the etheric energies in the body. Breathing is our number one contact to the outer world. It is even more important than eating or drinking. Breathing tells us whether a creature is dead or alive.

The average Westerner breathes much too shallowly and

quickly; the lungs do not get enough air, the supply of oxygen is hindered—and fear and depression frequently result. The Greek word *psyche*, which we translate as "soul," means the same as "wind" or "breath." Etymologically, breathing and psychic well-being are deeply linked.

In the beginning it makes more sense to concentrate on deep breathing rather than on exotic breath rhythms which strain the system. These have their value, and Yoga teaches numerous different breathing techniques, but they are better left for the advanced practitioner. Our first exercise therefore aims to develop the so-called "Yoga-breathing" before we get on to the subtleties of breath lore.

Phase 1

For the first few times, perform this exercise standing upright. Keep your feet at shoulder's width apart, your arms relaxed at your sides. It is better if you perform this exercise naked in front of a big mirror, because you can then study the phases visually and more easily detect mistakes.

Breathe for a while completely normally without influencing the breathing in any way. Your mouth is closed, so the breathing is done through your nose—even if you have a cold!

Phase 2

Now place both your hands, one over the other, on your abdomen immediately below the navel. Take a breath and try to feel your abdomen press against your hands. Do not consciously distend your stomach muscles; the movement must come about *by taking in air rather than by muscular force.* Now *breathe out,* still pressing your hands *gently* against your abdomen until *all* of the air has escaped. One cycle lasts for five such complete breaths. Perform at least four cycles in a row, allowing a short break of three to four normal breaths between each cycle.

Women usually women have more difficulty with this kind of breathing than men because they are more inclined towards chest than abdominal breathing. In this case, they would be advised to persist longer with this *second phase* until it becomes second nature.

Phase 3

Now place both your hands, one over the other, on your chest. Proceed exactly as in the *second phase, but this time breath mainly from the chest.* If possible, avoid any movement of the abdominal muscles.

Men usually have more difficulty with this kind of breathing because they are more inclined to breathe from their stomachs. In this case, male readers are advised to pay more attention to this *third phase.*

Phase 4

Still standing upright, breathe *first with your abdomen.* When it is comfortably full, continue breathing in, but now direct the air into your chest area. Once your chest is comfortably expanded, you will find that there is now a little more room in your abdomen; continue breathing in and fill this space with fresh air. Finally, with the expansion of your ribs, you will have a little more space in your chest; complete your breath by filling this space. All this happens with *one smooth in-breath.* When *breathing out,* you follow the reversed sequence: first release most of the air from the chest, then from the abdomen, then empty the rest of the air from your chest and finally empty your abdomen completely. Contract the abdomen as much as possible without strain. Imagine that you want to press the area from waist to the ribs back onto the spinal cord.

For clarity, both phases are summarized once again:

Breathing in: abdomen—chest—abdomen—chest
Breathing out: chest—abdomen—chest—abdomen

One cycle consists of six such full breaths. Practice with at least four cycles, taking a short break of three to four ordinary breaths between each cycle. You can begin to manage without these breaks as you get used to breathing this way, which won't take long if your lungs are healthy.

Basically this breathing is a caterpillar-like wave motion which ensures thorough respiration. It prepares you for the fifth phase, *which is the last level of this exercise.*

Phase 5

This phase is identical with the *last phase* apart from one difference: *when breathing in, the perineum is contracted, and when breathing out it is loosened again*—as you learned to do in the exercise "Strengthening of Pelvis 1." Follow *the same cycles as in the fourth phase.*

There is another version of Yogic breathing which you probably will not find even in specialist literature. In this, the muscles of the perineum are not contracted in the breathing in phase, but the muscles of the abdomen are slightly tensed. This tension seems at first paradoxical because you are supposed to be breathing into the abdomen, but, if you try it, you will find that a slight contraction of the perineum automatically follows and increases the breathing capacity. In my experience the first version is preferable, but the latter might be useful for people with prostate problems or weak vaginal or abdominal muscles or who suffer from rupture.

In the long run this exercise not only leads to better respiration and revitalizing of the organism, it also strengthens weak abdominal muscles in both sexes and may well help with potency and orgasm problems.

To achieve these benefits it is not enough to perform the exercise only once or twice a day. Deep breathing must become instinctive. If you are used to breathing in a shallow, staccato fashion, you now have to re-educate your body, and this can only be done by continual practice. At first this may seem hard, but practice proves exactly the opposite; deep breathing is the *natural* way to breathe, and it is so beneficial that the body very quickly grows accustomed to it. This may take a few days, at most some weeks, but, once you have succeeded, you will wonder how you ever breathed differently!

The psychological effects of deep breathing are also remarkable: calmness, relaxation, increased concentration and heightened vitality often result. What is more, the effect is noticed and attracts other people around you. You become a center of calmness, able to stand apart from the hurly-burly of everyday life. Of course, breathing alone will not make you master of all life's problems, but it is astonishing how little it takes to make the whole of reality appear in a completely different light.

Strengthening the Pelvis 2

Strictly speaking, this exercise not only strengthens the pelvis, but it also arouses the sexual *magis* and directs it to the will of the magician. It has the added advantage that it can be performed anytime and anywhere.

Contract your perineum about five or six times in rapid succession. Make these contractions as quickly as possible, then relax completely and repeat the exercise again after a quarter of an hour at the earliest. You can do this standing, sitting, lying—even when walking or running. Whether sitting in a bus or attending a top-level government reception, nobody will notice you practicing—even during conversation.

You should practice this exercise several times a day for at least a year; the more often, the better the result. After some days, it will become second nature and you will perform these contractions almost unconsciously.

In moments of great danger or terror people often contract the muscles of the perineum automatically. This is a natural protective mechanism; apart from the biochemical activation of the glands and other neurophysiological effects, the focus on the perineum has the advantage of "centering" one's attention. The next time you are in danger or suffering from fear, contract your perineum consciously and observe how it calms, or rather "clears," your mind. In combination with other techniques given here, it will often be enough to solve your immediate problems, or at least cut them down to size.

Breathing 2

This exercise is an example of how we try to combine as many techniques as possible to minimize the time and effort necessary for each exercise. To that end, this exercise will be expanded later by adding further elements. The form introduced here is known in Hatha Yoga as the "bellows breath." It combines a strengthening of the pelvis and abdomen with a thorough oxygenation of the system; it also builds up considerable *magis*—especially important in sex magic—furthermore, it improves clear-sightedness. When the breath is maintained over a longer period, it results in hyperventilation of the brain and can induce trance.

This exercise involves a more rapid and vigorous rhythm, like a bellows. You contract the perineum as you breathe in, as before, and loosen it again with each exhalation. Imagine that your perineum is a sort of energy-pump like the heart (Taoist Yoga actually calls a point close above the perineum the "coccyx pump"). Do not overstrain yourself, because this exercise, if performed correctly, takes a great deal of energy at first. Later on, it is the other way around; the exercise will become invigorating and strengthening. Do make sure that the in/out breath and contracting/loosening are in time with each other.

Don't bother to count your breaths; just time yourself for a cycle of five to ten minutes before resting. Do not perform this exercise more than three times a day to start with, and take a break between each cycle that is at least twice as long as the cycle itself.

Warning: People with heart problems or damaged lungs should perform this exercise with the utmost care (ideally under medical supervision). If there is any doubt, do not attempt it. The same precaution would apply to any exercise which stimulates the circulation and breathing.

Once again let me stress that you should never overdo these exercises! Pay attention to any discomfort when you perform them too eagerly or too long, and recognize it as a signal to finish the exercise and take a good break. Unfortunately, no book can replace personal tuition, but these tips should be sufficient for practical work.

Do not forget that you will eventually have to develop your own exercises to suit your own individual strengths and weaknesses. The examples given here are only guidelines. Should you ever feel competent to pass on your knowledge to others as teacher or "guru," you will do it in your own personal way shaped by your own experience. You are your own best teacher, and the same will be true of your disciples. But a great deal of experience—both failures and successes—will have to be encountered until that obvious platitude becomes a vital truth! Be eager to experiment. Say what you like about sex magicians; you cannot accuse them of being boring! Give your imagination free rein; only then will the magic within you and your environment become *alive*. Start *to live within magic—* instead of having to struggle to get *into* magic.

Strengthening the Sexual *Magis* for Male Sex Magicians

The following practices serve partly to strengthen the pelvis and partly to aid the general consolidation and circulation of the abdominal muscles. Furthermore, it is quite beneficial for the prostate gland and for increasing sexual potency in general.

1. Douching the Testicles

After a shower or a bath, spray your genitals with water as cold as possible until you feel the scrotum contract from the cold. Pay special attention to direct the water stream up to meet the perineum. Should you suffer from potency problems, this exercise has a very helpful effect, especially if repeated up to four or six times a day.

If you want to be really thorough, you can take a "half-bath" as frequently practiced in India, before each meal and before going to bed. In this, the legs below the knees, the arms below the elbows, the genitals and the perineum all are given a cold shower. Furthermore, allow first a trickle, later on a small stream of cold water to flow down the spine; splash cold water onto the crown of your head and onto your neck; fill your mouth with cold water and finally splash water about a dozen times into your open eyes. This sounds rather long and drawn out, but it is simpler than it sounds—the whole thing should only take about three minutes. Of course, circumstances don't always allow you to shower six times a day, but do it as often as you can. You will soon notice the physical benefits of the half-bath: more efficient cooling of the body, increased vitality and potency, better digestion, stabile circulation and less risk of heart attack. On a psychological level, the half-bath makes you more balanced, more concentrated and more calm, and it particularly helps meditation; so you should ideally take a half-bath before you start this practice. Furthermore, along with other exercises given here, it noticeably stimulates the sexual *magis*.

2. Washing the Penis

Whenever possible after urinating, male magicians should wash the penis with water as cold as possible. By doing so, they flush out harmful uric acid that can lead to premature aging and loss of vitality, and they also improve physical hygiene. Contracting the muscles to eject the last drops of urine further helps to promote sexual vigor.

Unfortunately, not many public toilets and workplace lavatories provide suitable washing facilities. In this case, you could carry a discrete plastic water bottle with you. Yogins and Tantricists perform this exercise regularly because they know its great value.

3. The Langota

If, after all these washing instructions, you now hear that we also recommend wearing a loincloth, you might think we have gone a bit too far! We are not trying to impose Indian culture; we simply aim to take from the East what may be most useful for Westerners without having to surrender our own cultural integrity. Anyway, it is up to you whether you follow our recommendations or not!

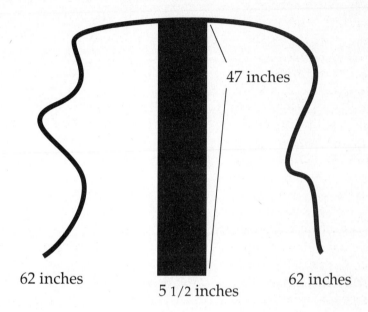

47 inches

62 inches

5 1/2 inches

62 inches

Langota

The *langota*, also spelled "lungota," is the Indian variant of the loincloth and is a very practical and hygienic garment. Usually it is made of thin cotton so that you can also wear underpants with it if you set great store by convention. When fully dressed, the langota is invisible anyway. Appearance and measurements of the langota, together with instructions on how to wear it, are given in the illustration.

This loincloth has the advantage that the penis is supported vertically and the testicles are held firmly without pressure. This immediately results in improved posture. Furthermore, carrying the penis in this manner is extremely helpful for controlling sexuality: ascetics find that the langota helps them to sublimate the libido; sexually active people will discover that it increases sexual endurance because this position slightly desensitizes the penis through the course of time to give greater control. Men with a hernia, prostate weakness and potency problems are especially advised to wear the langota

a) Belt part has to wind round the belly several times and is tied at the front in a loop.

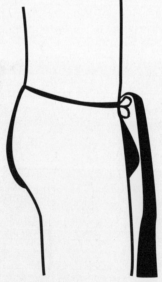

b) The main part of the loincloth is drawn between your legs in front of your body and is pulled through behind the strap; the penis lies upwards against your body; your testicles are pressed slightly downwards.

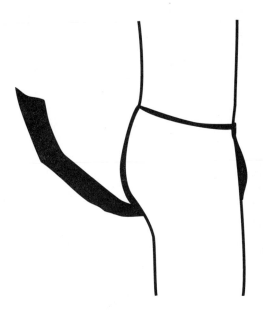

c) The loincloth is drawn through your legs towards the back again.

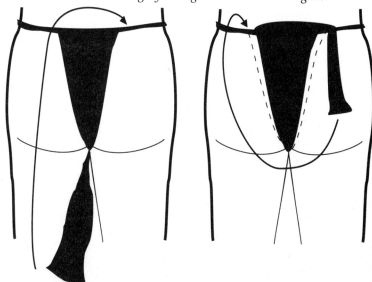

d) and e) The loincloth is pulled through the strap several times and eventually se-cured to a snug fit (do not knot it!).

f) The completed Langota

4. Circumcision

There is much debate—in the East and in the West—about the value of circumcision. Nevertheless, research has shown that the incidence of penile cancer is significantly higher among non-circumcised Hindus than among circumcised Moslems. Also, women with circumcised partners suffer significantly less cancer of the uterus than those who have intercourse with non-circumcised partners. From a hygienic point of view, everything favors circumcision, because bacteria, sebum and secretion quickly gather under the foreskin and can cause problems if there is inadequate hygiene.

In my opinion, circumcision has specific sexual advantages, too. It reduces the oversensitivity which causes premature ejaculation and increases the duration of the sexual act by increasing control. For this reason in particular, circumcision is highly valued in Eastern countries and in the Islamic-Semitic world. The operation itself does not hurt and causes few problems.

Extended sexual stamina is not prized purely for athletic reasons but rather because prolonged sexual arousal makes for better magic—simply because there is more time to do it. In addition, sexual *magis* is greatly magnified by lengthy arousal. If you are in doubt, it is worth discussing the matter with circumcised men, or reading further about this subject, to help with your decision.

Strengthening the Sexual *Magis* for Female Sex Magicians

The following exercises are recommended to strengthen pelvic and vaginal muscles, to increase psychological well-being, to achieve more conscious control of sexual *magis*, and finally to strengthen the sexual *magis* itself.

1. Rinsing the Perineum

This is similar to the "testicle douche" (see above). For female magicians, the perineal-shower and half-bath have the same positive effect: increasing the circulation of the abdominal area and strengthening the muscles of vagina etc.

2. Washing after Urinating

This is similar to the way a man washes his penis (see above). Women have to apply cold water more accurately to ensure contraction of the muscles and ejection of the harmful uric acid, which can also accelerate aging.

3. Abdominal Gymnastics

Here we include exercises which tone up the abdominal organs and muscles; for example, "leg raises" while lying on one's back and Yoga exercises like the "plow" and the "half spine twist" etc. You will find more information in any good book on women's gymnastics or Hatha Yoga.

Women who have given birth to several children should pay particular attention to this part of their body, because childbirth tends to slacken the muscles and, according to Chinese meridian lore, cause leakage of *chi* or sexual *magis*. This is even more applicable during menstruation.

Secondary Comment

On the subject of *menstruation and sexual magic,* the following needs to be said: nearly all cultures have specific taboos concerning

Woman Doing Half-Spine Twist

the menstrual phase of women. Menstruating women are often se-
cluded from communal religious ceremonies, sometimes even
spending the time in separate isolation huts. In general, they are
considered to be "impure," whereas, in reality, most women are at
the peak of their sex-magical power during menstruation. This is
precisely how the taboo has arisen; since these powers are rarely
handled in a controlled manner—even among primitive peoples—
and since so few female or male shamans have the relevant knowl-

edge, most patriarchal societies are simply not capable of handling such "bundles of power."

Experience of Western sex magic shows that menstruating women are an immense source of power in a ritual. Male sex magicians should rejoice in the opportunity to work with a menstruating female magician, because this can multiply many times the efficacy of sex-magical operations.

Conversally, many female magicians have to struggle with ingrained prudishness and feelings of inferiority before they can use these energies to best advantage. Luckily, the women's liberation movement has done much valuable pioneer work in this respect. Woe betide the careless male who calls down the fury of a "bleeding goddess"! Female sex magicians should therefore, apart from practicing the exercises recommended here, meditate deeply upon the significance of menstruation if they really want to employ their sex-magic powers in the optimum way.

4. The Dynamic Dance

Men can profit greatly from dance, despite the fact that it is far more popular with women than men in our culture. This may be just a question of education and convention, but here in the West the female seems far more drawn to rhythmic physical movement than the male. This is illustrated by the fact that ballet companies have trouble recruiting good male dancers, whereas qualified female dancers are much more easily found.

However, what we are recommending here is neither ballet nor ballroom dancing as such. Some everyday forms of dance such as Brazilian samba or flamenco are well suited for our purposes although they could count as ballroom dances. Equally recommended are jazz dancing, all African dances and Oriental belly dancing, which has become very fashionable during the last few years. Belly dancing in particular is a superb discipline which helps to strengthen the pelvis and abdomen as well as increasing the general libido.

For magical purposes, it is not so much the actual type of dance as the way it is done. The point is not so much to perfect certain steps and rhythms as it is to develop feeling and physical control not directed by the rational mind. Dance was always considered a holy art in temples and ritual places, from the simple roundel and circle dance to the highly complicated dance forms of India or Thailand. Indian mythology presents creation itself as a dance. Just think of Shiva's *Rasa Lila*. But Kali-Dhurga and other deities also maintain the cycle of creation, death and reincarnation by dancing. Everywhere in the world, there are ritual cult dances—in Siberia, Africa, Australia, among the Indians of North America and of course in the Afro-American Creole cults of Latin America and the Caribbean. Europe, too, has a rich dance culture, which stretches from north to south and from west to east. Not the least important reason for this is the immense *trance-inducing* quality of dance, but what matters to us now is rather the increase of body consciousness.

It is best to dance on your own, unobserved and, ideally, in front of a large mirror, although this is not essential. You should not be judgmental about your movement but rather develop a feeling for how you move. Pay special heed to the movements of your pelvis and legs, in swinging your hips, twisting your knees, moving your buttocks etc. Start with rhythmical up-tempo music until you are warm; then add some calmer pieces of music more suited for meditative and slinky motion.

Watching African women dancing, one is amazed at their blatantly sexual movements. This is even more remarkable when, as I once observed in Senegal during a national holiday, it happens in front of a luxury hotel in the middle of a city. All the more surprising was the fact that the dancers were elegantly dressed ladies from the highest echelons. Decked in their traditional garments, they danced in front of their husbands, who were dressed in an equally exclusive manner but in European style. These dances left nothing to the imagination! We Europeans often have to struggle to relearn this naturalness toward the body and sexuality because religion, education and environment have thoroughly suppressed it for us. But the point is not to succumb to illusions about "happy and noble savages" nor to give up one's own cultural identity—but rather to experience it more fully.

For this reason you should perform your ritual dances only on your own or in a small group of like-minded people who dance along with you. Try it on your own until you have lost your inhibitions. When possible dance naked, or at least in loose, comfortable garments, certainly without a bra, even if you fear pain from a well-developed bust. Any such discomfort will stop after a few practice sessions, as soon as your body takes control. Make the dance into a symbolic courtship, an act of copulation. Contract and relax the perineum during the dance. Let your abdomen, your clitoris, your vagina "talk" and let them move of their own initiative without conscious control. You will discover that you can become fully aroused even without a partner—an effect unknown to most Western men. When dancing try to feel every fiber of your body; follow the flow of energy and direct it by visualization into the abdominal area. Dance as long as you want but at least until it has made you sweat a little. Don't get into a full trance, but dance yourself into a gnostic or magical trance if you feel like it.

Should you be sexually aroused by the dance, don't be too hasty to relieve the sexual tension immediately afterwards by masturbation or intercourse. Rather, aim to increase this inner pressure by consciously experiencing and exploring your sexual energy without using those outlets.

This certainly does not mean enforced abstinence! Rather just let several hours pass before further sexual activity. You will probably find that your sexuality does not suffer, but rather gains, in power and ecstasy. This can be very helpful for psychological frigidity and orgasm problems, about which more detail will appear later.

After a while, you can go on to use the dance ritually and magically—providing that you have the necessary knowledge. For example, when working with "power animals," by using erotic energy to charge a sigil or assuming god-forms—not only the static ones of ceremonial magic but even more so the god-forms in motion, who have their own steps, ways of walking and rhythms. Before going on to such practices, however, you should dance for some weeks just for the sake of it in order to develop freer access to bodily feelings.

5. The Static Dance

Perform this exercise as often as you can. It is relatively inconspicuous and may even be performed at work; for example, on the toilet. Sufficient practice is, however, conditional on your already having a well-developed feeling for the energy of dance. Until you have practiced the dynamic dance, this exercise is completely ineffective.

Basically you dance as before, but now you minimize your *outer movements* and direct the sense of movement *inwards* as much as you

can. Seen from outside, it looks more like shaking or quivering—
something which may also occur with the dynamic dance once a
certain depth of trance is reached. In the beginning, you may just
tremble spasmodically with your whole body without much feeling
of deeper motion. But little by little you will master this hard-to-
describe technique and even feel that you can dance ecstatically
"inside" while appearing completely calm and motionless on the
outside! It is a combination of inner muscular awareness and
developed imagination which can be experienced but not really
described.

Deep Relaxation—Level 2

This exercise is for male and female sex magicians alike. It is an
advance on level one of deep relaxation, so that level should be mastered before you go on to level two.

Begin as you did with deep relaxation level one, while locating
yourself within your magical protective symbol. This time, instead
of abandoning yourself to the relaxation, you concentrate all your
sexual *magis* in the hypogastric region or "Hara," about three fingers' width below the navel. The Hara, also called the "earth center
of Man" (Dürckheim), is the body's center of gravity, the place
where the "inner center" is built and *sensed*. Asiatic martial arts pay
particular attention to the way that the male or female fighter
should stand "in the Hara" or act "from the Hara." If you are unfa-
miliar with this concept, you should read the relevant literature or,
even better, practice the Budo or Wu-Shu arts themselves. The information given here is just enough to get you started with your practice.

How do you concentrate the sexual *magis* in the Hara? This begins as an act of imagination, but soon you realize that the procedure has nothing to do with "fantasy" but is a real, objective
occurrence.

Start to visualize it as follows: in your relaxed state, direct the
warmth into the perineal region. Once it feels really warm, draw the
sexual *magis* up the spine until you reach the Hara point. Do not
force anything; you may only succeed after some weeks, so practice
patiently and, most importantly, with a *completely relaxed body!* Do
not try to aid it with muscle contractions or forced breathing; on the
contrary, you should breath as calmly as possible and more shal-

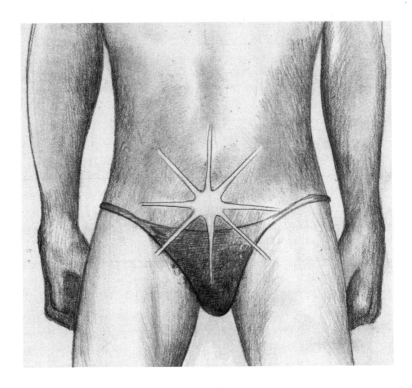

Position of Hara

lowly as you relax. It is a mixture of physical and mental manipulation of energy. Once you feel a bundled, concentrated warmth in the abdominal region, you will know that you have succeeded. It is not enough to pretend that the warmth is in the Hara; *it is essential that the sexual* magis *really does rise.* This exercise prepares for the "Lesser Energy Orbit" of acupuncture and Taoist Yoga, which will be covered later in more depth.

If you have diligently practiced your perineal contractions, you will find level two of our sex magical deep relaxation quite easy. Even if you have immediate success, you should still perform this exercise for several weeks before you go on to level three. Care now will pay off later during the work with the meridians. The intensity of your energy accumulation says a lot about your present state of vitality.

Sexual Delaying and Accelerating Techniques 1

As sex magicians it is important that orgasm does not catch us by surprise. The following techniques are mainly to be used at times when needed, but you should initially experiment with them so you can call on this experience whenever you really need it.

Delaying an Orgasm

Many women are disappointed by their male partners' problems with premature ejaculation. In general, men reach orgasm quicker than women, but this is not necessarily the case. There are also plenty of women who "come too early," but it is less of a problem because women find it easier to go on helping their partner to achieve satisfaction than do those men who limit themselves to purely phallic sex.

Right from the start, sex magic helps to remedy this problem, because the very act of concentrating on magic helps to delay orgasm. But if you still have problems with achieving orgasm too early, two main techniques can be suggested: concentration and mantra.

It is worth mentioning also that the previously explained techniques and practices—showering the testicles, circumcision, wearing the langota, etc.—can also be very helpful for delaying orgasm. Further tips will follow in the category "impotence/frigidity."

1. Concentration Exercises

Concentrate on something else whenever the orgasm threatens to overwhelm you. There are plenty of jokes about porno stars who think about their income tax returns or do complex mental arithmetic to calm themselves down at the critical moment. You could do likewise, but we want to remain here in the frame of magic and so recommend direct concentration onto magical aims. Apart from that, there is little to add about the actual procedure. But do note that magical concentration during the sexual act is not purely a *diversion*, or "stop-gap" solution to a problem but a valuable act in its own right. You might even get the impression that magical concentration becomes so important that it is difficult to maintain sexual excitement! But this, like so many other things, is just a matter of practice.

The simplest method is concentration on the sexual *magis* gathered in the Hara, as described above in level two of the deep relaxation, but without the initial relaxation itself. This concentration has the advantage that, apart from its orgasm-delaying effect, the sexual *magis* can be brought under better control for the sex magic act.

Closely related to Tantra is the invocatory approach to sexuality, which will be dealt with more in the next chapter. With this in mind, many sex magicians concentrate on invoking their tutelary deity or other desired power during intercourse. This may seem a bit strange at first but, if one believes that magic works best when integrated into everyday life, then it is clear that one should use magical practices whenever possible. Sex magicians like Aleister Crowley maintain that *every* act should be a magical act. In fact, Crowley's sex-magical diaries, especially those from his time in New York, prove that the Master Therion ritualized all his sexual activity as part of a sex-magic operation. Precise ways of using invocatory techniques will be shown in the next chapter.

It is also quite useful is to concentrate on etheric energies—including of course the already mentioned perception of the sexual *magis;* but the sex magician can equally concentrate on the magical vibration in the room, on protective symbols, magical glyphs or sigils, etc.

2. Mantras

Independently of the above-mentioned concentrations, the sex magician can fix attention on a mantra to delay orgasm. For the moment, it is irrelevant whether the mantras make sense or not. It has to be said, though, that mantras in general are valued by magicians because of their trance-inducing qualities. For now, it is largely a matter of taste whether you use a mantra from the Sanskrit tradition or use Hebrew phonetics. Feel free to experiment with them, and you will detect the differences and qualities of energy yourself. The repertoire of possible mantras is huge; the following are only suggestions.

Om, Hram, Hrim, Hrum, Om Mani Padme Hum, Lam, Vam,
Ham, Ram, Soham, Om Namo Shivaya
(Indian/Tibetan)

Ialdabaoth, Iao, Abrasax, Zasas Zasas Satanata Zasas
Io Pan Io Pan Io Pan Pan Pan
(Hellenic/Gnostic)

Yod-he-vau-he, Adonai, Ehieih, Agla, Al,
Elohim, Elohim Tzabaoth
(Hebrew)

Hagal, Tyr Tyr, Man, Fa, Ur, Sig, Is, Laf
(Armanic Runic tradition)

Shiki Fu I Ku Ku Fu Shiki Shiki Soku Ze Ku Ku Soku Ze Shiki
(Japanese)

Lah Illa Lahu, Alam, Alamas, Alar, Alamar, Ta Ha, Tasam, Jas,
Kaha Ja As, Cham, Cham Asak
(Islamic/Sufi tradition)

Beyond these, any magician and shaman will learn to build up his or her own "words of power"; for example, using the *mantrical spell method* of sigil magic.

But what does one do if the main problem is not so much premature orgasm as overlong excitement without orgasm? The next section will attend to this question.

Accelerating the Orgasm

The problem of not achieving orgasm despite strong sexual excitement mainly occurs with women, but is also known to many men. It can mostly be cured by regulated breathing, skilled muscle control and faster movements during sexual intercourse; that is, unless the problem concerns frigidity or some basic incapacity to orgasm.

A simple start is just to relax and ease the body—we come back later to psychological relaxation and "switching off the intellect." Sometimes a small break of about half an hour works wonders. Also helpful is calm, relaxed breathing, as far this is possible during strong sexual excitement. Occasionally it is enough just to want to *avoid* an orgasm—in order to produce it!

First, concentrate your breathing on the genital region and then try to move the sexual magis down into your legs and feet. Pay less attention to genital stimulation, but rather give yourself over to the feeling of warmth and comfort which will soon flow through your body.

Should an occasional inability to reach orgasm be caused by sexual satiation, abstain from sex for a while or restrict yourself to intercourse without orgasm. This can rapidly solve the problem.

If your excitement is not strong enough, it may be connected for a number of reasons with the relationship between you and your partner. We cannot go into all of them here. Simply provide more stimulation, whether physically (for example by masturbatory enhancement), or mentally (by specific fantasy). Quicker, stronger, more ecstatic movements, not specifically directed at reaching orgasm, may also arouse the excitement faster towards climax. The most important thing is not at any cost to concentrate directly on your desire for orgasm! Rather please your body and let it decide for itself when to peak.

Rhythmic contraction of the muscles of the pelvis and genital region is also helpful. If this is done with a pumping action similar to the contraction of the perineum—another useful practice—then you should be careful to take longer rest breaks. A change of position can also help, as well as experimenting with novel sexual practices and games.

We cannot go into all the possibilities here; they would fill a book by themselves. You will find further tips in later sections which also touch on this subject, but if you want to go deeper into the purely physical, non-magical aspects, you should read the relevant specialist literature now widely available.

What to Do About Impotence and Frigidity

Although orgasm plays an important role in sexual magic, the ability to achieve orgasm is not an absolute condition for success. Every sex magician, male or female, however, should aim to regain the ability and overcome any psychological blocks that nearly always lie behind such problems. The next few pages pave the way towards *psychological practice for sex magic*.

At the root of this inability, you usually find deep fears and trauma, although sometimes the cure is purely physical—diet, body movement etc. With men, impotence is often a reaction to the mostly unconscious fear of women and pressure to perform. The reasons for female frigidity are less well researched, but similar themes are found. In both cases there is *fear* of orgasm, described as "fear of flying" or "fear of letting go."

For many people, the moment of orgasm is the only time they can open up completely and "let themselves go." This makes it a moment of vulnerability, with fear of losing one's grip and becoming a helpless victim. The worst aspect of such fear is that the person affected is nearly always completely unconscious of it and will strongly deny it. A person who has tried everything possible to overcome impotence or frigidity, who has run from psychiatrist to psychiatrist and tried every psychopharmacologic drug and sexual position, still cannot see that, deep down, he or she does not want to have an orgasm because of subconscious fear of losing control.

We cannot hope to solve such problems in these few pages. There is no instant cure in any case. However, working with magical protection may help to demolish unconscious fear. More generally, the techniques described here do help to harmonize one's physical and psychological needs.

Furthermore, one has to differentiate between general impotence or frigidity and specifically hetero-, auto- *or* homoerotic forms. Many otherwise normal men and women are incapable of orgasm in one particular set of circumstances. No one is surprised if, for example, a heterosexual cannot be aroused by a homosexual partner or vice versa. But what of those who cannot successfully masturbate? Or those who can masturbate but cannot achieve orgasm with a partner? Masturbation in particular carries a heavy burden of guilt, thanks to education and religion. Only 50 years ago, it was equated with sodomy and outlawed. But other types of sexuality can also be "inoculated" against and may therefore lead to repulsion, loathing and inability to reach orgasm.

Whatever the form of impotence or frigidity, the same basic rule applies; namely, that the causes usually lie very deep and the persons affected can seldom detect them without help from others. Nevertheless, there are two techniques which can often prove very helpful.

The first is very simple: abstinence! In cases where the problem arises because of too much pressure to "perform," persistent sexual abstinence can work like a magic potion. This applies especially to men; frigid women are more likely to have lengthy spells without sex simply because they don't feel like it, but they too can profit greatly from conscious abstinence, deliberately holding back until they begin to miss making love.

The second method consists of busy sexual activity while deliberately *avoiding orgasm*. This may be done autoerotically, hetero- or homoerotically, with special attention paid to any specifically difficult areas. Depending on how deep the problem is, you should avoid orgasm in this way for at least three to six months. During these months, deep relaxation, particularly level two, should be assiduously practiced, together with perinal contractions and the "lesser" energy circulation (to be described shortly).

The term "impotence" is often misused. In general it is used to describe inability to enjoy orgasm as well as inability to have an erection. In strict medical terms, however, four types of impotence are distinguished.

1. *Impotentia coeundi:* incapacity for erection and/or ejaculation. This may have genital-organic causes; for example, tumors, abnormal smallness of the genitals or abnormalities of the foreskin. Even general organic diseases may cause *impotentia coeundi;* for example, diabetes, paralysis or obesity.

Another reason can be long-term poisoning with alcohol or nicotine, narcotics like morphine and cocaine, or lead and hydrocarbons, and such glandular disorders as Basedow, Addison or Cushing obesity may also be a cause.

Relevant psychological causes include, besides those already mentioned, sexual neurasthenia and—surprise surprise!—*hypochondria*.

Relative and *paralytic* impotence are less serious forms. The first means a dislike of a certain partner or, very importantly, a certain milieu; the second means exhaustion of the erection center through excessive sexual activity. Medicine even recognizes *"professional" impotence* as a male weakness caused by mental pressure and overexertion. It is frequently found among artists and scientists as well as among businessmen, professors and politicians.

The very description of these causes gives clues as to ways of curing this trouble, but do not hesitate to ask for professional advice on these matters if need be.

2. *Impotentia concupiscentiae* means lack of sexual desire in general. With women, it is often the basis of frigidity.

3. *Impotentia generandi* is sterility. In the case of women, the *impotentia generandi* means inability to carry a child through to the full term, as opposed to full sterility, which means fertilization itself is impossible. We need not deal with *impotentia generandi* in this book.

4. *Impotentia satisfactionis* means the "unsatisfying impotence" of

men where ejaculations occur but orgasm does not. This is nearly always caused by emotional disturbances.

It is striking that the *Pschyrembel* (251st edition), the German clinical dictionary, our source for this information, comments laconically on frigidity as "sexual coldness of women, incapability of reaching an orgasm." The reason for this short explanation is largely because of less research into female frigidity. Women, even more so than men, tend not to speak openly about certain problems. The other reason is that some forms of impotence, as listed above, apply equally to men and women alike.

Our final comment on male impotence is that its importance is often exaggerated. Even without a proper erection, intercourse satisfying both partners is perfectly possible because sexuality is not limited to mere penetration. Too much phallic emphasis is very one-sided and unwise. Experiment instead with oral techniques, with caressing and massaging, with mutual masturbation etc. If you remove the pressure for orgasm and compulsory ejaculation, many a problem will sort itself out.

Further hints will also be found in the section "Psychological Practice"

Deep Relaxation—Level 3

Level three of sex-magic deep relaxation leads us into Taoist and Kundalini Yoga. Its aim is to prepare us further for working with the Lesser Energy Orbit.

You proceed as in level two, directing sexual *magis* from the perineum into the spine and then up to the Hara.

Please note that we are not concerned with the so–called "chakras" in this book, and that the Hara is *not* identical to any of the chakra centers. The reason for not going into chakras is simply that there are a number of conflicting theories. Chakra lore is not absolutely necessary for understanding sex magic, and it would only complicate matters to bring them in. If, however, you already work with the chakras, please feel free to continue using them!

Having allowed the sexual *magis* to build up in the Hara for a while, now direct it further up the spine. Drive it up a little bit further every day, until, after a few weeks, you can bring it right up to the crown of your head. But do not stop there; instead of letting the energy remain at the crown as is common in Kundalini Yoga, you redirect it downwards *through the front* of your body via the roof of the mouth.

To assist this, you have to create a "bridge" by pressing the tip of your tongue lightly against the hard palate. One meridian (the Governor, the so–called *Renmai*) runs up through the spine across the crown of the head and down onto the hard palate, while another (the Functional, or *Dumai*) begins in the tip of the tongue and leads down the front of the body to the perineum. Tongue and palate therefore form a bridge for this energy. Should you forget to make this link, headaches, nausea, dizziness and hallucinations frequently result because the energy builds up in the head instead of flowing freely.

Draw the energy down the front of your body along the center line, back through the Hara and back into the perineum. Then let it rise up the spine again to continue the circuit. Don't bother initially about any special breathing; later, when you have gained more experience, you will discover how to direct and support the circulation with your breathing. When you are ready, you will feel by yourself how best to do this, so there is no need to give instructions now. The beginner is advised *not* to concentrate on breathing, because we know from experience that this is usually more a distraction than a help.

The Lesser Energy Orbit in Everyday Life and in Magic

Once you have mastered the Lesser Energy Orbit, you can practice it without the initial deep relaxation. You should practice as often as possible, because it helps you to center yourself and is excellent protection against lack of concentration, fear, insecurity, changes in mood—even against magical attacks.

Don't practice the Lesser Energy Orbit only when lying down; you should also perform it sitting, standing and even when walking. You may perform it on the bus as well as in your office, during a conversation or when watching television without attracting any attention. It is well worth practicing during unpleasant conversations with superiors, business partners etc. in order to maintain self-esteem. It can also be helpful as a cure for impotence or frigidity.

The Lesser Energy Orbit harmonizes the sexual magis like no other exercise, making it absolutely essential if you are really serious about your sex magic. It is beneficial in so many different ways that it would be silly to ignore it.

If you want to know more about the Lesser Energy Orbit, I recommend the book *Tao Yoga* by Mantak Chia.

Unfortunately, Mantak Chia does not mention one important fact: some people seem to have a polarity that is the exact reverse of the one described here. Such people may experience nausea and headaches, as well as general physical and psychological distress. These symptoms immediately disappear when the flow is reversed to go up the front and then down the spine. Should you be in any doubt, experiment with both directions of flow to find which suits you best.

The Lesser Energy Orbit is a vital prerequisite for sex magic with a partner as described in the next chapter.

Nutrition

If you have problems with orgasm, impotence, etc., you should make sure you are getting sufficient easily digested and vitality-supporting food. There are no absolute laws but just a few guidelines. Richly spiced and very salty dishes are not recommended. Make sure you get a sufficient supply of vitamins and albumen, and avoid excessive carbohydrates. Many sex magicians report that meat, as fresh and lightly cooked as possible (but *not* pork) increases sex energy; but on the other hand, there are vegetarians who claim exactly the opposite. Eventually, only you are able to find your own optimum diet through trial and error.

Overeating is generally considered to decrease sexual performance, and so are excessive alcohol, drugs and nicotine: one or two glasses of champagne may be very stimulating, whereas two bottles may well have the opposite effect. Hindus are generally forbidden to drink alcohol, so that even small amounts of wine will eroticize them in the ritual of *pancha makara* and lead to a quicker gnostic trance. On the other hand, Europeans with heavy drinking habits should refrain from drinking alcohol in connection with mild hallucinogens.

On the Subject of Aphrodisiacs

Douglas Adams, in his novel *The Restaurant at the End of the Universe*, jokes about mankind having asked only two basic questions since time immemorial: 1). What is the aim and the meaning of life? and 2). Where can I get an effective aphrodisiac?

There's many a truth spoken in jest! The fact is that the search for an effective aphrodisiac has led numerous people astray. Medicine only recognizes Spanish fly as effective, but it is so poisonous that its working dosage can actually be lethal.

The consumption of oysters, highly praised by the roué, is said to be effective with young people—at least with those suffering from paralytic or exhaustion impotence—because of the high zinc content in oyster flesh. In general, though, such recommendations are notoriously unreliable. You may swear by a dozen egg yolks in red wine, or a certain liqueur, but the vast majority of experiments suggest a placebo effect rather than any objective result from these "medicines." Mind you, there's little wrong with such "faith healing" as long as the drugs used are not actually harmful. Hormone injections may help if there is a genuine hormone deficiency, but this should not be administered without proper, professional supervision. Above all, you must avoid trivializing what could be a genuine problem by overlooking serious frigidity, impotence or a partner's sheer unwillingness, while seeking some sort of salvation in such obscure decoctions as ammonium carbonate, powdered rhino horn, testicle extracts, ect. Indeed, the psychological attitude towards sex is much more important than any aphrodisiac medicine chest.

On a different level there is, however, an undisputed aphrodisiac power in certain scents, and it is hardly surprising that you find highly skilled "odor-magicians" in the perfumery trade. One recipe for such an "irresistibility perfume" has been left to us by Aleister Crowley: musk, ambergris and civet essence blended in equal parts and applied on the scalp in such small quantities that the scent can no longer be *consciously* perceived. This is said to work wonders. Some magicians of my acquaintance can confirm the efficacy of this recipe, although there are others who disagree. Although Crowley recommends the mixture specifically for men, there is no reason why it should not suit women too: after all, musk, ambergris and civet are traditional ingredients in many well-known perfumes for women on account of their aphrodisiac qualities. Because of their relatively strong scent, they should ideally be used in very small amounts to have an effect purely on an unconscious level; this is much more effective than walking around in a cloud of perfume!

Note that aphrodisiac perfumes should use, where possible, natural substances. Genuine civet and ambergris can still be obtained at outrageous prices, but musk cannot because the musk-ox has practically died out. Those successful magicians I mentioned all without exception make do with synthetic musk in their perfume.

Finally, there is a legal drug which is said to have aphrodisiac effects, especially in the form of a liqueur. It is the Mexican plant damiana *(Turnera diffusa)* available at pharmacies and herb shops and which, when smoked in large amounts, has an effect similar to that of mild marijuana. I personally cannot confirm the aphrodisiac effect, but many sex magicians swear by it.

Recipe for Damiana Liqueur

• Soak 30g dried damiana leaves in about half a liter of good vodka and let the mixture steep for at least five days.

• Filter the fluid through a paper coffee filter into a bottle. The rest of the alcohol-soaked leaves should be soaked for another five days in about two liters of distilled or pure spring water.

• Afterwards, put the water extract through a filter and heat it to about 70°C and dissolve about 16 tablespoons of honey in it.

• Mix the alcoholic with the watery extract and leave the mixture for a further month. In the course of time the fluid will slowly clear and develop a golden color. A sediment also forms; it is harmless, but, if you like, you can decant the clear fluid and throw away the sediment.

• It is recommended to take one or two liqueur glasses full in the evening, but we naturally do not encourage regular consumption of alcohol over a longer period. The liqueur may also be taken as a sacrament in sex magical rituals.

Mexican women use damiana tea as an aphrodisiac because it stimulates the sex organs and increases sexual sensitivity. The tea is drunk one or two hours before intercourse and is said to be very effective if the damiana leaves are mixed with saw palmetto *(Serenoa repens)* in equal proportions.

The American sex magician Louis Culling, who knew Aleister Crowley personally, also recommends this tea. Let two heaped spoons of damiana steep in a cupful of water for five minutes, then allow the fluid cool before filtering it. Drink it in the evening for at least two weeks for significant results.

Damiana Smoking Mixture

To conclude the subject of damiana, here is a legal smoking mixture very popular in the United States. It has a mild aphrodisiac effect similar to that of marijuana. This mixture is called Yuba Gold, and is mainly smoked with a water pipe.

4 parts damiana leaves *(Turnera diffusa)*
4 parts scullcap herb *(Scutellaria)*
1/2 part lobelia herb *(Lobelia)*
4 parts passion flower herb *(Passiflora coerulea)*
1 part spearmint leaf *(Mentha spicata)*
(From: Richard Alan Miller, *The Magical and Ritual Use of Herbs*, pp. 15 ff.)

Damiana may also be smoked on its own, but it makes the throat feel slightly rough. To get an effect like marijuana, quite large quantities are needed. Anyway, this herb has the advantage of being completely legal, and no harmful side effects have yet been found.

Secondary Comment

Magic is largely a matter of perception: since magicians work on the so-called "etheric" level, the perceived effects of magic are often subtle. To judge the success and the failures of magic, we first have to know what to look for. This is not as obvious as it sounds. For this reason, many writers on magic put a great deal of emphasis on training the sense organs. This training plays an important part in this book, too, but another aspect, which has been nearly always neglected, must first be dealt with.

This neglected aspect is the art of perceiving and interpreting omens. The effect of magic is seldom dramatic; the inattentive observer may even miss it. If you, for example, perform a money ritual, only in the rarest cases does it result in a sudden lottery prize or in finding buried treasure. Sometimes a rich relative dies, and this creates its own moral-ethical dilemma, but much more frequently some lucrative business opportunity will show up, a likely sponsor will appear, or orders and commissions take an upturn.[1]

The more subtle the effect, the more difficult this becomes. Seeming coincidences, often very fleeting, need to be recognized for what they are and exploited; otherwise they disappear again. Often the desired result comes a few days after the magical operation and catches the magician by surprise. He or she is not quick-witted enough to seize the opportunity and "ground" the trend or make it permanent. If, for example, you want your employer to give you a better job, he may mention such a prospect the same day, or the week after. Whenever it happens, it is not easy to insist on an immediate "grounding" of the offer in a formal written letter—this demands diplomatic, organizational and argumentative skill. Instead you may agree to vague promises which, a week later, prove to be nothing but hollow words. This problem of grounding can only be mastered by increased awareness, quick-witted action and psychological preparation. This also involves a certain understanding of the symbolic language of the subconscious.

You should always pay attention to "coincidences"; be open but not too expectant. Avoid lurking with a stopwatch, impatient for success after a magical operation. The magical control of success is one of the most difficult disciplines of magic, and for this reason a carefully written magical diary is indispensable.[2]

Psychological Practice

Thought Control and Concentration

We pointed out at the beginning of this chapter that separation into purely physical, purely psychological and purely magical exercises is nothing but a convenient fiction. The main advantage of such separation is that it helps us to deal more closely with each aspect of the matter. How you bring together the different practices and techniques is eventually up to you, but you should do this only when you are sure that you have mastered each separate part.

We hardly need explain the importance of thought control and concentration. People who work without concentration make mistakes. They do not handle these energies with the necessary care. On the one hand, they reduce their success and, on the other hand, they risk harmful consequences.

In the *Bhagavad Gita*, it suggests that it is easier to rein a team of wild horses than to bridle one's own thoughts. Eastern cultures have dealt with this problem in depth and have developed a multitude of techniques and exercises for thought control. Any good book about Raja or Astanga Yoga, or about meditation and relaxation techniques will provide useful information about this subject. The discussion here is therefore limited to essential techniques particularly relevant to sex magic.

How to Quieten the Mind

The man-in-the-street—and plenty of inexperienced scientists too—believe that it is impossible to make the mind go blank, but experience proves otherwise—not that it is easy. Depending on individual ability, you may need hours or even years to achieve it. But never mind; regular practice has its own benefits and will lead to fertile changes on magic and etheric levels even if actual vacancy of the mind is slow in coming.

For all exercises in this section the same rule applies: they are best performed in a firm, comfortable posture with *vertical spine*, usually sitting or kneeling, but not lying down. Only in this position can the etheric energies flow unhindered. You don't have to force yourself into the lotus position, which is painful for most inexperienced people; but, if you do master it, so much the better.

So, take a firm, comfortable position which you will be able to endure for some time without moving and make sure that you will not be disturbed. Close your eyes and breathe deeply and calmly until inner peace sets in. Now all you do is observe your breath, breathing in and out without any further thoughts. When thoughts appear, as they surely will, do not struggle to drive them away. Just let them come and go without clinging to them or judging them. Perform this exercise for at least 20 minutes.

Creative Concentration

This exercise fosters concentration and, in addition, clarifies patterns of consciousness and subconsciousness.

Write a letter to anyone you like; it may be a living, dead or fictitious person—whatever you want. The letter should be at least three 8-1/2" x 11" pages in order to stretch your imagination. To bring in the concentration training, we include some conditions:
- You are not allowed to use the words "the," "and" or "or."
- The letters: "a," "l" and "f" may not be employed.
- The letter has to be written in grammatically correct English— do not worry if the style is a bit strange because of these conditions.
- Unusual abbreviations which don't make sense must not be

used.

You will possibly struggle over this letter for hours and curse the day you picked up this book! However, many trainees on my seminars find that, while brooding over the task, it suddenly "clicks" and the text starts to flow. What happens is that your reason has given up and simple intuition effortlessly carries out the task which you were beginning to think was impossible. Should this happen to you, try to observe it from the "back of your head," so to speak, without interfering in the process or interrupting it. The purpose of this exercise is to develop a feeling for the energy quality of this state. Should you already have experience in ceremonial magic, you can perform a Mercury or Thoth invocation beforehand to intensify your contact with this vibration.

The second part of this attention training consists of correcting the letter for mistakes immediately after writing. Thorough practitioners may recopy the letter several times until it is completely mistake-free.

Put this "faultless" letter aside for several days before examining it again, or get a friend to examine it for mistakes. Then you correct the mistakes found (there will always be some) and rewrite the letter again.

Detail your progress very accurately in your magical diary during this exercise. When reading about it, this exercise may sound a bit ridiculous, but you will come to understand why we include it: this exercise is invaluable for bringing linguistic and intellectual patterns into consciousness. The skills you acquire with this exercise will benefit you later with more complicated sex-magic operations. Furthermore, you may find that you succeed best when you approach the exercise in a playful spirit—an important principle which applies to the whole of magic!

You should now develop your own, individual exercises along these lines. It does not have to be a letter; it could be a *curriculum vitae* where you avoid, among others, the word "I." Crowley used to give his disciples the task of avoiding the word "I" for a week. Each time a disciple caught himself using it, he had to cut his forearm with a razor blade. This was a very drastic method and not necessarily more effective than the one describexd here, so it is not recommended.

The following shows how the principle of this exercise can be used in other, various ways.

Work with Linguistic Patterns

Level 1

For three days, note how often you use, for example, the word "and." Count it and try to keep a tally. Perform this several times and preferably choose words which are largely free of associations—for example "or," "the," "than," "if," "whether," etc.

Level 2

For three days, avoid a certain word when talking. Choose this word according to the same criteria as in Level 1. Record your mistakes thoroughly and repeat the exercise several times.

Level 3

For three days, avoid one special letter when talking. For the first time, choose a consonant which is rare, for example "j" or "z," but not "q" and "x." Proceed as described above and repeat this exercise with different letters. After a while change over to vowels.

Level 4

Design your own individual exercises which are combinations of the first three levels.

By the time you reach Level 3, you will certainly know what is meant by attention training! If your professional situation does not permit you to perform these exercises continuously, put aside certain times of the day for them and increase the number of exercise days proportionately.

Working with Emotional Patterns

Level 1

For three consecutive days, look out for and record some specific feeling, for example "boredom," "anger," "fear" or "restlessness." The term "emotion" is here used in a loose, colloquial sense! Keep an accurate record as before, and repeat several times with different emotions.

Level 2

For three days, avoid a certain emotion, and don't "cheat" by choosing a very rare one! This may sound difficult—it is indeed. If the emotion arises, the best evasive technique is to distract your attention or call up a different emotion. Repeat with another emotion, as before.

Level 3

On three consecutive days at specific pre-planned times, evoke a chosen emotion, even if you do not feel at all like it. Perform this at least 24 times each day during working hours. You only have to experience the chosen emotion for two or three minutes. Then you must banish it even if it arises spontaneously, because the aim is to *control* the emotion and not to indulge it. Once again you must carefully record success or failure as well as recording any other impressions or results.

Level 4

Choose two opposing emotions (like love and hate, or joy and sorrow) and experience them for three days. For the first half of each day, you experience one emotion; for the other half, its opposite. Try to keep the emotion present continuously in the background so that it colors your behavior even when you are at work or communicating with others.

Once you have got the idea of these exercises you can create your own individual training program, working with other patterns of perception, thinking or ideology. It all helps to develop a true magical personality, especially when combined with the other exercises in this book.

These exercises provide useful feedback to the Mirror of the Soul exercise described earlier. They help you to design your own questionnaire to suit your own patterns. Both techniques offer useful ways to explore and develop your sexuality. As with the other exercises, there is plenty of room for adaptation and further development.

Another useful tip when it comes to developing your own exercises is to imagine that you are creating an exercise program for an imaginary disciple. Distancing yourself from the exercise in this way serves to free the imagination to create a better program.

These initial exercises are deliberately not too sexually oriented. In the beginning, it is best to concentrate on the seemingly "unimportant" behavior and emotional patterns, because they can harbor a great deal of unconscious tension that must be dealt with first. Habits are the foundation of the personality; so, if we want to change the personality itself, we should begin with these humble first steps.

Meditation

The Buddhist meditational technique of *sattipattana,* or observing your own breath while letting the mind go blank, will be familiar if you have followed this exercise program. In recent years, this technique has become common in the West through the influence of Zen Buddhism.

A second meditation technique focuses on images and meanings. It also prepares you for the training of the imagination dealt with in the next chapter.

Having surrounded yourself with your magical protective symbol, assume the posture described for the first meditation. Then relax and still your mind. Now visualize your Lesser Energy Orbit as before, except this time the upward flow of energy should be seen as colored *red*, while the downward flow is *white*. The more intense and brilliant the colors, the better. Now bring in your other inner senses, feeling the red energy as a powerful stream of blazing fire and the white energy as cool liquid. At the same time, "smell" how the red energy exudes a strong, sensual scent, whereas a more gentle, soothing scent emanates from the white energy. In order to leave you free to choose your own imagery, these scents are not described any more precisely than that. More will be said about this in the secondary comment which follows.

To encourage the energies to pulsate in harmony with your breath, use a mantra, which also includes the sense of sound in the exercise. The mantra used consists of the vowels *A-E-O*. When breathing in, concentrate on the upward-flowing *red* energy and mentally intone the vowel "*A*." Since you cannot easily breathe in while humming the vowel, learn to use your "inner hearing." When you stop breathing in, mentally intone the vowel "*E*" and feel the red energy in the crown of your head (or vertex chakra, if you want to work with it) transforming itself into white energy. Then breathe out, mentally intoning the vowel "*O*," while concentrating on the downward-flowing *white* energy. Then pause with your lungs empty and your mind blank before taking the next in-breath.

As you progress with this meditation, try to allocate equal lengths of time to the four phases: breathe in—hold breath—breathe out—lungs empty.

This meditation combines Eastern Tantra and Western Alchemy in a classic magical practice. To reinforce this combination, try to reflect on the following associations, both during your meditation as well as at other times.

Red stands for fire, male, hard, penetrating, Adam, lust and sun.

White stands for water, female, soft, receiving, Eve, devotion and moon.

Allow these associations to resonate inwardly when meditating but *do not think about them consciously.* Hold them until they become imprinted in your mind like a formula. This mental "programming" will help you later to exchange energies during sex-magic workings with a partner. It also stimulates your imagination and your ability to think in associations and correspondences—an essential foundation of traditional ritual magic.

Secondary Comment

Magical practice requires that we create our own universe of symbols. According to the Hermetic axiom "as above—so below," everything is connected. This idea is beginning to find acceptance now in modern quantum physics and cybernetics as well as in the information-theory models of the universe. So the magician will include all phenomena—for example, metals, numbers, colors, herbs etc.—in symbolic categories so that the energy of these symbols can be used in rituals. Therefore, there are classical lists of correspondences in which, for example, the metal gold, the number six and the color yellow are assigned to the sun; while the metal silver, the number nine and the color white are assigned to the moon. One could think of these correspondences as aids for concentration, or "oscillation generators," which use symbolic association to evoke specific types of awareness and energy for magical purposes.

If you look at tables of magical correspondences, you will note that there are two kinds: those which concentrate on a precise listing of individual elements and those which use more general descriptive terms. As examples of the first kind, Bardon lists under "Jupiter" six different incense mixtures: saffron by itself, or saffron mixed with linseed, orris-root, peony blossoms, begonia leaves or birch leaves; while the cabalist James Sturzaker lists no less than 29 (!) such plants, and even Spiesberger lists eight.

By comparison, Crowley in his *Liber 777* gives the following terse description: "saffron, all generous scents." At first this generalization is a bit daunting: Why isn't Crowley more specific? Is he trying to be mysterious or secretive? The truth of the matter is that correspondences are largely subjective and always very individual. The more an author goes into detail, the more arbitrary the correspondences seem to be. Why exactly should birch leaves (Bardon) or rhubarb (Sturzaker) be assigned to Jupiter and not to Venus or Saturn? Broad descriptions like Crowley's are superior because they convert the individual element to a common denominator. Not everybody will perceive a particular scent as "magnificent" (Jupiter). Maybe somebody perceives it as "virginal" (Moon) or even as "foreboding" (Saturn) and so on. It is not so important to use saffron incense with Jupiter; what is important is to use an incense which arouses the association of "magnificence."[3]

With his deliberately imprecise classification, Crowley is pointing out that symbolic language does not tolerate over-accurate definitions. This applies even to practical workings. If you try to be too exact in your aims (for example, a spell to win precisely $5,023.21 on the 15th March at 2:36 p.m.), you will almost certainly fail. The unconscious works with images and symbols, and it is their very fluidity which makes it possible to attract the right circumstances out of the huge pool of probabilities. If instead we ask for a "big sum" to arrive "in the course of the next three months," then our request is more organic and better in tune with the magical universe. We must learn to accept the indeterminacy of the magical universe and to work with it instead of trying to fight it. For many people, this means reversing their old opinions, because our technological civilization is based on the greatest possible precision. Magic tells us that precision means limitation, whereas indeterminacy means potential.

If you want to work magically, practice thinking and feeling in images. When Kekul["discovered" the benzene ring in a vision, he did not immediately see the finished formula but rather a snake biting its own tail. His creative achievement was to see the connection between this symbol and the benzene atom. A magician would say that he knew how to translate one correspondence into another—and this is exactly what we must learn as magicians.

Finally, it must be emphasized that we should not overdo the individuality of our own correspondences. It is useful to follow traditional correspondences for metals, numbers, colors, gems and deities because they have a certain consistency. To use them is to tune into the traditional "current" of these magical symbols, making it easier to work with other magicians from a common basis. However, the old notion that correspondences are "objective" in the sense that there are "true" and "false" attributions simply doesn't stand up to trial. This error has caused a great deal of damage because of its tendency to encourage the crusader mentality of divine rights and exclusive knowledge. If we study other magical cultures, we find that they use entirely different correspondences and systems, but they are no more nor less successful for that. Shamanic magic, for example, uses neither astrology nor the kabbalah, whereas the shaman's power animals or fetishes are largely unknown in hermetic magic.

It would be foolish to ignore such differences because of our longing for "unity" and even worse to falsify them. There are many examples of this, as when authors try to Christianize the Chinese *I Ching*. There is no need for this, because the desired unity can actually be found to some extent in such common structures as our equation: "will + imagination + magical trance = magical act." Such formulae might have their variations, exceptions and occasional contradictions, but they usually serve better than an obsessive clinging to the details of older magical systems. On the one hand, these basic formulae offer us the structural advantages of framework, and, on the other hand, they leave us free to dress it up with our own choice of materials and outward details.

A description can easily be "literally" incorrect but completely true as myth. The story of the expulsion from Paradise may not be historically true but the messages behind it—for example, the loss of unity, innocence and security through the separation of Good and Evil—are certainly "true." Myths provide valuable assistance with the symbol-logic of magic, and magic is often rightly called "applied mythology."

Training the Etheric Sense
The Complementarity Model

The importance of etheric perception has already been discussed; it only needs to be emphasized that the term "etheric" is only a metaphor and not some pseudoscientific hypothesis. The concept of an ether is far from new; it was already popular in the nineteenth century. Since most esotericists and magicians are already familiar with it, it is used here without claiming any quantitative, scientifically measurable reality for these "etheric" energies. Unfortunately, a sort of pseudoscience has flourished among certain esoteric schools for a good hundred years now. You can find "scientific" dissertations about the nature of these magical energies. In earlier times, the "animal magnetism" of Mesmer bore the brunt of this approach; then the "electromagnetic" model took over and still haunts many semi-educated parapsychologists. People nowadays also try to use mesons, quarks and the uncertainty principle to explain magical phenomena. If this is merely an attempt to woo science, then I consider it totally meaningless. Otherwise, there are some points in favor of this approach.

Humanity naturally wants to bring contemporary conceptions of the world into magic to avoid endless debate about epistemological contradictions. From a psychological point of view such attempts serve to placate reason and remove the sense of being raped by the "irrationality" of magic. From a magical point of view, this is sensible, because a satisfied mind allows the subconsciousness more space than does the frantic rationalization of scepticism, which puts all sorts of obstacles in the way of *magis*. It is not important whether the models are scientifically "true"; what matters is that they are *mythically* true and that they satisfy the individual and provide working hypotheses. Think again about what was said before about "objective" and "mythical" truth on the subject of correspondences.

These reservations must be born in mind while the following "complementarity model" is briefly outlined. This model should be somewhat easier for the modern, scientifically oriented reader than medieval systems with their alien cultural and religious assumptions. The complementarity model was developed by Peter Ellert and J rg Wichmann and was introduced in the now defunct German magic magazine *Unicorn*, among others.[4]

This model cannot be "proven" according to our present state of knowledge, but it has proved very useful in practice and has been developed through practical use. Here it will serve to cast light on etheric or magical perception which we know from experience to be less a question of "psychic" talent than one of inner attitude.

The model is quite simple. The so-called "wave/particle dual-ity" of light is well known: sometimes light reacts as if it had a wave form; at other times it seems to consist of particles. It depends largely on the test conditions, and hence on the observer. Thus it would be wrong to understand light as being either a wave only, or a particle only, because both states complement one another. They are "complementary" to each other.

The complementarity model claims that this idea is applicable to the mind/matter dualism which has for centuries inflamed the pas-sions of occultists and magicians. Instead of considering mind and matter as being fundamentally distinct, the complementarity model regards them as different sides of the same coin! Here again, it de-pends on the state or awareness of the observer whether certain en-ergies appear immaterial or material. So we can conclude that we first have to change our own perception if we want to sense "etheric energies." It is not that etheric energies are sometimes present and sometimes not; it rather depends on the magician whether they are perceived as such. Unlike light and more like gravity, etheric ener-gies are everywhere present. There will be times when the magician finds it more difficult to "tune in" and perceive these energies, but this has nothing to do with the quality of the energies. Note also that the term "energy" is just a loose expression for want of a more pre-cise word to describe something experienced partly as a "power" and partly as an "entity."

The important thing to remember is that we need to develop our ability to enter this receptive state or "gnostic trance" if we wish to perceive and use the magic which lies everywhere behind reality. In this connection, shamans talk about "moments of power" which have to be "grasped"; these are times when no special effort is re-quired to contact the *magis*. Such moments are rare, however, and, if we rely entirely upon their occurrence, we will fail as magicians.

The perception of etheric energies demands from most people a sort of ideological superstructure. Medieval books on magic under-lined the importance of "faith" for magical success. Nowadays the word has gone out of fashion; it is taken to mean "believing some-thing is true when you know it is not." But faith is an archetypal real-ity and cannot therefore be wiped out by intellectual trends. The principle of faith has therefore crept in again through the back door and pops up under the term "paradigm." "Paradigm" is a term taken from grammar; originally (according to the *Fremdw rterduden* or *Loanword Lexicon*, third edition), it was understood as a "pattern of a certain class of declination or conjugation which is exemplary for all equal inflectives; a pattern of inflection." The term has taken on new meaning through the impact of modern quantum physics and the "morpho-genetic fields" postulated by the English biologist Sheldrake. It stands now for the fundamental worldview. As already said, faith has crept in again through the back door!

It is important that you build up a model to explain the world to yourself—a model which to some extent satisfies your intellect but which also heals any contradictions between the rational-materialistic, scientific view and your magical experience. The following sentence derives from Chaos Magic: "belief is just a technique." As already mentioned, it does not matter which of the models you choose so long as it convinces *you personally*. I recommend first that you become familiar with as many models as possible, because each system has its limits and flexibility is needed for magic.

Before starting the actual training of the etheric sense, you should meditate on the complementarity model outlined above and internalize it. You will soon notice how much it helps your practical work.

Seeing the Aura

There are many treatises on the nature and function of the aura, and they usually contradict one another on almost every point. They have in common the basic idea that there is an invisible field of energy round any organism which can be made visible by suitable exercises or tools, such as Kirlian photography or aura goggles. We do not want to take sides here but will simply accept the lowest common denominator: namely that objects have a sort of etheric energy which can be perceived as a field of power or "energy shell."

Do not be confused by these aura picture-books which show multicolored pictures of auras. These works may mean well, but in my opinion they cause more harm than good. What was often originally intended as an illustration only is soon taken as a description of "objective" fact. As a consequence, there have been whole generations of frustrated esotericists failing in their attempts to see the human aura exactly as laid down in this literature.

If five different people see an aura, it will nearly always be perceived in five different ways. Consider an example from aura-diagnosis, because it underlines what really matters. Five seers examine a patient's aura at the same time. The first one sees "yellow spots" in the region of the liver; the second one sees "gray fissures"; the third one sees only a "hole"; the fourth one sees a "spider" in the liver; and the fifth one sees a hump-like bulge on the left shoulder. It is apparently a complete mess of contradictions. What is interesting, however, is that all five might equally diagnose "cirrhosis of the liver" despite their completely different perceptions. How does this apparent contradiction resolve itself?

The fact is, each seer has "deciphered" his individual symbolic observation and translated it into a medical term. For one of them, it may be enough just to recognize some disorder in the region of the liver; the next one may work with a complicated "color scale" which is interpreted in accordance with experience. It does not matter, therefore, what you actually perceive; what does matter is seeing in the right way and drawing the correct conclusions—a viewpoint we can hardly accept because of our scientific prejudices. Basically, everybody has his or her own individual key to symbols; hence the proliferation of different oracular techniques. Nor must we be misled by the fact that aura viewers sometimes perceive exactly the same picture. It is either a case of similarly structured inner symbology or else simple telepathy. This happens quite often between people who have either an extremely good or extremely bad rapport—and frequently the wrong conclusions are drawn.

It is a little known fact that many people, particularly beginners, do not see the aura in color but simply in black and white! People who do not know this may see the aura very clearly, but reject their perception as wrong because of Theosophists' claims that the aura has to be in color.

Seeing the Aura—Exercise 1

Put a large, white sheet of paper onto an empty table with good, even lighting. No shadows should fall onto the paper even if you lean forward. Now place your two forefingers side by side with the fingertips resting on the paper. Adjust your gaze "out of focus" so that the outlines of your fingers become a bit blurred. Draw your fingertips apart *very slowly and observe the gap between them*. Do you see a sort of veil? If you do, you have already succeeded in seeing the aura! Do not dismiss it as just an optical illusion. Accept the statement at face value for the time being, even if it needs a pinch of salt!

The 180° Gaze

This is one of the most important magical exercises, and it therefore merits special attention. It helps you not only to see the aura better but also to perceive other etheric energies more easily and reliably.

During the first exercise, you were told to let your gaze go "out of focus"; this is now extended further. For the 180° gaze, you widen your field of visual awareness to at least 180 degrees. It is obvious that this is not a sharply focused gaze; objects towards the edge of your field of vision will of course remain blurred, but even at the center it remains slightly out of focus because you are not concentrating your gaze on any one spot.

Should you have difficulties with this, try the following tips:

• Keep your eyes open as long as possible without blinking; any watering of the eyes is completely harmless and normal, but stop the exercise if the burning sensation becomes unbearable.

• Do not look at any special object, but rather be mentally aware of what you can see toward the corners of your eyes;

• Hold up both forefingers at arms' length straight in front of you; then move them slowly outwards in an arc until they are roughly level with your ears. All the time follow the fingers with your awareness but without moving your eyes.

• It helps sometimes to press the eyes slightly forward during this exercise. This automatically takes them out of focus.

The next exercise puts this 180° gaze into practice.

Seeing the Aura—Exercise 2

Place two empty water or wine glasses on an empty table, approximately eight inches apart. Seat yourself so both glasses are comfortably in view.

Now be aware of both glasses at the same time, using the 180° gaze. After a while, shift your attention to the gap in between rather than watching the glasses themselves. Take note of everything you perceive: perhaps a shimmering in the air, colored threads of light pulsating between the glasses, or moving shapes. Do not make judgments; just observe. Record your observations in your magical diary and repeat this exercise as often as possible—at least a dozen times.

Seeing the Aura—Exercise 3

Now for a bit of "green magic"! Take a walk in the woods and observe the trees with the 180° gaze. Do the same with the gaps between the trees. Follow a path for a while with a fixed 180° gaze, remembering not to move your eyelashes and keeping your eyes open as long as possible! Again, don't pass judgment or rationalize what you perceive.

Repeat the experiment at night, too. A small hill is an ideal spot where you can look at the aura of an entire wood with the sky as background. *Very brave adepts* can spend a whole night in the woods, practicing the 180° gaze as often as possible and remaining in the same general locality so they can note the changing etheric energies during the course of the night. If you are really dedicated, you can even spend 24 hours in the wild practicing this exercise. If it is also possible to intensify the practice with fasting and temporary sleep deprivation, you will get amazing results in a very short time.

The previous exercises have concentrated on the optical or quasi-optical perception of etheric energies. You can develop similar exercises to train the other senses too. For example, you can feel the aura of trees with your hands, especially if you sensitize your palms by rubbing them strongly against each other before starting. You can also "smell" the aura, or "hear" it and so on. Unfortunately, there is not enough space here to go into all the possibilities in depth. There is plenty of literature on the subject of "training of the senses," however, a selection of which is given at the end of this chapter.[5]

Crystal Ball and Magical Mirror

Vision plays an important role in shamanism especially. It would be misleading to go into the details of shamanic vision here, but any magician should at least know that shamanic visions are always accepted as "true" and not just as illusions.

Two disciplines have always played an important part in western magic: crystal gazing and work with magical mirrors. Both methods are important in sex magic, particularly if two partners work together and one of them has a mediumistic talent. These comments are basically an anticipation of the next major section, "Practice of the *Magis*," but they are introduced here because they are relevant to the previous exercises.

The crystal ball is hardly ever made of real crystal; it is more often made of glass, blown as faultlessly as possible. Although balls of rock crystal are cherished because of their inner sparkle, balls of a decent size, especially if they are as "flawless" as possible, are way beyond the means of most people, . The ball should in any case have a diameter of at least six inches, the bigger the better. Place the ball (which is usually supplied with a stand) about 10 to 12 inches away and make sure that no obvious light is reflecting on the surface. Then watch the crystal ball with the 180° gaze. After a while (maybe not before the eighth session, so be patient!), the crystal ball will become milky to your eyes, and eventually you will be able to recognize pictures, figures, events and so on in this "fog." This may sound easier than it really is. In fact, it usually needs a great deal of practice, and even that does not guarantee results. In my experience, success with a crystal ball or a magical mirror demands a particular magical talent.

Magical mirrors work on the same principle as crystal balls when they are used for visions, but apart from this they have other uses too. A magical mirror typically consists of a black concave glass in a wooden frame. Like the crystal ball, it has to be placed at a comfortable distance away and be as free from reflections as possible. Then one uses the 180° gaze as before.

The magical mirror is often ritually "charged" and used not only to "communicate with the world of spirits" but also for the evocation of demons and making them manifest; for directing ritually polarized energies towards other people for healing; and for intercourse with succubi and incubi and so on.

Often, before working with a crystal ball or magical mirror, sex magic is performed to heighten the sensitivity or to "charge" the objects. Both techniques, the crystal ball and the mirror, are attributed to the element of water (because they work with vision) and are therefore very receptive to the watery sex-magic energies. Particularly good times for crystal-ball and mirror magic are traditionally the times of full moon and new moon, and the eleventh day before and after these phases.

The orgasm is often a strongly visionary experience, and it therefore makes sense to use sex magic to support this "clairvoyance." The post-orgasmic phase is especially conducive to visions—to the extent that older writers like Gregorius and Spiesberger considered sex magic as a basic prerequisite for mediumistic works. In our experience, astral travel is also much easier when linked with sex magic.

Dream Work

Dream work is of the greatest importance in magic, and especially so in sex magic. The reason is obvious: the censor which keeps the consciousness separate from the subconscious in the awakened state is switched off during the dream phase. Etheric energies can therefore manifest themselves much more freely in dreams. Thus the magician sometimes uses the dream state as a gnostic trance, particularly lucid dreaming. It takes a long time to get to this point, so you should start practical dream work as soon as possible. Sex magic, by the way, plays the same sensitizing role in dream work as was described above in visionary magic. Begin keeping a dream diary, and keep it separate from your magical diary. Only dreams with a specific magical significance should also be recorded in your magical diary. Once you have started this dream diary, you will notice how the number of dreams remembered increases within a very short period of time. If you put them all in your magical diary, it would degenerate into a dream diary with occasional "magical intervals." If you have difficulty remembering your dreams at all, this can easily be remedied by taking these steps:

• Each night before falling asleep, tell yourself aloud that you will be conscious of your dreams and will remember them in full detail the next morning.

• Always have writing materials handy beside your bed.

• Try not to move after waking up until you have recalled your dreams.

• Work backwards, taking the last dream first. It often helps to grope your way back, starting with the most recent, and so "freshest," details first.

• After recalling the dreams as completely as possible, write everything down at once. Short notes are usually sufficient, but do not neglect the details. Trivial details frequently prove significant later on. Should you have difficulty in finding words to describe your dream, just try to *draw it*. The sketch does not have to be artistic; it will still be a powerful trigger for your memory if you want to re-experience the dream later. Write it all down, leaving space between the lines for adding any details which come back to you later. In the worst case, you will have to rewrite your notes.

• Also keep a book of your personal dream symbols, with an alphabetical index. Enter each symbol featured in your dreams, including objects such as "hammer," "piano" or "saddle," or situations such as "wedding," "execution" or "party"—also any people encountered. Next to the symbol, put a reference to the relevant dream; for example, its number or its page number in your dream diary. After writing this for a few months you will have some very informative statistics on your most frequent symbols.

• You will find that the use of a good handbook will help you to pursue your dream work systematically and conscientiously.[6]

• Do not forget that dream work is essential groundwork for the astral traveling frequently practiced during sex magic. Astral traveling has an energetic quality which can easily be confused with the quality of dreams (or more accurately with the quality of daydreams.) People who do a great deal of dream work will be able to travel much easier on the astral.[7]

• Work towards having a so-called "lucid dream," in which you are semiconscious, at least once a month. Once you have reached the stage where you can participate consciously in a dream, you can begin to perform magical rituals and exercises in this state, and these can be very effective. You can encourage this ability by relevant suggestions or sigils (see below), and especially by using sex magic.

• Allow yourself occasional holidays from dream work rather than let it become boring. Continuous dream work for months on end can sometimes lead to sleep disturbance which affects your health. This danger is unfortunately never mentioned in the relevant handbooks—so make sure your sleep remains refreshing and restful! On the other hand, once people get used to regular dream work there are usually no unpleasant effects.

• Pay particular attention to your dreams after important magical operations—such dreams frequently contain advice, instruction or warnings. These are direct messages from your subconscious.

• Also try to encourage sexual dreams by suitable suggestions before falling asleep, because these dreams often cast light on the less known parts of your sexuality.

• There is also a phenomenon known as the "astral course": a series of dreams (sometimes only two or three, sometimes as many as a hundred) which accelerate your magical knowledge and cause a "quantum leap" of your consciousness which can last for many years. Such dreams are admittedly very rare and should therefore be seen therefore as a sort of blessing, even if something of a mixed blessing, because they can turn your everyday life upside down and may advise you to do things quite against your nature.

The above list is not exhaustive. A fuller account has to be left to a broader introduction to the whole of magic, a book which is already in preparation. The exercises described are a sufficient starting point for practical sex magic, however.

Finally, here are some further topics which can be useful in connection with sex magic.

Seeing the Aura With a Partner

This exercise brings together some elements with which you are already familiar from earlier exercises. What you must do is to try to sense the Lesser Energy Orbit while your partner is circulating it. This may be done by feeling with your hands. Having sensitized them by rubbing the palms briskly together, you let your hands play over your partner's skin at a distance of about four inches. You should feel a slight tingling or warmth. Alternatively, you can sense the energy in a quasi-optical way, where the technique is identical to seeing the aura: Use the 180° gaze and look slightly "around" rather than straight at your partner. This succeeds best when the partner is naked and standing in front of a plain, light colored wall—so avoid the flowery wallpaper in the hallway!

If you have ever met shamans, you might have noticed how they squint sidelong at people when they first meet them. They are scanning the aura.

The abilities developed by these exercises serve as general training for the intuition, and this is useful for spiritual healing. All our exercises have a magical basis, even if they are frequently used in other, non-magical disciplines.

In sex magic, seeing the aura plays an important role. Without it, the exchange of ritually polarized or aroused energy would be virtually impossible.

How to Handle Sexual Fantasies

Modern sexology has considerably enhanced the status of sexual fantasies, pointing out that we are essentially "dream-animals," and that sexual fantasies are no mere substitute for sex; they are rather an integral part of sexuality itself.

Sexual fantasies can certainly liven up sex and help it to reach new heights. Unfortunately, the imagination is seldom properly trained, and so the result can degenerate into vicarious satisfaction:

Sensing the Lesser Energy Orbit

if you allow sexual fantasies to dominate your sex life it can lead to unfortunate physical as well as mental results.

An excess of sexual fantasy is often one of the reasons for impotence and frigidity. Too much fantasy means it is all "in the head," and we lose touch with our bodies. The only remedy is to abstain completely from fantasy for a while. Rather than any bad influence on one's morals, this dissociation is also the real danger in pornography. To avoid any misunderstanding, I am simply talking about the possible dangers of overdoing fantasy or over-reliance on pornography. One must be conscious of these risks in order not to jeopardize the very real benefits of sexual fantasies.

Sexual fantasies are like daydreams: a means for easy access to the subconscious and a route to gnostic trance. Sexual intercourse with incubi and succubi, which we will deal with later, takes place on this level.

Stick to the following rules when dealing with sexual fantasies:

• If you have sexual inhibitions and have difficulty facing up to your sexual desires even in private, you should indulge regularly in sexual fantasy as a sort of "dry run" to reduce your inhibitions until you learn to experience and value yourself as a sexual being. However, make sure you live out these fantasies *physically* by, for example, masturbating or grinding your hips in order to stop it from being "all in the head" as described above.

• Should sex become impossible without fantasies, or if you suffer problems with potency or orgasm without them, take it as a serious alarm signal and abstain from any sexual fantasy for a while. The same applies to pornography, against which there is no particular objection so long as it does not become the sole factor in your sexuality.

• Use your fantasizing ability to explore sexual practices which you do not like or which you positively loathe. By doing so, you use the power of imagination to build the broader, less rigid personality which sex magicians need. However, this could degenerate into mere vicarious satisfaction unless it is also transferred into physical action.

Sexual fantasies are a good way to train the imagination, because the pleasure they provide is a powerful inducement to success. That is why the concentration is mainly on sexual imagination in the next section, although the imagination should and can be trained in other areas as well.

Practice of the *Magis*

The final section of this chapter will be devoted to practical work with the *magis* and will therefore venture deeper into actual magic. Since the ground principles have already been explained, the concentration is now on specific techniques.

1. The Gnostic Trance

Gnostic or magical trance has already been mentioned. Now it is time to look at it a little more closely.

Basically, gnostic trance is divided into *inhibitory and excitatory* trance, following the guidelines in *Liber Null*.[8]

Peter Carroll, the author of *Liber Null*, writes:

> In the inhibitory mode, the mind is progressively silenced until only a single object of concentration remains. In the excitatory mode, the mind is raised to a very high pitch of excitement while concentration on the objective is maintained. Strong stimulation eventually elicits a reflex inhibition and paralyzes all but the most central function—the object of concentration. Thus strong inhibition and strong excitation end up creating the same effect—the one-pointed consciousness, or gnosis." (p. 31)

You should become familiar with as many different routes to gnostic trance as possible, because this not only increases your ability to enter trance states, but also helps you to choose the right technique for every occasion.

The following lead to *inhibitory trance:* sleeplessness, fasting, exhaustion, meditation, vacancy of the mind, sensory deprivation, trance-inducing concentration and the death posture.

The following. meanwhile, lead to *excitatory trance:* pain, dancing, drumming, chanting, emotional stimulation (for example, fear, anger and horror), hyperventilation, sensory overload and sexual excitation.

Exercises such as seeing the aura, the sex-magical deep relaxation technique, workings with mantras and performing the Lesser Energy Orbit, as well as dowsing, or working with the crystal ball and magical mirror, may all lead to gnostic trance. However, as mentioned above, we here want to concentrate on using sex to enter trance. Another quote from *Liber Null:*

Sexual excitation can be obtained by any preferred method. In all cases there has to be a transference from the lust required to ignite the sexuality to the matter of the magical working at hand. The nature of a sexual working lends itself readily to the creation of independent orders of being—evocation. Also in works of invocation where the magician seeks union with some principle (or being), the process can be mirrored on the physical plane; one's partner is visualized as an incarnation of the desired idea or god. Prolonged sexual excitement through karezza, inhibition of orgasm, or repeated orgasmic collapse can lead to trance states useful for divination. It may be necessary to regain one's original sexuality from the mass of fantasy and association into which it mostly sinks. This is achieved by judicious use of abstention and by arousing lust without any form of mental prop or fantasy. This exercise is also therapeutic. (pp. 32 ff.)

Whether you prefer excitatory or inhibitory trance is up to you; sometimes one can slip easily from one to the other. Excessive sexual activity can, for example, cause inhibition through exhaustion, but it may equally turn into overstimulation and produce excitatory trance—or the already described *eroto-comatose lucidity.*

Further analysis of the different types of trance is not of much practical value. Normally, you do not mechanically decide on a certain type of trance and then carry out your decision; the decision is rather made on an intuitive level, which is much more useful and sensible. The differentiation into these two forms of trance provides a *structural* insight into the nature of the magical trance, and this is the reason for mentioning it. They are basically two different starting points that lead to a similar end result. Neither form of trance is "better" than the other, but the quality of each energy will "feel" different. You need a great deal of experience to master the question of trance. Experience cannot be imparted by any book; you have to gather it yourself.

Note that both types of trance involve some form of "superelevation." Among English adepts, the following saying has gained currency: "In magic, nothing succeeds like excess." The idea of this is not simply to frighten the middle classes! Remember the African medicine man indulging in all forms of physical and psychological excess so as to reach the sources of his magic. This does not mean overtaxing ourselves to the point of physical and psychological ruin; it is just that there is no room for half-heartedness in magic.

Discover for yourself how far you have to go to get the desired success.

2. Suggestion and Affirmation

Perhaps you are already familiar with the "positive thinking" techniques of suggestion and affirmation. More efficient techniques will be described later, but you should first have practical experience in using suggestions and affirmations before you train the *magis*. Magical techniques need to be "grounded" properly by practical application before they are used in sex magic. If this step is neglected, the energies set free by sex magic can get out of control.

Suggestions and affirmations can be either *verbal* or *pictorial*. Verbal suggestions about reaching some desired aim are repeated to yourself in a state of gnostic trance; for example, during great sexual excitement at the moment of orgasm or immediately afterwards. It is important that your formulations are *positive*. Do *not* say, "I will not be sick." Say instead, "I will be healthy." Experience has shown that the subconscious can overlook words such as "not," "none" or "never" in a suggestion. You can probably guess what happens!

Verbal affirmations work on a similar principle, but they are worded as if the desired state has already been achieved; for example, "I *am* healthy." This does not work for everyone; you often get problems because of the obvious inconsistency between the ideal and the real. The resulting doubts can jeopardize the entire operation.

The pictorial technique can well be combined with verbal formulations, but its actual stress is on *pictorial imagery*. In the above example, you could imagine yourself jumping around as fit as a fiddle. The more vividly the picture is built up, the better it works.

At first you might assume that there could be no difference between pictorial suggestion and pictorial affirmation, but in fact the difference is great. Pictorial affirmation is a sort of "pictorial suggestion plus the eradication of all possible obstacles." The image is built up until a sort of "success trance" follows; this is then maintained over days and weeks until the desired aim is achieved.

Some readers may think that pictorial affirmation is no more than systematic self-deception, because each doubt about possible success, and so each obstacle, will be "killed through optimism." To think so would be wrong. As a matter of fact, it is a magical practice as ancient as the protective circle—momentarily keeping at bay all disturbing influences in order to boast the energy for success. Critical or pessimistic people need extra strength of mind to master this "reality dancing," as shamans would call it.

Imagine, for example, that you are in a delicate financial situation. At the peak of the orgasm during a sex-magical Mercury ritual, you concentrate on the affirmation: "I am rich. Money is flowing towards me." Afterwards, you perform a banishing and end the ritual itself, but your magical operation will still go on for several weeks. You go back into everyday life again, but you get into the habit of stroking your wallet and enjoying the sight of the money it contains, even if it is not much. Then you might go to a restaurant and give particularly generous tips to the staff. You simply cannot be stingy, because you are "already rich." Most beginners make the mistake of going back to life as they did before—in this case still acting poor or bankrupt—and hoping for a miracle to lift the burden from their shoulders. Not so the experienced affirmation magician! After your meal, caress the rest of your money again and talk to it in a low voice (not too conspicuously!), saying things such as: "You are welcome any time. I like you. You are beautiful. We two belong to one another." Afterwards, close your eyes in ecstasy and murmur something such as: "What wonderful, rustling thing is it that comes towards me? Aha, it is MONEY!!!" Do this even if you see no money at all in your inner eye; go on until you succeed. Take the tip about "ecstasy" seriously. The more you can create this feeling, the greater your chances are. Keep it up for weeks on end until you are in a total money trance and, as experience proves, money has no alternative but to come to you. It won't necessarily do so in the dramatic form of a winning a lottery or an unexpected inheritance, but perhaps in the form of particularly lucrative business offers. Force your luck in this playful manner, and you will find it a great deal of fun! A silly exercise? On the contrary—in this manner are millionaires made!

In my experience, affirmation is better suited to bringing about a certain *condition* than some specific, concrete *event*. It is easier to put yourself into a millionaire "state" than to imagine winning a million specifically in the lottery. Feel like a millionaire and behave like one until you really start to need the appropriate money for your millionaire behavior. Then, as experience has shown, it will not be long in coming.

What was said about the difficulty of bringing about concrete events with the help of magical affirmations needs one small qualification. If you maintain a magical affirmation over weeks and months, you may begin to experience more of these "moments of power" mentioned earlier, during which any magic effortlessly succeeds. During such moments, it is possible to formulate very concrete and precise aims and to achieve them in a very short period of time—particularly if they are related to the original affirmation.

Magical affirmations have the disadvantage that they usually need to be maintained for a long time, and it is not always easy to maintain several affirmations simultaneously. On the other hand, they demand very little effort, they need no magical tools, they can be employed at any time regardless of astrological influences, and they are generally quite an "elegant" form of magic. They lend themselves to use with sex magic because they are based on happiness and optimism and have the same ecstatic basis as sex magical operations.

When performing sex-magical workings, make sure you finalize your affirmations *before* the operation so that sex magic can give your affirmation a strong push. If the affirmation is to last for several weeks, repeat the sex-magic operation several times during that period.

3. Sigil Magic

Because we deal with the sex-magic aspects of sigil magic later, those readers who have already mastered sigil magic may leave out this section and continue with the section entitled "Training of Imagination."

Here, only the basic elements of sigil magic that are needed for our present purposes will be outlined. If you want to know more about this interesting topic, I recommend my book *Practical Sigil Magic*[9]; in it, you will find much more practical detail and background.

The Basics of Sigil Magic

The foundations of sigil magic as we know it today were laid by the English magician and painter Austin Osman Spare (1886-1956). Spare was a contemporary of Aleister Crowley and was for a short time a member of Crowley's magical order, the A∴ A∴ (Argenteum Astrum). Early on, he read about Sigmund Freud's psychoanalysis and adopted Freud's model of "consciousness" and "the subconscious," between which lies a psychological "censor."

We use the word "sigil" to describe those magical symbols created according to Spare's method. Basically, a sigil is a magical glyph with a specific meaning, or a sign which symbolizes a certain state of trance or will. Unlike traditional sigils, such as those used in planetary magic, these sigils are purely personal. They are developed and designed by the magician himself or herself according to a precisely formulated sentence of desire. The actual technique is explained later.

Once a sigil is created, it is charged or activated by one of several techniques. After this "charging," it is then banished. After this, the sigil has to be forgotten so that the subconscious is free to convert the sigil, with its encoded sentence of desire, into action. The encoding allows the sentence of desire to slip past the psychological censor and become implanted directly into the subconscious. Since the sigil is a pictorial representation abstracted to the point that its literal content cannot be openly recognized, the moral authority of the censor sees no reason to prevent the subconscious from receiving it.

This suggests that sigil magic is largely free from ideological dogma. There is no need to believe in demons and dark powers, in astral larvae, etheric energies or deities if you want to work sigil magic. All you need is pen and paper.

The Statement of Desire

The most important prerequisite for successful sigil magic is the correct formulation of the statement of desire. As with suggestions and affirmations, the statement of desire should always be formulated in positive terms without using negatives. Precise formulation is not always easy, because it not only demands (as does any magic) that you know exactly what you want, but also that you can express it explicitly yet without excessive detail. There is no point in defining a sum of money to the nth decimal place when performing a money-magic operation. Remember what we said about the vagueness of symbols, images, analogies and correspondences!

But even seemingly explicit formulations can lead to odd surprises. For example, a participant at one of my seminars told me about a colleague who was a passionate showjumper. This colleague decided to perform an operation to win a particular event.

He formulated the following affirmation: "I will win the tournament." One would think that this was quite explicit enough—but what happened? In fact, he rode worse than usual and only came fourth. And his reward for that? As a consolation prize, he was presented with a bottle of aftershave with the trade name, "Tournament"! Be thankful for such experiences because they wake you up. From such mistakes you learn the most!

Once you have constructed the statement of desire, write it in capitals on the upper half of a piece of paper. It is advisable to begin each operation the same way; for example, "THIS MY WISH..." or "IT IS MY WILL..." Avoid vague formulations such as "I would like to..." or "I would wish to...," etc., because they take the necessary power from the operation.

As an example, take the following sentence: "THIS IS MY WISH TO EARN THREE HUNDRED DOLLARS TOMORROW."

How to Construct a Sigil

(Word Method)

Now delete each letter which appears more than once, leaving only the first one. In the example, the following letters remain:

T, H, I, S, M, Y, W, O, E, A, R, N, U, D, L

These letters form the raw material with which you construct the sigil. This is done by simply linking the letters into a monogram. Not all of them need be the same size (see figure 1). If you have a close look at the illustration, you will be able to find all the letters from the above row.

Now the sigil should not be too complicated, because we need to visualize it when charging it. Hence we can simplify it further, so long as we can still recognize each single letter in the finished product. An example of such simplification is shown in figure 2. Look closely and see that you can still recognize each letter. Do you recognize the Y, M, and S?

Remember: this is only an example, so do *not* use this sigil yourself. From what was said previously, it should be clear that the sigil has to be constructed by you personally. As a matter of fact, the construction of the sigil is even more important than the charging! Because, although consciousness and reason formulate the state-

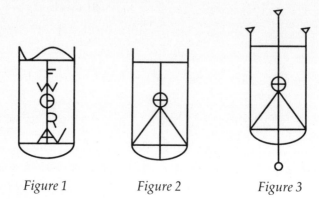

Figure 1   Figure 2   Figure 3

ment of desire, the subconscious is already involved in it through the artistic and graphical translation, which can itself be a sort of "pre-charging." Theoretically, it should be possible to perform magical operations for other people by means of one's own personal sigils, but the sigil of a magician only works for the person who constructed it. This is the difference between a sigil constructed on these lines and a traditional sigil from, for example, Agrippa or Paracelsus.

You may if you like decorate the finished sigil a bit so that it looks more "magical" from a subjective point of view; this is entirely up to your own artistic feelings. You may even color it. In any case, it is advisable to put a frame around the finished sigil—for example, a circle, square or triangle—because it gives it a more finished look and helps you to concentrate on the symbol. An example of a decorated and framed sigil is shown in figure 3.

Please note that the sigil must not be too simple. If you cleverly managed to combine all the letters into a simple square, it would make it very difficult to forget the symbol after charging it; therefore, make sure it is complex enough to be forgotten.

Before we go into charging or activating sigils, we will describe a second method of constructing them. In each case, the technique of activating them is the same.

Constructing a Sigil by the Pictorial Method

For the pictorial method, you must be able to represent your statement of desire by a simple image. This suits some people much better than the linguistically oriented word method, but there are others who cannot manage the pictorial method. Experiment with both and find out which suits you best.

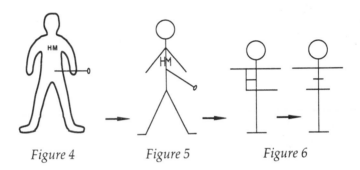

| *Figure 4* | *Figure 5* | *Figure 6* |

Do not write out the statement of desire this time; instead put it straight into pictorial form. For example, you want to heal a friend called "Joe Mayer," who has stomach pains. As with the traditional wax images, you draw a figure (a simple matchstick man will do!) using its initials (figure 4). Now you draw a sort of "astral acupuncture needle" pointing towards the region of his stomach. Through this needle, the healing energy is directed to the part of the body concerned (figure 5). Again, *this sigil needs to be simplified and stylized*, as with the word method (figure 6).

To illustrate the procedure more clearly, here is another example for a binding spell to bring two partners (A and B) together. Figure 7 shows two different possibilities for a finished sigil, which demonstrates that there are unlimited possibilities for designing sigils.

Activating Sigils

Perhaps we should define the term "charging" more precisely. If we "charge" an object—for example an amulet, a fetish or a talisman—it means that we direct energy from *inside ourselves* into the object.

But if we "charge" a sigil, it is more like "loading"; for example, you "load" a program into a computer or a cartridge into a gun. To avoid this confusion of terms, we prefer to talk about "activating" sigils.

On the other hand, there is also an intermediate process. For example, you can put a sigil on an amulet and then activate it by sex

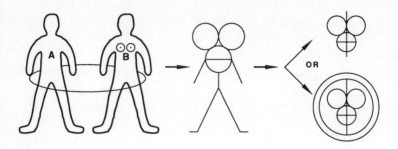

Figure 7

magic, and afterwards you can additionally charge the physical amulet with sexual *magis* by an additional act of will or by anointing it with sexual secretions. We will deal with this in more depth later.

Only the method of activating sigils by means of sex magic will be described here. As experience has shown, this is the quickest and most efficient technique.

Once you have constructed your sigil, copy it onto a separate piece of paper and destroy all the earlier drafts. Then go into your bedroom and lie on your bed with the sigil. Masturbate and concentrate on the sigil during the climax. In the beginning, you should stare at the drawn sigil with eyes wide open. With experience, it is sufficient to visualize the sigil as realistically as possible. But remember, you must have the sigil in front of your eyes at the moment of orgasm! At this point, you must no longer be thinking about the original statement of desire or the actual meaning of the sigil! It helps if you let some time pass between the construction and the charging of the sigil, so that you are no longer sure what the sigil was originally meant for. It is also possible to have sigils in reserve to be activated in the future, but of course this is only suitable for long-term actions where a few weeks more or less do not matter.

The final banishing is of the utmost importance! The simplest way of doing this is by *laughing*. Laughter is an excellent magical protection anyway. During attack, laughing quickly takes the wind out of an aggressor's sails and weakens his energy. So as soon as you have charged the sigil at the moment of orgasm, start laughing as loudly and intensely as you can, and then *immediately think of something completely different which has nothing to do with the magical opera-*

tion. By doing this, you distract the consciousness and the psychic censor and "seal" the awakened energies as if closing a pressure cooker. Obviously you will by now have turned over the piece of paper so the sigil is no longer visible: *It is just as important to forget the sigil!*

Forgetting is the biggest problem with this technique. In the beginning, it is sufficient to forget the symbol itself. Later, you should try to banish the entire operation from your memory. On the other hand, you do want to monitor any successes. The best way is to enter the operation as usual in your magical diary and then glue a piece of paper over the entry. Here you may write down the expiration date after which your sigil is no longer valid, and you can then remove the piece of paper. This may sound a bit ponderous, but it doesn't take long and it does guarantee a record of many successes.

As the above description implies, you can set a time limit for magical operations, and it is advisable to do so. Make a deadline for when the operation has to be considered finished, and after which point you should take stock of your success or failure. According to experience, most operations either work immediately (from a few days to about two weeks) or only after a period of six months. In general, I give my operations a period of nine to twelve months, depending on the desired aim.

These tips should be enough to set you going on practical sigil magic. Further details can always be found in the literature mentioned. Of course, sigils can also be charged with a partner, but in the beginning you should concentrate your sex magic on autoerotic techniques, at least until you have developed a feeling for the sexual energies and also have more experience.

Sex-Magic Training of the Imagination

Introductory comment

The term "imagination" is likely to be misunderstood. In a magical sense, it is more than simply a pictorial "visualizing" process. Magical imagination is much more a sensual act, which means that the images have to be perceived vividly and with the greatest possible realism. Whether you perceive an image "optically" or in terms of other quasi-senses does not matter—ideally you perceive it with all your "inner senses" simultaneously.

You have already learned a number of imagination exercises,

and you have also been given suggestions for some additional reading. The following material deals with imagination at the specifically sex-magic level. To save time and encourage thoroughness, these exercises are based on other, previously described exercises.

The Sex-Magic Invocation 1

With these exercises, you will enter the fields of ceremonial invocatory magic, but with the minimum of equipment.

For male magicians:

Meditate for one week on the solar principle in all its aspects. Watch the physical sun in the sky and adjust your timetable to its rising and setting. Enter completely into the solar principle; for example, wear a lot of golden jewelery, pay attention to yellow colors, behave in a "sunny" manner and so on. The other important thing is to abstain from *any* sexual activity during this time of preparation!

Here are some examples of solar correspondences or "keywords" so that you can create your own individual one-week "Suncosmos": gold, fire, phallus, light, yellow, the number six, warmth, fathering, wealth, reason, consciousness, male, day, active, singe, burn, physical health . . .

Once you have spent a week in a permanent sun-trance, choose one day at noon when you are completely undisturbed and free to go into the open country to perform your Sun evocation. Should it be impossible to work outside, you may do so indoors provided the sun is visible.

Having sensitized your palms by rubbing them briskly together, stand facing the sun and raise your arms with your palms toward the sun. Let yourself be flooded by the rays of the sun, taking them in through your palms with each inhalation. Then concentrate the energy in the Hara with each exhalation. Do this for at least a quarter of an hour—in any case until you feel completely flooded by solar energy. If you wish, you can combine the whole thing with an invocation to the Sun (which you should write yourself).

When you are fully charged with energy, excite yourself sexually by masturbation. The use of aids like pornography or fantasy is forbidden, and you should also do without aphrodisiacs the first time—your week-long sexual abstinence should make this easier. Little by little, you become the Sun God himself, reaching this climax with your orgasm.

Note that it is not the purpose of this exercise to achieve any specific external effect; the whole aim is to waken and anchor the Sun principle in yourself. This is of the utmost importance for later ritual sex magic and sex mysticism. Do not banish by laughter this time, but let the experience end slowly after the climax. This can sometimes take several days.

It is obvious that during your Sun working you should be magically protected by one of the techniques described earlier. Experienced ceremonial magicians might start and end the operation with the Lesser Banishing Ritual of the Pentagram. If you do this, do not forget the final dismissal. You can formulate this yourself, but it should have roughly the following content: "I dismiss all the entities which are banished by this ritual." This helps the "astral ecology" and ensures that unpleasant visitors do not hang around.

During the following days, and maybe weeks, pay attention to every occurrence which seems to reflect the Sun principle and keep a careful record.

For female magicians:

Meditate for one week on the lunar principle *in all its aspects.* Watch the physical moon in the sky and adjust your timetable in accordance with it. Enter completely into the Moon principle; for example, wear a lot of silver jewelery, pay attention to white and silvery colors, behave in a "moon-like" fashion etc. The other important thing is to abstain from any sexual activity during the time of preparation!

Here are some examples of lunar correspondences or "keywords" which are presented to you so you can create your own one-week "Moon-cosmos": silver, water, vagina, darkness, white, the number nine, coolness, conception, vision, intuition, dream, softness, subconscious, female, night, passive, extinguishing, stroking, psychological health . . .

Once you have spent a week in a permanent moon-trance, choose a night when you are undisturbed and free to go into open country at midnight to perform your Moon invocation. Should it be impossible to work outside, you can do so indoors provided the moon is visible.

Having sensitized your palms by rubbing them briskly together, stand facing the moon and raise your arms with your palms stretched toward her. Let yourself be flooded by the rays of the moon. With each inhalation, take them in through your palms, and, with each exhalation, concentrate them in the Hara. Do this for at least a quarter of an hour—in any case until you feel entirely flooded by the moon energy. If you wish, you can combine this with an invocation to the Moon (which you should write yourself).

When you are fully flooded with the energy, excite yourself sexually by masturbating. The use of outside aids such as fantasy or pornography is forbidden, and you should not use any aphrodisiacs the first time—your week-long sexual abstinence should make this easier. Little by little you should become the Moon Goddess herself, culminating in the orgasm.

Note that it is not the object of this exercise to achieve any specific external result; the whole idea is to waken the Moon principle and anchor it in yourself. This is of the utmost importance for later ritual sex magic and sex mysticism. Do not banish by laughter this time, but let the experience end slowly after the climax, even if this takes several days.

Obviously, you should protect yourself magically by one of the techniques already described. Experienced ceremonial magicians might start and end the operation with the Lesser Banishing Ritual of the Pentagram. If you do this, forget the final dismissal formula. You may formulate it yourself, but it should be on roughly the following lines: "I dismiss all the entities which are banished by this ritual." This is good for the "astral ecology" and makes sure that no unpleasant visitors hang around.

During the next few days, or perhaps weeks, pay attention to every event which seems to reflect the lunar principle and keep a careful record.

The Sex-Magic Invocation 2

This invocation brings us to true sex-mystical integration. It is the magical equivalent to work with the animus/anima in C. G. Jung's depth psychology. However, this working is also a preparation for sex invocation geared to specific results.

For male magicians:

Proceed as for the previous sex magic invocation, but this time follow the instructions given for female magicians. Instead of the

Sex-Magic Invocation

solar, you will work with the lunar principle. The purpose is to deal with your own feminity, which supports your entire sexuality and helps to stabilize your magical power. Remember that all magicians work with light *and* shadow, with the male *and* female principle, with Yin *and* Yang!

It is also important that you feel the female *physically* inside yourself, until your very genitals seem to change their form!

For female magicians:

Proceed as for the previous sex-magic invocation, but this time follow the instructions for male magicians. Instead of the lunar, you will work with the solar principle. The purpose is to deal with your own masculinity, which will bolster your entire sexuality and help to stabilize your magical power. Remember that all magicians always work with light *and* shadow, with the male *and* female principle, with Yin *and* Yang!

It is also important that you feel the male *physically* inside yourself, until your very genitals seem to change their form!

The Sex-Magic Invocation 3

For male magicians:

Proceed as in the first sex-magic invocation, but this time work with the *Mars* principle. Since you cannot always find Mars in the night sky, you may have to imagine it.

To give you some ideas, here is a brief list of traditional Mars correspondences: iron, fire, red, dry, hot, five, drive, aggressive, piercing sexuality, war, will, assertion power, vehemence . . .

For female magicians:

Proceed as in the first sex-magic invocation, but this time work with the *Venus* principle. Since you cannot always find Venus in the night sky, you may have to imagine it.

To give you some ideas, here is a brief list of traditional Venus correspondences: copper, water, green, damp, cool, seven, feeling, passive, dissolving sexuality, softness, premonition, abandon, gentleness . . .

The Sex-Magic Invocation 4

This exercise has the same inverted approach as "Sex-Magic Invocation 2. "

For male magicians:

Proceed as in Sex-Magic Invocation 3, only this time follow the instructions for female magicians, which means that you work with the *Venus* principle.

For female magicians:

Proceed as in Sex-Magic Invocation 3, only this time follow the instructions for male magicians, which means that you work with the *Mars* principle.

Have you noticed the difference between Sun and Mars, and between Moon and Venus? In some respects, these energies are similar to each other. It is important that you feel for yourself what is the same and what is different between their energy qualities so that you learn to differentiate between them correctly. Experienced planetary magicians will be familiar with these differences, and beginners are advised to look into the astrological symbolism in relevant literature.[10]

What matters most is your own individual experience. You start with the basic duality between the male and female sexuality, and you go on to discover that Sun and Moon represent more *abstract* and *spiritual* aspects of the principle, whereas Mars and Venus incorporate the more *specific* and *physical* aspects.

You are advised to support these invocations by drawing down the appropriate energies and becoming one with them by imagining yourself in the corresponding form; for example, as the Sun God with shimmering blond hair and magnificent golden physique. or as the Moon Goddess with long silvery hair and ethereal, shining features. This combines both invocation and imagination training.

A Further Tip for the Advanced Practitioner

It is obvious that invocations are not an end in themselves. In the beginning, you practice becoming familiar with the energies. Later you assume whichever god-form is required *to perform and accomplish some magical result*. If your magical aim fits a certain planetary principle, you work with it. You *become* the energy and are, as its ruler, able to direct it to the desired aim.

This is the magic of the will as opposed to the prayer of mysticism. On the one hand, you beseech the Jupiter principle to grant you something; on the other hand, you become Jupiter yourself and order what you wish. Both methods have their advantages and disadvantages, and sometimes it is a question of the appropriate time-quality which method you chose. It has to be said that not all invocatory work has to be done by sex magic; nevertheless, experience has shown that this shortens the work of months into a few weeks. Also, the magician's subconscious tends to accept sex-magic associations more thoroughly and quickly.

The Technique for Charging Talismans, Amulets and Fetishes by the Use of Sex Magic

Talismans and amulets are among the most developed disciplines of western magic. Fetish workings are less well known because they are seldom referred to by this name. A brief summary of the talismanic discipline will be given for beginners; advanced practitioners may skim over this section.

Basically, a talisman is charged for something, whereas an amulet is charged against something. For example, one may produce a talisman *for* health or an amulet *against* illness. This, by the way, does not contradict our rule never to formulate statements of desire in a negative way, because amulets are actually charged in a positive fashion. (As regards the formula used in charging an amulet—it will not be charged "against illness" so much as to "fortify one against illness.") A magical fetish, in comparison, is what shamans call a "power object"; it serves basically as a form of "storage battery." There are, for example, curse fetishes in which anger and hate are stored, healing fetishes, weather fetishes and of course sexual fetishes, which are charged by sexual energies.

Talismans, amulets and fetishes can be made of any material. In general, planetary talismans and amulets are made of the metal which is attributed to the appropriate planetary principle. Fetishes are often made of wood or stone, but other materials—paper, silk, leather or natural fibers—are also used.

Talismans, amulets and fetishes are an *externalizing* of the adept's magical personality. One puts part of one's power, and therefore of oneself, into this external object by "charging" it, and this part can then work independently. Therefore, one must deal carefully with the charged objects. If they are lost or stolen, a part of this power and personality is out of control, or in the hands of enemies. This can have dangerous results. Conversely, one should take equal care not to touch talismans, amulets or fetishes of other magicians without permission, because most good magicians take special precautions against such interventions and attacks. Even if there is no special protection, bad consequences may result if the energy of the other magician and your own do not get on with one another. These power objects can remain effective for centuries, particularly if they have been charged animal sacrifice or by sex magic.

Secondary Comment

Sex magic and the magic of animal sacrifice are very similar in their energetic quality, but sex magic avoids the negative effects of blood sacrifice. These negative phenomena exist mainly because animal sacrifice suffers from the law of diminishing returns. Such sacrifices have to become greater and greater, because they gradually lose their effectiveness. In the end, one has to wade through pools of blood to achieve even the smallest result.

Love and death are counter-poles of life, so it is hardly surprising that the energies liberated by sex are akin to those of sacrifice. The equation of orgasm and death is traditional. In French, an orgasm is often called *la petite mort*, "the little death" or, more literally "the little female death." In Kaula Tantra, this view is reflected when a male adept and his Yogini perform sacred sexual intercourse on top of a corpse, and the communion between Shiva and Shakti takes place in this tension between love and death.

This point also plays an important part in our perception of sexual roles. Whereas the life-giving principle has always been ascribed to men, especially in the patriarchal society characteristic of many Sun cults, the image of women as those who give birth has been repressed; they are instead demonized as those who devour. Such prejudices seem absurd to the modern pragmatic thinker who does not understand the reasons behind their development. On the one hand, these reasons can be found in subconscious fears: men's fear in face of women's greater power of sexual performance, fear of being devoured by the archetypal "vagina dentata", fear of female energy-vampirism etc. On the other hand, the adoption of a compensatory superior role contributes to the problem. As sex magicians, we must realize there are two sides to the "male/female" complex. Man is the active, conquering progenitor/father and life-giver, or solar principle, while the woman is the passive, conceiving one who gives birth—a lunar but also earth principle—who incorporates the primordial "chthonic" depths and is therefore the one who devours. However, we also find the roles reversed: man as soldier of destruction and death, to whom the woman forms the constructive counter-pole, being life giver and life preserver. It would be equal nonsense to call either view the only "true" one in the interest of some ideology, just as it would be stupid to deny the real differences between the sexes. In any case, orgasm is experienced by both sides as a "little death," as disintegration of the Ego, as loss of other reality, as pure ecstasy, even as an out-of-the-body experience as described, for example, in the *Tibetan Book of the Dead*—whose sex-magic aspects, by the way, are far from being fully explored.

We will meet the subject of death again in the discussion of the Hermaphrodite Ritual of the *Chymical Marriage*. Suffice it to say that the magical sacrifice of animals should be seen as a poor substitute for a sex-magic ceremony, rather than the other way around. Occasionally, the sacrifice of animals is in fact connected with sex magic, as at the ritual of the Goat of Mendes, or sometimes even at the black mass, both to be discussed later.

Animal sacrifice was certainly an early substitute for human sacrifice, but we should not forget that any sex-magic ceremony which avoids actual physical impregnation does indeed "sacrifice" a potential human existence—which is one reason for the prohibition of masturbation and contraception by the Catholic Church. In these terms, most sex-magic operations are a symbolic human sacrifice. If we propose the hypothesis that, on an archetypal level, the subconscious mind understands it in exactly that way, it could explain the strong inner tensions from which sex magic gets its efficacy. It also explains why animal sacrifices are generally not needed in sex magic.

Strictly speaking, the sigils constructed and activated according to Spare's method are purely "astral" or nonphysical. Occasionally, they are also physically fixed by drawing them onto a virgin parchment, which makes them into talismans, amulets or fetishes. In that case, the parchment is sewn into a silk or leather pouch so that the sigil really can be forgotten.

The general sex-magic technique for charging talismans, amulets and fetishes is to direct one's entire will-energy into the objects during sexual climax, so that the energy is stored within them as if in a charged battery. The actual technique is much less complicated than one might expect. It may be a simple laying on of hands, but more frequently the objects are anointed with the sexual secretions, which are considered to be particularly effective carriers of the sexual *magis* and which can therefore be administered as a sacrament, or "holy substance." Thus the sexual "elixir" becomes the medium for the energy which has been charged with the statement of desire. A popular technique is to project the energy into the object in form of an imagined beam or vortex.

Sexually charged talismans, amulets and fetishes are particularly effective, so the magician must take special care that they do not fall into unauthorized hands. Often they attract people by their archetypal ugliness—a piece of iron, for example, which is engraved with sigils and spread with sperm or menstrual blood is not usually a very esthetic sight—but such people would not know how to handle the energies stored in them. It is as if a child were to grab a power line with bare hands, whereas the magician is like the electrician who knows exactly how to isolate dangerous energies in order to turn them to good use.

Any experienced magician knows that magical objects are simply aids to support the imagination, and that ideally we could do without them. But this is not easy, because only the adept really masters the "techniques of the empty hand." Even then, the adepts will often hold on to magical tools, partly as a reminder of their own fallibility and partly to preserve the magical "batteries" as insurance against mental failure or loss of power. Never forget that these talismans, amulets and fetishes are *parts of yourself!* Treat them as parts of your own body and take care that you yourself remain in command over them!

You may produce talismans, amulets and fetishes in any of the sexual modes, but, for purely practical reasons, you will probably charge most of them autoerotically. Find out your own best times for sex-magic work. In general, the new moon and the last quarter of the waning moon are recommended, but many sex magicians report individual differences. Not everybody reacts equally strongly to the lunar phases, although you might discover that sex magic increases your sensitivity in this respect. Constructive operations such as healing are often best performed at full moon. Nevertheless, it is probably best to orient oneself by one's own individual cycles rather than by some calendar. Once your intuition has been developed by magical practice, you no longer need an ephemeris to set the time for ritual because an inner voice will tell you with far greater accuracy.

Telepathy and Other Psi-Phenomena

Magic is often confused with psi ability. Journalists especially like to ask the magician to "do some spells, please," meaning that they want to see "miracles": a glass shattered by mere thought power, a spectacular levitation or materialization—especially of money—and other such nonsense. I personally do not know any serious magician who would agree to something like this, and certainly not through fear of failure. The reason is that real magicians are rarely interested in such phenomena because they are at best a side effect to the true aims of magic. So-called "paranormal abilities" do occasionally appear in magic—in particular divination and precognition—but they are not the aim of magical practice. They actually distract the magician more than being of use, and it is no coincidence that Yoga also despises the psi abilities (the so-called *siddhis*) as distractions, although every real guru has some experience of them. Perhaps the reason that these phenomena occasionally occur although uncalled-for is just through lack of vigilance. The fact that they are most easily aroused in a playful way, whereas any grim striving for mastery usually ends in frustration, also supports the argument. You should always recognize such phenomena as soon as they appear, but you should not cling to them or make the mistake of looking out for them.

Telepathy is particularly prominent in sex magic with a partner, and female magicians often report greater sensitivity for divination.

One type of telepathy and telekinesis which is relevant for magic is magical remote influence.

Remote Sex-Magic Influence

Doll Magic and Healing

One of the most important areas in magic is remote influence. This can serve a range of purposes—from constructive ones like healing to destructive ones like death charms. The "trick" is to imagine the person you want to influence as vividly as possible at the moment of climax. During orgasm, the desired energy is directed towards the person concerned by an act of imagination.

Experience has shown that this works best between persons who have a strong emotional link. If necessary, such emotions have to be artificially invoked, as, for example, when the operation is performed for a client and the person to be influenced is not known personally.

Doll magic, another well-known technique, is not, as is commonly believed, peculiar to Voodoo. In the European Middle Ages, dolls made of rags and wood were used to impersonate a target person. Nor is doll magic only used for destructive and death spells; doll magic is equally suited to sympathetic healing. The doll may be made of any material: beeswax, wood or rags are common, but leather and even stone are also used. The important thing is that the doll is magically linked with the target. It is quite difficult to obtain a strong link by mental power alone, so normally locks of hair, nail parings, blood or other secretions from the target are fixed on or built into the doll. Nowadays, magicians like to integrate a photograph of the target into the doll—to provide its face, for example. According to the law "as above—so below," the doll *becomes* the target person, and anything that happens to it happens also to the target. If the target suffers from some illness, the magician may treat the doll as a patient and give it power by means of sex magic

Even sexual intercourse with the doll is possible; this has proven to be a powerful love spell—if you dare to incur the karmic consequences of interfering with the will of another. Less frequently, the doll serves as the material basis when dealing with succubi and incubi, which we consider in the next chapter. If a doll is used, then it either serves at the beginning to help the evocation or it is used to store energy. In the latter case, the doll becomes a real sexual and magical fetish.

There is only one basic principle to doll magic: *once the doll has been identified with the target person, you treat it exactly as you would treat the target itself.* Therefore, all descriptions of special rituals and techniques are superfluous as long as we heed the basic requirement "will + imagination + magical trance," without which no effective magic is possible. To influence a person in a remote magical way you must have a one-pointed will, your imagination has to clearly visualize the desired effect, and you have to be in a magical trance when doing it. Sexual excitement and orgasm readily get you into this trance—and that, once again, is why sex magic is so powerful.

The magical mirror is very popular for magical remote influence. The necessary energy is either built up in the mirror, and the mirror is then directed towards the target like an antenna, or else the target is visualized in the mirror, and you then manipulate this image in the desired way. Since sex magic is so effective with visionary techniques, this is obviously a good approach.

The *deflection doll* is an excellent form of protection against undesirable remote influence. In this case, the principle of doll magic is reversed: you build a doll which represents *yourself.* It is this doll which will bear the brunt of any attacks. The most efficient way to charge the doll is by masturbating and adding the sexual secretions whilst you "calibrate" it with a sentence of desire to receive and store all magical energies which are directed towards it. The point of storing the energy is very important, because otherwise the doll would redirect it faithfully towards you! Thus you create a dummy which gets the thrashing instead of yourself. The deflection doll should be kept in a prominent place—for example, in your temple. Every now and then you should discharge it; for example, by holding it under running water for half an hour.

Should you master the technique of total shielding, which is equivalent to an astral invisibility spell, you can even build several deflection dolls with the purpose of sending them out at the peak of a magical war as a diversionary tactic to veil your own activities. This has the advantage that your shielding spell will not immediately be recognized, and the antagonists will therefore aim at the wrong object and give themselves away. Thus you create a whole army of "silent allies." However, such screening skills demand a great deal of combat experience. There is also the risk that you will have to bind part of your *magis* because of being quite distant from your deflection dolls, and you will also have to be attentive so as not to stumble into any traps set by your adversary. If nothing else, this will keep you awake, and you can be sure that you won't be bored!

A Tip for Healing Spells

Surprising though it may seem, it is the peak of so-called black magic to try to heal someone who has not asked for it. Illness is more than just a nuisance to be avoided at all costs; it can be an important part of one's fate, a stimulus to change. The sick person may well have worked toward becoming ill in order to learn some particular lesson. You will often find that, deep down, sick people do not really want to become healthy again. Perhaps the sickness helps them to hold on to certain experiences which they might not otherwise have; for example, getting attention or compassion. Perhaps their illnessnes are intended to bring about changes, decisions or redirections of energy. Therefore, don't be so foolish as to heal anybody without asking! There is hardly anything worse than the do-gooder who means so well that they constantly interfere with and suffocate others with their "love." Over and above this, such action would be highly inadvisable from a sex-magic point of view because, in effect, even if not in intention, it would amount to an attack that could well trigger subconscious defence mechanisms. It is not enough to want to do "good" at any price because of some naive sense of morality or unacknowledged guilt; make sure that the patient really wants your magical help and will accept it. You do not necessarily have to call it "magic" to his or her face. If the word "magic" might alarm the patient, call it a "healing prayer" or a "paramedical remote suggestion." The main thing is to make sure that the patient wants your help first. It is a completely different matter if there has been an accident where the patient is unconscious; then you must let your true will make the decision as to whether you accept the responsibility and attendant risk.

Never forget that equal balances equal; the stronger the energies with which you work, the stronger are the reactions—for good or evil! Since sex magic involves great power, we have to take appropriate care.

Astral Travel and Doppelgänger Magic

Astral traveling and doppelgänger magic are both enhanced and facilitated by the use of sex magic. Sexual trance is a powerful stimulus to astral projection, whether the trance is achieved by extended sexual abstinence or by creating eroto-comatose lucidity through overstimulation and exhaustion. In the latter case it is necessary to work with a partner, both of you being naked so the partners can sexually stimulate each other by massage and caressing the erogenous zones, holding back shortly before climax. This should be repeated several times until a point of dreamy exhaustion is reached. Then the activating partner stands or sits at the feet of the entranced partner and stretches out the arms, the palms toward the lying partner. The lying partner, with eyes closed, tries to feel his or her own astral body being drawn out of the physical and towards the palms of the other as they inhale. The active partner imagines this too. It is important that the astral body of the lying partner should be "sucked" out on the inhalation and simply held and stabilized during the exhalation or when holding the breath. This stabilizing is every bit as important as the drawing out of the astral body because it helps to consolidate the experience and give the astral body more substance.

The projection may occur in a number of ways. Usually the astral body rises out of the physical body while remaining horizontal; sometimes it leaves the body through the head or feet.

Don't be put off by authors who insist that there must be a connection between the astral and physical bodies—the so-called "silver cord," said to run either between navel and navel or between the back of the astral head and the forehead of the physical body. As a matter of fact, this phenomenon is very rare. Tests in Australia and England have shown that only three percent of all astral travelers perceive the silver cord. If you do perceive it, that's fine; if not, don't worry.

Once you feel you have left your physical body, start transferring your consciousness into every part of the astral body. *Do not make the mistake of immediately looking around with the eyes of the astral body!* If the astral body has not been sufficiently consolidated, and it hardly ever is during the first attempt, the ethereal perception can collapse. Rather, try to "build up" your astral body step by step, beginning with the feet and proceeding to the head. Keep to the same order as given for the deep relaxation, but instead of the suggestion of relaxation and warmth, you should focus on firmness and consciousness. Only when you have properly "animated" the entire astral body can you concentrate on astral-sensual perceptions. Try to hear, taste, smell and feel with your astral body—and last of all try to see. Scrutinize your environment with your astral body without comment (the physical eyes are closed) until your perceptive focus has improved. In the beginning, you will probably have the same impression that you got with the 180° gaze—a somewhat blurred but many-sided optical perception. In this case, you should first concentrate on the aura of your standing partner (who is still concentrating on efforts to draw out the astral body) and "scan" it before eventually directing your attention to his or her physical body. You then look at this body astrally with all its details. Once you can achieve and hold that perception, your astral sight will have been stabilized sufficiently. The standing partner will nevertheless have to keep up his or her efforts because now you enter a tricky phase which may cost you all of your power.

For now you turn your astral body and look at your own physical body. Have a look at it as you did before with your astral body, beginning at the feet and ending at the head. *Last of all, you look at your face.* This is the crucial test for two reasons. First, it will finally convince you with a hundred percent certainty that you really have succeeded with your astral exit, because hardly anybody is able to imagine his or her own face in full detail without difficult training for years. Second, seeing one's own face is such a shock for many beginners that they shoot right back into their physical body and may have to fight the resulting mental block for years to come. I myself practiced astral projection (although not in a sex-magical way) at the age of 14 and achieved the desired success after only three weeks of regular practice (without the silver cord, by the way). However, when I looked down from the ceiling and suddenly saw my face in every detail, that was it! It was ten more years before I managed another astral projection. This experience, which has been confirmed by several other magicians, has convinced me that it is of the utmost importance to prepare this test carefully.

Once you have fully succeeded with your astral projection, you may travel around with your astral body as much as you like. You can give your partner some pre-arranged signal, such as raising the left forefinger of your physical body, to signify that the work is done and that he or she can relax. If your astral form is stable enough, small motions of your lying physical body won't disrupt your astral exit. There is therefore no objection to giving such a signal.

Unlike the astral body, the magical *doppelgänger* does not necessarily have the same shape as the physical body. Once the awareness flows out of the physical body, it may then be shaped at will by the magician. It may take the form of a blue ball, a hailstorm, or even an animal—a very popular form among shamans. The technique for projecting the doppelgänger is the same as for astral traveling. Once again, sexual stimulation helps you to master this technique within the shortest period; it would otherwise need many years of training.

Later, when you master astral projection without the help of a partner, you will no longer do it during a sex-magic ritual except for some specific purpose. Pure astral "tourism" just to satisfy one's curiosity is possible but not advisable. First, such dabbling can weaken one's ability to project astrally and, second, an astral body or doppelgänger projected by sex magic is so highly charged that it cries out for purposeful expression. In my experience, this means practical magic.

If at first you don't succeed immediately with astral projection, don't worry; just keep practicing, either with a partner or on your own. Nobody can guarantee success within a certain period; all I can promise is that it works much quicker with sex magic than without.[11]

How to Handle Magical Weapons

If you want to work with traditional magical "weapons" such as the dagger (will), wand (fire), sword (air), cup (water), pentacle (earth) etc., you should charge them by sex magic. Alternatively, you could obtain a special set of weapons for sex-magic ritual operations. These weapons could be just the same as the usual, but it would be better if they were specifically geared to sex magic. The wand, for example, might have the shape of a phallus; the cup might be like a vulva; the pentacle might show a couple copulating in a field of wheat etc.

When you charge your personal magical weapons by sex magic, you should do it autoerotically so that they are infused with *your own* sexual *magis* and no one else's. If, on the other hand, you share a temple or altar with a sex-magic partner, you may well charge the temple or altar together, whether in a hetero- or homosexual way. The same can be done with objects such as fetishes which you share in your workings. Apart from this, the same principles apply to sex-magically charged weapons as to magical weapons in general. They should be made by yourself using the best of your skills, or at least they should have come to you in some unusual manner. Take care that they don't get into the hands of unauthorized persons who might abuse their power. If you have no experience of ceremonial magic, you will first have to get some practical ritual-magic experience before consecrating or charging your magical weapons. Describing all this here would take us too far from our subject, although the next point will look briefly at the basics of ritual and banishings.

Sex Magical Ritualistics and Banishings

Unlike many other magical authors, I believe that there is more to magic than ritual working; indeed, ritual is not even the most important part. Ritual is certainly highly developed and very popular in Western magic, and I do not deny that it has a great deal of power. I myself have made much use of it and still practice it today. But I have made an interesting observation: the more advanced a magician is, the less frequently he performs rituals. As Peter Carroll rightly says in *Psychonaut*: the sign of a true adept is the technique of the empty hand, which includes doing without rituals. During recent years, when interest in magic has been intensified (and we do not mean popularized), it has been shown again and again that magic can flourish without costly rituals and grandiose ceremonies.

Still, ritual has its place and probably always will have, because it is an archetypal act, maybe even one of the first acts which originally differentiated human from animal. In the beginning, it was a means of organizing and concentrating energy, but soon it fell into the hands of people interested in political power and influence, and they monopolized it for the priesthood. Well-ordered workings with several magicians together are impossible without a basic ritual structure. This is especially true for beginners, and for groups which consist mostly of beginners, or groups which are not able to raise beginners quickly enough to their group level. Ritual is an ideal means of channeling energies, and with repetition it also helps to wake the desired energies. So beginners are strongly advised not to overlook ritual magic; they will need such ritual experience when it comes to sharing sex magic with a partner.

Western ritual usually incorporates the following elements:

a) preparation
b) clearing and banishing
c) meditation on the desired energy
d) invocation of the desired energy
e) performance of the magical act of will
f) sending the energy out or giving thanks
g) banishing
h) writing up the operation

Points *a* and *h* are self-explanatory and do not need a separate explanation. Point *b* will be dealt with later. Point *c* is illustrated when magicians stimulate themselves sexually to produce the necessary tension. At point *d*, the energy is focused with an appropriate chant or use of imagination, and at *e* the orgasm leads into the real act of will. In phase *f*, the original balance is restored, and *g* is a repeat of *b*. This structure applies to both magical and mystical rituals, whatever their purpose. The whole procedure is supported by formulas and gestures, by magical weapons and fetishes etc., but this book is not the place for such details.

To point *d*, it has to be added that invocations of deities and rulers of elements are usually accompanied with a hymn or chant which should ideally be written by oneself. These invocations have their own typical structure: 1) calling the desired energy, 2) description of its attributes and its glory, 3) declaration of becoming one with the energy in a moment of ecstasy, 4) confirmation of this oneness during the magical act of will, and 5) thanksgiving and dismissal of the invoked energy. While, for example, phases 1 and 2 are characterized by the "you" form (for example, "I call you, Mercury!" "You are magnificent, Jupiter!" etc.), in phases 3 and 4 the "I" form is frequently emphasized (for example, "I am Mars!" or "I, Venus, thus call forth...!"). In the final phase 5, the "you" form is used again. In sex magic specifically, the different phases are supported by different levels of stimulation so the orgasm, if included, usually happens in phase 4.

Although there are some exceptions, this structure is basic to nearly all magical rituals and ceremonies in the Western tradition. Sometimes it begins with an admission ceremony, particularly in Masonic-style groups. It may also happen that the working is done without protection, as in so-called "spontaneous" magic; or the order may be reversed, as in the blasphemous masses of chaos magic designed to free one from stereotyped behavior and expectations. Not all magicians are conscious of this ritual structure, but they follow it intuitively and are glad to stick to it when they work with colleagues from other systems. The technically oriented reader might be interested to know that a clearly structured magical ritual has the same advantages as a clearly structured computer program: the ritual "software" brings the "hardware" (body, *magis*, energetic potential) in alignment so that it can be employed purposefully. Frequently, the ritual structure provides a thread of continuity which leads the magician through the form even in a very deep trance.

Banishing, as explained earlier, is both a concentration on essential elements and an elimination of disturbing influences. It involves building up protective symbols, charging them and creating a harmonic balance (for example, the invoking of the rulers of the elements and archangels in the Lesser Banishing Ritual of the Pentagram), and driving out unwanted energies or entities by appropriate symbols and mantras. In other words, magicians build a border and enclose a universe inside which they have unlimited power—because of being initiated into the laws of magic.

The finest magical protection is to make sure you are firmly in your Hara and that your Lesser Energy Orbit is flowing strongly. Everything else is just an aid to ensure this! This explains why the real adept or master of magic only rarely needs physically performed rituals. To be in one's center is to be in harmony with the universe, so that everything in accord with one's own will happens anyway. This is a stage where magician and mystic become one.

With this, this very lengthy chapter is concluded. Because of lack of space, many things could only be touched upon. To the beginner, some things may seem bewildering, whereas the advanced may consider them trivial. Since magic in our society is in such a poor state, with no common standards to define the reader's level of magical knowledge and practical experience, it is necessary to compromise. People who really understand the basic structures of magic do not need detailed knowledge, because they can correctly deduce everything from first principles. Beginners are not aware of this freedom: instead of working it out for themselves, they search desperately for further rules and added complications to which they can cling. No magical teacher should encourage this. The arrogance with which earlier writers looked down on the "stupid, ignorant non-initiate," while at the same time withholding the decisive knowledge, is no better than post-pubescent sadism—something we should all grow out of. One limits the power of magic if one makes it overly easy—but, on the other hand, magic makes such demands on discipline and flexibility that it is unnecessary to put deliberate obstacles in the way. The true secrets protect themselves and cannot be given away or desecrated—on the contrary, only by "revealing" them constantly are they truly protected. Everything else leads to distortion and mutilation of the original wisdom. It is about time that magic became once more the unified art and science which it used to be—an art and science with the power to embrace life's many contradictions!

Notes

[1]Compare the part on money magic with my essay, "Geldmagie, oder mit Dreck fängt man keine Mäuse," *Anubis. Zeitschrift für praktische Magie und Psychonautik* 1 (1985), pp. 13–21.

[2]Also compare my essay "'Zufall natürlich!' Das Problem der magischen Erfolgskontrolle," *Unicorn* 7 (1983), pp. 225–229.

[3]George Ivanovas offers an overview of different scent correspondences in his article "Räucherwerk—Nahrung der Götter," *Unicorn* 5 (1983), pp. 80–84. Please note that his listings of Crowley's correspondences for Mars and Venus are exchanged.

A special introduction into the area of magical correspondences may be found in my article, "Mythen in Tüten—Vom magischen Umgang mit Analogien," *Unicorn* 11 (1984), pp. 221–229.

[4]Compare Peter Ellert and Jörg Wichmann, "Der kleine Gott. in jedem Quark begräbt er seine Nase. Ein Komplementaritätsmodell von Magie und Naturwissenschaft," *Unicorn,* 13:1985, pp. 100–105.

A simplified description of this model can be found in Peter Ellert's introduction to Peter Carroll's *Psychonautik. Liber Null Teil II,* Bad Honnef: Edition Magus, 1984, pp. 11–13.

[5]Particularly worthy of mention are:

Ralph Tegtmeier, *Der heilende Regenbogen. Sinnvolle Spiele, Experimente und Meditationen zum kreativen Umgang mit den geheimnisvollen Energien Klang, Farbe und Licht,* Haldenwang: Edition Schangrila, 1985, and *Musikführer für die Reise nach Innen. Kosmische Klänge zum Entspannen und Meditieren,* Haldenwang: Edition Shangrila, 1985.

Franz Bardon, *Initiation into Hermetics,* Wuppertal: Rüggeberg, 1971.

[6]The best book on this subject still is Strephon Kaplan Williams, *Jungian-Senoi Dreamwork Manual,* Berkeley, PA: Journey Press, 1980.

[7]Compare also my article "Der Doppelgänger als magisches Faktotum," *Unicorn* 2 (1982), pp. 79–81.

[8]Peter J. Carroll, *Liber Null and Psychonaut* ,York Beach, ME: Samuel Weiser, Inc., 1987.

[9]Compare my detailed study on this subject, *Practical Sigil Magic,* St. Paul, MN: Llewellyn Publications. 1990; see also its bibliography.

[10]A future project of mine is a book on Planetary Magic.

[11]Compare my essay, "Spaltungsmagie: Der Doppelgänger als magisches Faktotum," *Unicorn* 2 (1982), pp. 79–81.

PRACTICAL APPLICATIONS

Orgasm—Yes or No?

In the '20s, there was much discussion about avoiding orgasm, particularly in German magical literature. The authors, who were largely influenced by Eastern Tantric ideas, looked for a "new" (though really ancient) form of sexuality and love. Out of this grew the method of "karezza," which became highly respected among occultists.

From modern Tantric literature we know the importance of avoiding orgasm. It has been argued for thousands of years that male semen is much too valuable and loaded with energy to be wasted. Tantricists try to achieve the *Unio Mystica*, or "union of Shiva and Shakti," by means of ritual in which orgasm is avoided. Kundalini, which slumbers in the root chakra, is awakened and directed upwards through the middle of the spinal cord *(Sushumna)* to become one with its female counterpart in the "thousand petalled lotus" or crown chakra. One modern Tantric text, the *Anandasutram* by Anandamurti, says, *"Shiva shakti atmaka brahma,"* which means "Brahman (the highest deity) is the union between Shiva and Shakti." Thus, God or the highest principle is understood and experienced as the unification of male and female and as a surmounting of the sexual poles. We find this concept in Occidental alchemy and mysticism, too, whether in the union of "Adam, the Red" with "Eve, the White", the androgynous cult or those heretical sects which combined male and female on an equal basis. There were, for example, the "gnostic syzygie" (union, conjunction) of Simon and Helena, and the Holy Mary and minnesinger or troubadour cult of the courtly and post-courtly period.

Chinese culture developed (almost certainly through Indian influence) the "Inner Alchemy" of Taoism, which is also called "Taoist Alchemy" or "Tao Yoga." This deals mainly with the prolongation of physical life by avoiding ejaculation, but also with the mystical "union of heaven and earth." This alchemy is closely related to the meridian lore of acupuncture, which runs through the entirety of Chinese philosophy and works chiefly with the Ching Chi or "sexual Chi," which is similar to the "sexual prana" or "sexual *magis*." Unlike Kundalini Yoga and Tantra, Tao Yoga does not merely aim at directing the sexual energy up the spine; it also leads the energy down the front of the body back to its origin, where it is stored in the navel area (the Lesser Energy Orbit). Here again, as with Tantra, the exchange of sexual energy with a partner is possible.

So far, we have equated "orgasm" with "ejaculation." This indicates a dilemma that characterizes most Eastern sexual systems. Nearly always it is male sexuality which is considered; female sexuality is coyly avoided or concealed with vague and evasive phrases. There is plenty about the necessity of avoiding ejaculation, but little advice for female adepts. Now, it can happen that women ejaculate like men during climax—particularly, if the so-called G-spot or "Grafenberg spot" is stimulated—but this is not the rule.

We want to have a closer look at this subject, because it is still a source of misunderstanding and sometimes fatal error in magical practice. Let us start with the equation "male orgasm = ejaculation." The orgasm of a man can be identified most easily by ejaculation, and an orgasm can also be prevented by avoiding ejaculation—but is the subject really avoiding *orgasm?* Do ejaculation and orgasm have to be identical?

To answer the first question, we will first have to deal with the second one. Scientists and experts cannot yet agree whether orgasm and ejaculation are identical. Increased scientific study of female orgasm, which is more complicated than male orgasm, has simply added to the disagreement. Unfortunately, investigators tend to overlook one phenomenon which is known to many people who enjoy a healthy, trouble-free life; namely, male orgasm *without* ejaculation! Men who have experienced it know that it differs from the usual ejaculatory orgasm, because it does not only touch the genitals but involves the entire body. This nonejaculatory orgasm is also called "full body" or "valley" orgasm, whereas the usual ejaculatory orgasm is called "genital" or "peak" orgasm. The images of "valley" and "peak" show clearly the different energetic qualities of the two forms of orgasm. While the ejaculative orgasm "mounts" in a short climax, after which the excitation drops like sliding down a mountain slope, the nonejaculatory valley orgasm is characterized by a long-lasting level of excitation without peaks and valleys. This form of orgasm gives the feeling of being subjected to high voltage, and one is sometimes almost glad when it stops—not because it is unpleasant, but because it can be so unbearably beautiful that one fears the neural fuses might blow! Strictly speaking, this is a controllable form of the so-called "Kundalini syndrome," which Gopi Krishna describes in his classic book *Kundalini*. This state equates with Crowley's "eroto-comatose lucidity"—although the latter may be attained by a different method described later.

To my knowledge, no other author has talked about valley orgasm in such a precise and explicit manner as Mantak Chia in his two works, *Tao Yoga* and *Tao Yoga of Love*. We recommend them to anybody interested in body-oriented sexual wisdom. Chia states clearly that it is the ancient need to *avoid loss of semen* which hits the crux of the problem, whereas actual orgasm should not be excluded. On the contrary, through the valley orgasm the adept attains what Chinese Taoists call the "union of heaven and earth," which corresponds to the fusion of Shiva and Shakti in Kundalini Yoga and Tantra. Once this new state of orgasm is mastered, ejaculation becomes superfluous, and the energies contained in the semen are not wasted; they are refined and stored within the body.

Chia is not totally consistent, however. For example, he warns against using nonejaculatory sex as a means of birth control, because any accidentally released semen would be particularly strong and efficient for fathering after having been kept back for so long. On the other hand, he says on the same page that he himself ejaculated by masturbation when he was planning to father a son in order to get rid of the weak semen first and make room for new, fresh and fathering-efficient semen. Additionally, he indulges in several rather obscure calculations as to how many liters of semen an average, frequently ejaculating American loses during a statistically average long life. Mantak Chia warns somewhat naively that, because of the valuable raw materials and trace elements contained in the ejaculate, it should be obvious how dangerous the loss of semen is on account of such overexploitation of physical reserves.

Such quantitative justification simply tells me that the author has not yet made his peace with science. Trying to gain the respect of the white-collar gods of science is no solution; it is simply nonsense to explain premature aging and symptoms of disintegration by the minute amount of trace elements lost through ejaculation, all of which can be quickly restored with an average balanced diet. Even more bizarre are the practices described by Mantak Chia whereby the semen is ejaculated into the bladder and excreted with the urine—with no concession to "securing the trace elements"! So you must allow for such odd lapses in Mantak Chia's books, which in other respects are quite excellent.

Similar strange advice can be found in traditional Tantra and Yoga texts. In the famous *Hatha Yoga Pradipika* (the standard work of physical Yoga), practices are described, whereby the yogi learns to suck in fluids with his penis—supported by certain breathing techniques and muscle-contracting exercises—just in case some semen should be lost when performing the sacred act. This begs the question as to whether a yogi who has such body control, could not equally easily control the ejaculation itself. The suspicion arises that these exercises serve rather as general discipline and as a deromanticizing of sexual matters than any true "energy recycling"!

Interestingly enough, Mantak Chia and others do differentiate between "semen-water" and "semen." Chia considers the semen-water, which is that clear fluid which often precedes the ejaculation and sometimes follows it, as being so low in nutrients that its loss need not be taken too seriously. He also states that this semen-water is occasionally secreted in small quantities during valley orgasm, a fact confirmed by practice. But he does not expand further on this.

It seems to me that this conflict can be solved relatively easily from a magical viewpoint. True, the sexual act results in loss of energy, not only with men, but avoiding this is not so much a matter of saving physical semen as saving its *etheric components*. In other words, if you extract the Ching Chi, prana or sexual *magis* from the semen *after* ejaculation, what remains is relatively worthless. The organism can easily cope with this purely physical loss as long as the "sexual essence" is preserved. This does not involve fakir stunts with the urethra that could be quite dangerous for the entire bladder and genital region. It is sufficient to reabsorb the energy mentally with the inhalation and to feed it into the Lesser Energy Orbit. When performing an act of sex magic, the sexual *magis* is consciously directed to the "etheric level" in order to work there; this means that it is, as it were, "invested," so that it can come back to the magician in the form of the desired success. This is a conscious *transformation* or alchemical transmutation, hence not at all a waste as with normal, non-magical sex.

This confusion of the etheric with the material level is nothing new. It occurs typically when occultists try to woo the scientific community. They seek to justify their beliefs by looking for material factors which align with and explain the etheric ones; for example, the chakras were assigned to the glands, or electromagnetic fields are postulated to explain etheric forces. But this is also a very old phenomenon: it is striking how Yoga, with its concept of prana, should see so much harm in the material loss of semen. It is my opinion that a prejudice and misunderstanding has long been fostered, partly deliberately and partly unconsciously, and it serves to veil the real key to the sexual *magis*. It is not the material loss of semen which has to be avoided—but rather that *the etheric energy contained in the semen must be kept, refined and stored or transformed into magical success-energy.* In any case, magical sexuality requires a conscious handling of etheric forces.

We find similar ideas extant among the sexual-gnostics of late Hellenism, provided that we can trust the sources which derive mostly from their opponents, the Christian church fathers. According to these reports, the gnostics used to spread sexual secretion onto their palms and used it to absorb energy from the sun. As we will now see, Crowley's practice was also based on this principle.

Eroto-Comatose Lucidity

Behind this ghastly piece of jargon lies an experience which mankind has probably known for ages: that sexuality does not have to weaken but can, on the contrary, *activate and stimulate*. The pendulum seems to swing between two extremes: on the one hand, those who demand the strict retention of semen and, on the other hand, those who see a rejuvenating element in ejaculation because it activates the gonads and thus hormonally stimulates the entire body.

The term "eroto-comatose lucidity," which comes from Crow-

ley, has three parts. "Eroto" indicates sexual force. The word "coma-
tose" suggests coma, hence the state of unconsciousness: it actually
means the magical trance as we already know it. "Lucidity" is a state
of clairvoyance or heightened awareness. Hence Crowley's term
means nothing else but "magical trance induced by sex." Such a
trance, as long as the individual does not simply get lost in it as most
people do, does not only strengthen, but it also increases the creativ-
ity and "vigor." With Crowley, this is achieved by overstimulation
and excessive sexual activity, which amounts technically to a sexual
exhaustion-trance.

For artistic natures, this is nothing new. Austin Osman Spare
was well known for his sexual activity, as were Picasso, the writer
Henry Miller, and his colleague Georges Simenon. Actors, dancers
or musicians of any merit—regardless of gender—all know about
the "power-station sexuality" which slumbers within us. Sexuality
here is not used as a means of manipulating other people by exploit-
ing their desires; what is used is the vital power contained in sexuality which mankind has given so many names: *prana*, mana, *Chi*,
ether, Vril, Od, Kia, *magis* etc.

Crowley, in fact, trod in his practice a path similar to that of the
more materialistic authorities. Although he positively encouraged
ejaculatory orgasm in his sex magic, he always made a point of consuming what he called the "elixir" afterwards. He understood this
elixir to be the mixture of the sexual fluids of both partners or, in the
masturbatory act, as just the semen. He entered very carefully in his
magical diaries a description of the elixir's consistency and taste,
and he even recorded the prophecies which he deduced from these
data. This means that even the Master Therion was mainly interested in saving and consuming the material substance instead of
concentrating on its etheric nature.

The magician works with intense states of consciousness. Even
if avoiding full trance because of the loss of will involved, a magician will approach full trance as shamans do as far as possible in order to perform an important operation. Occasionally, the magician
contravenes this rule and deliberately seeks full trance, but not
without having invited a confidant to supervise the operation. The
obsession techniques of Voodoo, Macumba, Candomblé or Santería
work with full trance, which in these cases involves a purposeful invocation at the moment of loss of consciousness, because it is not the
aim to go arbitrarily into trance. The one full trance most easily at-

tained and most efficient is the moment of ejaculation and orgasm, even if it only lasts a second or two. Furthermore, sex magic is much less dangerous than other magical systems, because orgasm is a completely natural form of trance which does not require any of the severe and unnatural means frequently employed in shamanistic cultures to get into this altered state of consciousness.

A prerequisite for this use of orgasm is that it should be prolonged. If we "inject" the moment of climax with our magical sentence of desire, it helps if the moment does not pass too quickly. You may achieve this by trying to heighten and intensify the orgasm by mental power. The intensification is not itself the actual purpose, but experience has shown that you will prolong the orgasm in this manner. Anyway, further intensification is also quite desirable for its own sake!

Orgasm is the moment when the walls between consciousness and subconsciousness are sundered and direct access to the deeper levels of the psyche becomes possible. Ejaculation itself feels like a *push*, a hurling forward of the magical will and the *magis*. Since, with men, the ejaculate is merely the material carrier of this energy, as is the vaginal secretion with women, it is clear that we use the substance only for symbolic reasons and spread it onto talismans, amulets or pentacles to transfer the power in a symbolic and sympathetic-magical way. It should be obvious that the energy is *not* extracted from the sexual fluid if you want to *charge* an external object with the sexual *magis*, but, if you want to activate these objects, you must reabsorb the sexual *magis* contained in the ejaculate or secretion by imagination, store it in your body and perform the charging and activation in an etheric manner.

One advantage which a peak orgasm has over a valley orgasm is that the latter often depends on long training. Mantak Chia denies that such training is always possible, but practice has proved otherwise. Sometimes the will to avoid ejaculation is enough to direct the sexual *magis* into a valley orgasm. The following tips should help with the conscious magical handling of orgasm and sexual *magis* and are applicable to all forms of sex magic.

The Magical Use of the Genital Orgasm
(These clues are equally applicable to male and female magicians.)

In Western sex magic, the genital orgasm is the rule rather than the exception, as it is in Tantra! Enough groundwork has been provided in the previous section that you should be able to catch the precise moment of climax and use it for magic. Since masturbation is the easiest way, we will start with autoerotic techniques.

We have defined the magical act as "sentence of desire + imagination + gnostic trance." Formulating the sentence of desire comes first and must be considered an important part of the operation, but this has already been dealt with.

Orgasm itself is sufficient to achieve gnostic trance provided that control is maintained and one does not simply lose consciousness, as most people do at the moment of ecstasy. By thorough self-observation, you will come to know the signs that orgasm is about to occur. It is of the utmost importance that you do not immediately let go; rather you must hold back briefly at this point. This ensures prolongation and intensification of the orgasm, which is always more powerful after a short period of holding back. At the moment of the climax, you must be ready to activate the sentence of desire. For example, the sigil should lie ready in front of you or be readily visualized, the mantra should be spoken clearly at the right moment, the desired situation should be imagined with full intensity, or energy should be polarized in a special way and directed towards the aim. Rather than allowing yourself to be suddenly surprised and overwhelmed by the orgasm, you should train yourself in the techniques for delaying orgasm, to be described later.

The longer the orgasm, the more time you have for the magical operation. Do not be too demanding. If your orgasm usually lasts one second, prolonging to "only" two seconds would be an increase of 100 percent, which is already quite an achievement. You are not expected to use a stopwatch; the time is mostly subjective. It is well known that time perception during orgasm is altered, so that one second can be felt subjectively as an eternity—part of the pleasure of sex!

In summary, the procedure is as follows: you decide to perform a sex-magic operation and formulate your sentence or image of desire. Then you activate your sexual *magis* and, at the moment of peak orgasm, concentrate *exclusively* on the sentence of desire. This concentration is not a mere "attentive thinking about it," but an act of total imagination that ideally involves one's *whole organism*.

Now, the moment of genital orgasm cannot always be precisely defined; it raises some questions. Do you count only the period of the most intense contractions, and face the problem that you do not know if they were the most intense until after the event, or are you able do justice to the subtleties of orgasm by reducing it to a single climax? Indeed, the genital orgasm is a complex *process,* although apparently much shorter and one-pointed than the valley orgasm, and this process has to be used in its entirety. We do not start with the magical operation at the moment of the climax; we rather work towards it, bringing the climax of the operation and the climax of the orgasm together almost as two lovers might seek to climax at the same moment. This is a matter of experience that nobody can achieve for you. It may comfort you to be told that success can still be attained with only a "vague termination." This works better if the climax of imagination comes shortly *after* the sexual climax; it works less frequently the other way around. If in doubt, therefore, it is sensible to wait until the climax is upon you before throwing yourself into the imagined whirlpool of power—an image which can actually be experienced in this form! Fine tuning the operation to maximize the chances of success will then be a matter of practice.

Another advantage of this technique over nonsex magical practices such as positive thinking is that it is not necessary to hang on to nor repeat the mental images. If you look at the training programs of authors such as Bardon, Gregorius or even Aleister Crowley, you will probably be appalled by the demands they make. Who could ever perform all the exercises that Bardon lays down? It would require at least 10 years of practice to do his first 10 levels before even starting with actual magic! We do not want to encourage sloppy training or inadequate preparation—quite the contrary. Bardon's exercises may be excellent, but his time limits are exaggerated, and this overemphasis has not helped the cause of magic among German-speaking peoples. Frightening off one's disciples with impossible standards while not keeping to them oneself is not good magic. Bardon, for example, warned constantly against smoking, but I happen to know for sure that he himself was a chain smoker.

It is not necessary to begin with a perfect imagination in order to practice magic. In magic, as with any other field of knowledge, only practice makes perfect. To go back to the image of driving lessons, somebody who has just got his driver's licence will not have the same traffic experience as a driver with 30 years practice. The beginner can only get this experience by driving—not by studying automotive mechanics or by "armchair driving" at home.

So don't despair if you encounter obstacles—this is part of magical practice! At least sex magic does not require you to remain motionless in the lotus posture for an hour with a brimful bowl of water balanced on your head! That particular exercise, which was developed by Crowley and used to train neophytes in his order Argenteum Astrum, is an excellent way to develop control of thought and the etheric body, but it is not basic to every kind of magic, least of all sex magic! Don't torment yourself with extreme exercises; simply find your strengths and weaknesses and work on them, for not everyone starts magic with the same physical and mental skills. As shamans say of "power animals," "what the owl is for one person, the nightingale is for another."

Next, what about the "sacrifice of lust" during magical sexual intercourse? As stated in the introduction, sex magic is not for lecherous debauchees, but let us not forget that orgasm is for many people their only chance to truly "let go." Nowhere else can they relax and encounter a "touch of eternity"; that is part of the value of sex. If you, therefore, subject this last fragment of liberty to your will, the reaction could be one of revulsion and disgust. The practice would be seen as killjoy puritanism, even though it strives for exactly the opposite.

In fact, such an attitude indicates a serious lack. If sexuality is really the only free space which someone has to let go, then that person is missing out on his or her slumbering potential for power. To such people sexuality is a substitute for everything missing in life.

Nevertheless, even more balanced and fulfilled people criticize the loss of lust with sex magic and Tantra. Writers who cling to Christian-like sacrifice-cult thinking talk about "sacrificing" lust on the "altar of magic," or of fulfilling one's will when performing sex magic. The lust will then be sublimated and transformed into magical power. This attitude is not really necessary for success in sex magic, but its value should not be underestimated. After all, sacrifices are an ancient archetype which can be found in the cultures of all times. Many people have internalized or, more accurately, activated this archetype in its perverted form to such an extent that they are not able to enjoy anything without apologizing for it and look for some pretext, or rather pseudo-religious excuse, for having a good time. This is a lack which derives mainly from feelings of guilt, but this is not the place to go more into its actual causes. Nevertheless, nearly everybody has an inner "sacrifice priest" that should be respected and utilized.

We can say here that, as for magic in general, it is to a large extent rather a matter of belief than technique. Should you realize that you make more progress in sex magic if you work with the sacrifice-model, then do it! However, even then you should at least occasionally try to allow feelings of lust during sex-magical operations. Lust is an integrated part of sexuality—*and* of the gnostic sexual trance! Lust is something like an additional thrust which can inspire your sexual *magis*. (Playful magic is the most successful kind!) Once you realize that you have fun, and that you don't need a "lust sacrifice" in sex magic any longer, enjoy it as long as you are able to work your magic carefully.

Magical Use of the Whole-Body Orgasm
(These tips are equally applicable to male and female magicians.)

Normally, whole-body orgasm is the exception and genital orgasm is the rule. It is actually very difficult to achieve whole-body orgasm deliberately because it seems to need such a high level of energy.

Still, there are certain guidelines. Basically, there are two types of whole-body orgasm involving different types of energy. One takes place immediately before genital orgasm would normally have occurred and actually prevents it; the other happens immediately after a genital orgasm so that the energy level is left on a kind of plateau.

This sort of whole-body orgasm is sometimes confused with a special type of genital orgasm that consists of a rapid-fire sequence of minor genital orgasms, in which the energy level between "mini-climaxes" remains high without the drop you expect after genital orgasm. The main difference is that these orgasms are restricted to the genital area, extending perhaps to the abdomen, stomach, lower spine and nipples. The real whole-body orgasm, however, embraces every fiber of the body. In general, women experience serial genital orgasms more often than men, but if men do experience them, the orgasmic contractions are only rarely ejaculatory.

Don't be confused if you find little reference to the whole-body orgasm and its relationship with serial orgasm in the literature of sexology. Despite much effort during the last hundred years, sexual science has made little progress. The existence of the "Grafenberg spot" is still debated among sexologists and anatomists, as is the

ability of women to ejaculate; and most scientists still raise an eye-
brow when the whole-body orgasm is mentioned. This is no wonder, because it can hardly be demonstrated in a laboratory. It is
better to trust your own experience and the reports of reliable magicians, Tantrics and Tao masters in these matters.

In general, the chances of a whole-body orgasm can be increased
in two ways: either by holding back genital orgasm or by exhaustion
and overstimulation. The stronger the sexual excitement, the
stronger the sexual *magis* will be, especially if you hold back shortly
before genital orgasm and (with men) avoid ejaculation, particularly after longer periods of abstinence. The stronger your sexual
magis, the more likely the whole-body orgasm will occur. This
method requires discipline and bodily control.

The second method demands excess and therefore requires a
strong sexual drive. After a series of genital orgasms, the sex organs
become tired and desensitized, but, if you still manage to get excited, then a whole-body orgasm can be reached without achieving
further genital orgasm. The difficulty here lies in being potent
enough to reach this stage!

Although whole-body orgasms are called "valley orgasms" or,
more rarely, "plateau orgasms," this does not mean that they are
completely free of contractions—hence the difficulty in distinguish-
ing them from serial genital orgasms. The contractions of the whole-
body orgasm are, however, almost continuous—like being "elec-
trified"—with occasional explosions of greater intensity. These explosions can take place in any part of the body—for example, in the
little finger of the left hand, or behind the right knee etc. A whole-
body orgasm can expand the personal energy field ("aura") so
much that a mere thought is enough to cause further spasms of ecstasy, and the physical presence of the partner is no longer needed
for orgasmic feelings. These are the times which provoke ideas such
as "the highest form of sexuality is the renunciation of sexuality."
One gets an insight into the deeper meaning of asceticism—not so
much the abandonment of pleasure as the search for an ecstasy beyond all others. As the old Chinese writings say, people who know
the valley orgasm will never be easily satisfied with mere genital orgasm. But it would be silly to chase only the whole-body orgasm;
better to enjoy both types of orgasm and "have the best of both
worlds." A whole-body orgasm is like the experience of *Unio Mystica*, and in sex magic it is nearly always linked with it—but, on the

other hand, not every whole-body orgasm leads automatically to *Unio Mystica!* Even if a whole-body orgasm would always lead to *Unio Mystica*, not even born ecstatics could bear such an experience for long. All the great mystics knew periods of inner emptiness, and seldom was the *Unio Mystica* permanent—although it did sometimes last for months or years. (The *Unio Mystica* corresponds to the Indian *Nirvikalpa Samadhi*, the *Satori* of Zen, the union of heaven and earth in Taoist sexual Yoga, the union of Shiva and Shakti in Tantra, the Nirvana of Buddhism and the *Ain* of the Jewish Kabbalah.) The great mystics all needed earthing to prevent the neural fuses from being burnt out; otherwise Moses' vision of the burning bush would have led to death or insanity. For such reasons one should deliberately balance whole-body orgasms with genital orgasms in order to keep both feet firmly "on the ground" once a high level of sensitivity is attained. This is also the reason why magicians and shamans practise normal, everyday occupations besides their magic; it keeps them in contact with the material world without their slipping into the intoxication of self-deception, which is the chief danger of the magical path.

The first time a whole-body orgasm is experienced, it is usually with a partner; but it can also be attained without one *after* this first experience, although with greater difficulty. Both partners frequently have the same experience at the same time, if they are sensitive and in harmony. The mistake is to link this experience with the partner. All Chinese Tao masters share the opinion that this experience should if possible be had on one's own and inside oneself. For this reason, we give two ways of working in the last chapter of this book, which deals with the Chymical Marriage: with a partner and autoerotically.

Readers may wonder which form of orgasm is best for which magical purpose. So long as you are not sure of being able to reach whole-body orgasm, this choice is only theoretical; once you get to that point, you will realize that the question depends upon the individual case.

In general, whole-body orgasms are suited for mystical and healing work or for luck or love spells, whereas work in connection with magical attacks or protective blockades is better with genital orgasm. Exceptions are nearly always the rule, however; for example, magical protection may be strengthened particularly well by a whole-body orgasm, whereas some forms of healing—mainly for tumors, viral infections, or other diseases connected with the immune system—tend to react better to sex-magic workings with genital orgasms. You must not cease experimenting and building up your own system. Once again, the motto is "practice makes perfect."

Secondary Comment

Today's literature about sex magic relies heavily on practices which were already common in the O.T.O. or in its later development by Aleister Crowley. This literature differentiates the workings of the VIIIth, IXth and XIth grade, which was introduced by Crowley. (The X° of the O.T.O. is a mere "administrative grade" of no special magical importance.) The division is as follows:

VIII° O.T.O. = autoerotic practice
IX° O.T.O. = heteroerotic practice
XI° O.T.O. = homoerotic practice

This is the traditional sex-magic practice as performed under Crowley. After his death, there were several schisms and new formations of the order, some of whose representatives are in a state of bitter feud. There are examples:

• The Swiss O.T.O. of Hermann Metzger, which had until recently almost died out. They practiced sex magic almost entirely in a symbolic way. The order is mainly known in the German-speaking world because it published Crowley's writings in German in the '50s through its own publishers, Psychosophische Gesellschaft, and also ran an abbey of "Thelema" in Stein (Appenzell). Currently (1990), some attempts are being made at reviving and rejuvenating this partcular branch of the O.T.O. which seem to show a certain degree of success. There is, however, still the old contention with the American based Caliphate O.T.O. (see below) as to the claim to sole, legitimate representation and world leadership. Both organizations claim the right to institute the leader or O.H.O. (Outer Head of Order).

• The English O.T.O. of Kenneth Grant. Grant was expelled from the O.T.O. proper by the former leader and legitimate Crowley successor, Karl Germer, and formed his own organization with the same name. Grant has not only made himself a name by publishing his rather controversial books about the "Typhonian current," he has also changed the sex-magical grade system of his O.T.O.

•The former Californian, now "Caliphate" O.T.O. (inofficially so termed) of the late Grady McMurtry (Caliph Hymenaeus Alpha), who was appointed head of the American O.T.O. by Crowley himself, subject to the approval of Karl Germer. Germer never approved nor disapproved this provisional appointment, but the courts seem to have ruled in favor of the sole authenticity of this branch, at least in the United States. This is today's largest and internationally most active O.T.O. group, with working temples from the United States to Europe (including England, Germany, Norway and even Yugoslavia) and Australia, and it still adheres to Crowley's sex-magical grade system.

•The O.T.O. of Marcello Motta in Memphis, Tennessee. Motta wrote some quite useful comments on Crowley's works, but his legitimate right to form his own O.T.O. was only recognized by himself and a few followers. During a court case against the American publisher Samuel Weiser, whom Motta sued for a million dollars because of allegedly infringing his copyrights on Crowley's works (unsuccessfully, by the way), it became known that his organization had only seven members.

•Some smaller splinter groups, such as the "Haitian Voodoo-O.T.O." of Michel Bertiaux or an O.T.O. group in Frankfurt (Germany) with connections to the French Martinist and Illuminati scene, but with only a handful of members. There are also other O.T.O.-like organizations and groups in England and the U.S.A., about which nothing need be said, inasmuch as such "orders" often exist only in the fantasies of their founders.

•The *Lodge Fraternitas Saturni*, which was founded in 1928 and has since had friendly connections with Crowley's O.T.O. and which has also guarded their sex-magical knowledge. Within the official framework of the lodge, this knowledge has only very rarely been worked practically, but there have been quite a few sex-magical activities in an unofficial format. This lodge is not a branch or sister organization of the O.T.O. and never has been, as some authors are still wont to believe. Nevertheless, after Crowley's death, this order was for a long time the only large working organization which tended and guarded O.T.O. knowledge. Over and above that, there have been several "special offprints" by the FS about sex magic. These have become legendary and are frequently quoted in English literature. These offprints do not offer much that may be considered sensational, because their content basically derives from the dogmatic "recipe tradition" of the 1920s; for example, one of these writings contains recommendations for coitus positions at certain astrological solar positions. This order, too, has experienced its own schisms and squabbles. In this connection we must also mention the German *Ordo Saturni* founded in the late 70s, which also leans heavily on the O.T.O. and even more on the *Fraternitas Saturni*, from which it has originally derived by schism.

Since Aleister Crowley lived his life to the full and according to his own tastes, he introduced an XI° into the O.T.O., which was worked homoerotically Kenneth Grant seemed to have a strong prejudice against this, and he abolished homoeroticism in his own organization as being "perverted." Instead, the VIII° was subdivided into autoerotic work and masturbatory or oral practice with a partner. The IX° was left to heteroeroticism, the "supernal" ("natural intercourse") as well as the "infernal" ("unnatural intercourse," or anal sex); the XI° is also heteroerotic and is used for materialization workings at the waning moon, without any special sex practices being mentioned—though occasionally it is said that the XI° in Grant's order is reserved for anal intercourse.

We do not want to go into the tricky question of the relative legitimacy of different versions of the O.T.O., nor of their worth. Michael Eschner is right when he says, "All these groups have failed to break free from the 'old men's occultism' of the early twenties. They still have the same pompous style and use the same imprecise jargon."[1]

It is nevertheless interesting to observe how these self-appointed masters have reflected their own sexual fears when creating their systems. Consider, for example, Kenneth Grant, who is in my opinion widely overestimated for his purely speculative "lunatic etymology," which is rightly ridiculed in English magical circles. Grant has founded a whole non-style of Thelemic literature with this "etymology." Grant's outright banning of homosexuality from his order says a lot more about Grant personally than about his knowledge of the laws of sex magic. Even Crowley himself cannot be cleared from all accusations despite all he has given us. If sexuality really can burst all borders of consciousness and existence as he claimed, why was he content with just auto-, hetero- and homoeroticism, and why did he not deal with other forms of sex magic in his order? One may fantasize about hidden secrets behind his every action or statement—particularly if one reveres the Master Therion as World Saviour or God incarnate as the Crowely community is wont to do. Everybody may do as he or she wills, but I think there is more to be gained by recognizing that every authority, however great, has his or her own ultimate limitations. Crowley's threshold may have been far higher than that of most of his worshipers, but this does not alter the basic fact that we are all human.

Apart from its wooliness, this "granny occultism" is also marked by an extreme hostility toward women and a deplorable lack of psychological and magical finesse. But insufficient knowledge cannot be disguised by pompous noise, and sadly we must face the fact that most of the relevant early literature is no longer in print for a very good reason—it is just as well forgotten! The quest for the ultimate book of wisdom which unveils all secrets may be a beginner's inspiration, but when old hands who should know better fall for this dream, it is hardly surprising that sex magic has fallen into such disrepute.

You could say that orders such as the O.T.O., by providing a structure for sex magic, have at least given us a framework for practice. We do not want to abandon such structures, but to go further and place the *entirety* of sex at the disposal of magic without making arbitrary distinctions between "natural" and "unnatural" practices. Sex magic is as many-faceted as mankind itself, and it makes no sense to be bound by a grade system which has little in common with the reality of human sexuality. My advice is this: do not allow authors (myself included!) to dictate which sexual practices are "permitted" or "not permitted" in sex magic. This would merely revive the meaningless distinction between "white" and "black" magic which has led us up the garden path over the centuries.

Autoerotic Practices

Although nearly everyone has masturbated and most people start their sex life this way, many still have difficulties. These people start with feelings of guilt over an "indecent" act ("only inadequate people need it..."), grow into absurd health fears ("masturbation makes you go blind"), and end with moral condemnation ("self-abuse is the work of Satan")—indeed, the range of inhibitions is wide and colorful. In the meantime, word has got around that this intolerance is the fault of repressive education and the body-hating attitudes of the Christian churches. Unfortunately, this insight does not change the actual problem.

It must be stated clearly: *sex magic is impossible without wholesome autoeroticism!* We will leave it at that, because we cannot provide what should be left to sex-education books. Nobody is asking you to prefer certain sexual practices to others (although this can be interesting as a magical exercise), but any inability to perform a certain practice is an imbalance which should be worked with. Autoerotic practice is of central importance, because not only does it provide magicians with an ideal experimental and magical technique, but it also gives them independence from partners.

The man in the street often fantasizes that sex magic is *always* performed with partners, assuming that it involves wild and blasphemous "perversion" in Satan's name. The reality is quite different. Sex magic is mostly practiced solo. Even magicians who prefer to practice with partners rarely work exclusively this way. Sexmagical partner workings are not quite the exception, but autoerotic practices are certainly the rule.

In the following discussion, it is assumed that you are mentally and physically capable of masturbating.

One form of autoerotic practice has already been described under the topic of sigil magic. The principle of this technique remains the same: magicians stimulate themselves sexually and waken their sexual *magis*. At the climax of the operation (which nearly always means the orgasm), they direct their entire concentration to their magical act of will. This may be that a previously prepared sigil is "sucked in" and afterwards banished; or that the ritual climax is synchronized with the sexual peak by projecting the sex *magis* into a talisman, amulet or fetish; or directing it towards a client and so on. The condition for success is, of course, that the sexual *magis* is charged with high energy, which means that one's sexual excitement is intense—it is not enough to perform what is colloquially dismissed as "a quick jerk." If you have done the exercises given, the necessary intensity will be there anyway because you will have reached an inner sexual balance. Think again of the magic rule: "nothing succeeds like excess"! This does not mean that you should overexert yourself physically, but that your sexuality has to be really intense and powerful to be useful in magic. Everything having been said about the actual technique, the discussion can proceed with some more specific autoerotic practices.

Intercourse with Succubi and Incubi

There have always been many dark warnings about this subject, even from German authors such as Eschner and Jungkurth who base their works on Austin Osman Spare who, ironically, from what we know about his magical life, was a complete virtuoso in this practice.

Incubi and succubi are sex manifestations which are used for astral intercourse. Incubi are male, succubi female. Much nonsense has been written to the effect that, although succubi appear as female, they are "really" male—believe it or not, I have never found any sensible explanation as to why this should be so. It is indeed questionable to impose human sexual genders on etheric entities. We cannot operate using terms such as "male" or "female" in a sexual sense when we deal with demons (but of course, we can do so in a mythical sense). The whole problem is likely to be a late echo of the scholastic quarrel which occupied the Church for so long about the gender of angels and demons. It remains a fact that succubi appear as females and incubi as males, and that they behave according to their gender in astral intercourse. They are probably defined as demons because, first, they specialize in a limited area of action and do not have much independent intelligence, and, second, because dealing with them is not without danger. People like to ascribe everything dangerous to demons. Intercourse with incubi and succubi played an important role during the time of the witch hunts and has contributed largely to our prejudices. Many witches—whether voluntarily or by force—described intercourse with "Satan" and his vassals, and this practice was therefore damned as dangerous and wicked. If it is true, as some scientists have suggested, that the deadly nightshade and other drugs in witches' ointments were responsible for erotic visions, we may be provided with a pharmacological explanation for this phenomenon. But, all the same, intercourse with succubi and incubi can easily be performed without drugs.

If you wish to have intercourse with succubi or incubi, some rightful warnings are nevertheless appropriate. Magicians of both sexes agree that this form of sex is strenuous to the point of being exhausting and may lead to considerable loss of power if performed over a long period. I myself came to the conclusion that this is more a problem of adapting one's energy to the unusual conditions, as we often find when we begin lucid dreaming. People who begin with five or six lucid dreams one after the other are often reduced to exhaustion. Sleep seems to be unsatisfying; tiredness and in some cases depression ensue. But, after steady practice, these problems disappear, and one can fully enjoy the blessings of lucid dreaming.

In my experience, the same applies to intercourse with succubi and incubi. Lucid dreaming, however, seldom leads to obsession, but it may happen if you mishandle sex demons. The reason lies not so much in the inherent danger of these energy forms but in the magician's inability to "keep his or her own space" by defining clearly what he or she allows into his or her own universe, for how long and how much. Another point is the magician's inability to cope with the energies he or she taps, of absorbing and transforming them.

Obsession is usually dismissed psychologically as a form of schizophrenia on account of its symptoms, but this does not really explain the root cause of obsession, which, from a magical point of view, results from a person binding himself or herself to a type of energy which is experienced as a demon and being unable to loosen this bond. Most authors seem to consider that the best protection would be not to use these techniques at all, but this would mean throwing out the baby with the bathwater. It is as if your driving teacher advised you all your life to keep below 20 mph because higher speed demands more of your skills and your nerves. Therefore, to get back to magic, beginners should first attend to the elementary phases of magic and gather sufficient experience before they venture into the tricky area of sex-magical intercourse with demons.

For magical intercourse with incubi and succubi, you must first make sure your own internal energy is both stable and resilient. You should begin by limiting the number of operations, with a long break between each. This is not always easy, because intercourse with demons has an intensity which may lead to addiction. It is similar to psychological dependence on certain drugs; your organism does not need these substances, but your mind is insatiable and demands more and more and thus entangles itself in its self-created addiction. But, just as you do not need to become addicted to cocaine if you handle it moderately and sensibly, so also incubi and succubi don't necessarily have to become "resident." The Tantric idea that everything we meet is a product of our own selves helps a great deal here—it is applicable to demons as well as to deities! If you deliberately limit the acts of intercourse with incubi and succubi, you will also notice less tendency for the experience to become dull and uninspiring. This shows the true magician: able to dominate the deepest drives without simply suppressing them in an unimaginative manner!

You must always keep control during intercourse with incubi and succubi—especially if the experience is intense—just as with any other demon evocation. This is made more difficult because incubi and succubi appear mainly during dreams, deep trances or drunkenness. Fostering gnostic trance should therefore be the main preparation for dealing with these energy forms. A final thorough banishing should be self-evident—and even experienced magicians find this hard to do, because the intercourse leaves them somewhat dazed. *Absolute discipline is needed!*

You should on no account have intercourse with succubi and incubi if you are energetically weak or ill. Only very experienced magicians know the art of actually increasing their energy by this technique, although this should be the long-term aim of working with sex demons. It is interesting that it is mainly older magicians who get on safest with incubi and succubi, even if they start comparatively late with this practice. Only sparse information is available, though, because the people concerned mostly keep silent about their experiences.

The practical value of intercourse with incubi and succubi is otherwise quite limited, and therefore one can easily manage without this branch of sex magic. Only magicians with a natural leaning towards this practice—usually already apparent during puberty—reach beyond very intense experiences and are able to use incubi or succubi as suppliers of energy, or even as familiars to support their divinatory practice or for transfer of healing power etc. Nevertheless, one should give it a try, because it may open hidden sexual dimensions to you, and it is excellent preparation for astral intercourse with a human partner. Regular intercourse with sex demons also increases one's own sexual attraction, although partners without magical knowledge will experience attraction mixed with a kind of subconscious fear which is seldom admitted.

Finally, I want to give one very serious warning: obsession by incubi or succubi is usually the result of intellectualizing one's own sexuality in a way previously described on the subject of "sexual fantasies." Also, sexual frustration on the human level is a bad prerequisite for intercourse with sex demons. Working with incubi and succubi could be a substitute for human sex partners, but we advise against it. When somebody looks for a substitute, then there is a lack—and such a lack always means a shortage of power and the danger of becoming addicted to these "suppliers of energy." Once such an addiction has built up, it is very difficult to get rid of without a lengthy course of banishing rituals and exercises. In the last chapter, we will describe a more suitable technique for achieving sexual fulfilment without any human or ethereal partner.

The easiest way to call up an incubus or succubus is by sigil magic; for example, with the sentence of desire, "It is my wish to meet a succubus in my dreams this week." Should you still experience difficulty in remembering dreams, include a relevant suggestion in the sentence. Prepare well, because the intercourse is a very strange experience for the first few times and cannot really be put into words. It is experienced as "non-human." Frequently, a certain feeling of dissatisfaction is left, but this can have its own special charm.

You may also work ritually towards the desired intercourse; for example, by charging a talisman or fetish and carrying it on your body. "Sacrifices" (or, more accurately, manifestation energy put at one's disposal) in the form of sexual secretion are preferred. We have already mentioned that sometimes magically charged dolls or fetishes provide the material basis of the apparition, but this should only be used if one wants to bind the energy of the incubus or succubus materially for certain reasons—a so-called "spirit trap," mainly employed during exorcisms or combat magic.

Of course, intercourse with sex demons is not limited to dream states. You may invoke it in a ritual when you are in a sexual trance—this is sometimes even more intense than a dream experience. As long as you heed the above warnings, let there be no limits to your imagination.

The same principles apply to sex demons as to dealings with guardian spirits, elementals, familiars and other spiritual entities. Never, for example, fall for rash promises or "pacts" with these entities. Haggle really toughly with them, as if you were an Oriental carpet dealer! Seriously though, the more natural or "human" your dealings with such energies, the more protected you are from possible negative consequences. It may well be that the psychological and Tantric assumptions are right and that these entities are "only" projections of our own psyche, but at the time of contact they are certainly not experienced as such. Or, if they *are* experienced as such, you can be sure that they are only half-baked fantasmagoric figments without any significance—what is sometimes called "astral larvae"—and dealing with them is not only a waste of time but positively harmful to one's magical judgment and energy reserves. Take it as a rule of thumb that sex demons are either completely real (if only in a very fugitive manner) or they are a matter of hallucination.

Another form of autoerotic practice is sex magical fetishism. Strictly speaking, it should be listed here, but, because an entire section is devoted to so-called "deviant" practices, fetishism will be dealt with under that heading instead.

Autoerotic Workings with Atavisms

Finally we come to autoerotic workings with atavisms. I have already dealt with atavistic practices in more depth in my study *Practical Sigil Magic* (Llewellyn, 1990), so I will restrict myself here to essential sex-magic aspects.

By work with magical atavisms, we mean contacting prehuman forms of existence that are still genetically present in humans. The concept as we know it today was developed by Austin Osman Spare, but its basic structure is far older and can be found in one or another form in nearly all shamanic cultures. In general, we only deal with the animal forms that form part of our evolution, but there are attempts which lead back to even earlier stages of development.[2]

Spare believed (as do numerous shamans today) that the primordial source of all magical power lies in our prehuman past. The more we consciously go back in our evolution, the more powerful our magic becomes. This is, by the way, the actual point behind the sodomitic sex-magic practices handed down to us from antiquity; the goat of the witches' sabbath had the same function.

The descent into those earlier levels of evolution still stored in us—as each embryo's development in the mother's body shows— may be done by meditation, but sigils and relevant sex-magical rituals are more effective. Peter J. Carroll writes in *Psychonaut* how he once as a beginner experimented with sigil magic and charged a sigil to attain "the karma of a cat." In Spare's system, "karma" is understood as the sum of all life experiences and not, as the word is normally used, as a sort of balance of debits and credits which still have to be lived out. After he had nearly forgotten this operation,

Carroll met a cat on the street one evening. Suddenly, something clicked between him and the cat, and he ran screaming and hissing through the streets. As he told me personally, he has frequently had trouble with dogs ever since! This anecdote is an example of a quite effective but non-directed atavism. Most beginners would probably experience their first atavism in a similar form, so they are advised to start on the dream level first!

Once you have decided on a certain atavism, you can call it up by charging a sigil. With autoerotic workings, you may also proceed as follows: you stand within your protective symbol (or ritual circle) and bring yourself into a relevant animal trance, while at the same time stimulating yourself sexually. Strictly speaking, this is a form of "trance within a trance" that obviously needs a lot of practice. One difficulty is synchronizing the climax of the sex-magical operation with the climax of the animal trance. The result of this work, if performed correctly, will be a considerable strengthening of your magical power and abilities. Normally, you will use an animal trance to direct your *magis* during very important operations. Once this technique is mastered, you can manage without any other form of trance, because this one provides everything a magician's heart might desire! Please note that we do not dictate which animal forms to use—this you must decide for yourself. In general, shamans reject working with domesticated animals because they have lost too much of their original wildness. Most people end up with wild animals when they perform the shamanic power-animal dance.[3]

An atavism can be treated and used like a doppelganger, familiar or psychogone, but it is superior to them. It is also much more independent, so its control demands unbending will—but also a certain willingness to compromise. Later, a heteroerotic variant of atavism work will be introduced.

Heteroerotic Practices

Before going into the heteroerotic practice of sex magic, one important misunderstanding should be clarified in the following secondary comment.

Secondary Comment

It is a remarkable fact, but one rarely commented upon, that, in Aleister Crowley's sex magic, perverse ideas of "naturalness" have somehow crept in—ideas which would do little credit even to the Catholic Church. True, Crowley did see the role of women as being that of bearers of children, and consequently he was strictly outspoken against abortion, but his strong opinion has merely served to sustain an almost medieval attitude towards *contraception* that I can only term a product of the worst superstition. Even followers such as Grant and Eschner have the cheek to claim that contraception or wasted semen creates "demons" and other such nonsense. Behind this superstition lie ancient magical ideas such as those found in the Bible with its condemnation of "onanism" and its ecologically disastrous demand to "go forth and multiply"—but not everything ancient is good. I leave it to you to decide, but, from my own experience, I can say that these ideas have *no* practical foundation.

Historically interested readers may note that there are also totally contradictory traditions. The late-Hellenistic gnostics, for example, regarded reproduction as a sorry ploy by the demiurge Ialdabaoth (= Jehovah) to expand his territory and split up the "divine spark" inherent in every creature into smaller and smaller pieces by uncontrolled reproduction. Thus scattered gnostic sects developed, such as the Simonians and other "Barbelo" gnostics who reportedly forbade even their own believers' reproduction as being an unnatural and heinous deed and who favored ritual abortion—including ritual consumption of the fetus, if the sources can be trusted. This of course brought bitter opposition from the church fathers, the more so because gnosticism was the strongest competitor to early Christianity. I personally consider these gnostic attitudes as no more perverse than the opposite one which, under the pretext of being "pro-life," still has not faced up to the catastrophic consequences of overpopulation—blinded by the demiurge, as the hellenistic gnostic would say.

There is a certain irony in the fact that today's papacy would, at least in this respect, have been in cahoots with the "Great Beast" Aleister Crowley! If one takes the sentence *deus est homo—homo est deus* (God is Man—Man is God) seriously, it seems particularly perverse to dictate to a God-Man what to do about contraception, especially since this subject has always been a major weapon in the armory of human suppression. In this, Crowley betrayed his undeniable contempt for women—which did nothing to diminish his attraction for them! Men like him, who spread their "wild oats" throughout the land without a thought for the consequences, are throwbacks to an old or patriarchic eon, in my opinion. I only ask you to think seriously and without fear about contraception. Practices which need the mixing of the male and female secretions will, of course, not be possible with condoms.

Heteroerotic sex magic presents two possibilities: work with a partner who knows about sex magic or work with a partner who is not aware of their hidden role.

It seems obvious that the work should be much more effective when both partners are involved at all levels, but, nevertheless, magicians quite frequently work with partners who know nothing about their roles—as we see from Aleister Crowley's sex-magic diaries. There may be several reasons for this.

It may simply be a matter of expediency. It is not always easy to find partners who approve of magic, let alone the dreaded sex magic. Magicians, who should follow their True Will (Thelema), will mostly shake off yesterday's moral scruples on the matter. It is all a question of personal ethics. There are also magicians who reject such practices for technical reasons which we will deal with soon.

On another level, it can serve as an exercise in transcending patterns of loathing and fear. People who, for example, are scared of prostitutes will do it for *precisely that reason* if they take their magical development seriously. Such inner psychological tensions can set off a powerful gnostic trance with excellent results. Crowley, for example, while in New York, advertised as "artist looks for model" for hunchbacked, crippled, tattooed and in general "as ugly as possible" women in order (according to John Symonds) to work sex magic with them in a trance of loathing. In such cases, it would not be sensible to initiate one's partner into the practice of sex magic because too much nearness and sympathy would only diminish the loathing.

If a non-initiated partner is only used because no other is handy, then why was the work not performed autoerotically in the first place? Such operations can be a form of vampirism—a practice which I do not recommend because it can raise feelings of guilt. Nothing is more detrimental to magic than that! It is up to your own personal ethics as to how you handle this, but in any case do not make a regular habit of it. It could very subtly develop into an addiction, and it might also lead to emotional disturbances. Most magicians share the opinion that it is not compatible with the magical principles of ideological and sexual liberty to force people to do magic against their will, or to use their energy without their knowledge.

If both partners agree to sex magic, it is best if both are on the same level of energy; otherwise, the partner with less energy may experience an increase of energy at the expense of the stronger partner.

It is not practical to go into all the possibilities for heteroerotic practice here. There is little value in an endless catalog of techniques. It is preferred to teach you basic structures so that you can deduce the rest yourself. The emphasis will be on the sex-magic exchange of energy between partners, the intensification of magical acts of will through partner workings, heteroerotic work with atavisms, and the infamous "Moonchild" operation. Most of what is offered elsewhere in this book can also be adapted for heteroerotic workings anyway.

The Exchange of Energy Between Partners

One of the most common techniques is the exchange of energy between an ill and a healthy partner. This is mostly described from a male point of view, but there is no reason why it should not be practised by women—it happens often enough but nobody talks about it!

A quote from the Bible follows:

> Now king David was old and stricken in years; and they covered him with clothes, but he gat no heat. Wherefore his servants said unto him, Let there be sought for my lord the king a young virgin: and let let her stand before the king, and let her cherish him, and let her lie in thy bossom, that my lord the king may get heat. So they sought for a fair damsel throughout all the coasts of Israel, and found Abishag a Shunammite, and brought her to the king. And the damsel was fair, and cherished the king, and ministered to him: but the king knew her not.
>
> —I Kings 1:1-4

Observe the expressions "the king may get heat" and "the king knew her not." "Getting heat" certainly does not mean a mere transfer of body heat. Rather it has to do with an exchange of vital energy or "animal magnetism," as it was called in former times, which reveals itself mainly as inner warmth, just as a lack of vital energy is often accompanied by an inner cold which does not respond to external sources of thermal energy.

The biblical word "know" means sexual intercourse, so it is probable that "not knowing" was a basic condition for the whole therapy, because such practice can only have the desired success if the sexual *magis* is transferred *without* the explosion of sexual intercourse and orgasm.

Transferring Energy to Heal or Strengthen a Partner

When one partner is weak or ill and sees no other way to increase the energy level, he or she should lie down naked on a bed. The other partner, also naked, lies down after a period of meditation and absorption of power, so that physical contact is as close as possible. Both partners find a synchronous breathing rhythm, which should be as long and deep as possible: one inhaling while the other exhales and vice versa. Once this pattern is established, the patient concentrates on sucking in the *magis* of the partner on the inhalation and letting it flow through the entire body on the exhalation. The energy-giving partner concentrates on transmitting energy to the other person. Any sexual activity must be avoided, although a certain excitement very much supports the flow of energy. The transmission is performed as long as possible, at least an hour, unless the energy-giving partner is excessively weakened. Several transmissions a day are possible, depending on the stamina of the donor. In difficult cases, this practice is performed over several weeks.

Some Advice for the Energy-Giving Partner

It is a law for any magical healing technique that you should never give away your *own* energy. This means that the energy you give has to come from somewhere else. Make yourself into a channel for energy, but reserve your own energy for yourself—*anything else would be suicide!* Don't let yourself be blinded by compassion. There are many ways to tap healing energy. You may energize yourself with runic exercises or take energy from the sun, the earth, the four elements, trees, animals, crystals and so on. You have already been trained in suitable techniques, and you can learn about others in any good book on applied spiritual healing.

If you proceed as described above, it is not necessary to worry about large differences in age and energy between the two partners as in the King David story. It always has been an Oriental custom that men lie down with very young and possibly virgin girls without having sexual intercourse, so as to absorb their energy—this much was reported about Mahatma Gandhi. The same is found in our culture when grandparents are subconsciously drawn to taking their grandchildren to bed. Still, provided the energy-giving partner knows how to recharge his own energy and understands how to transmit the stored energy to the other person, one can do without such manipulation of unsuspecting victims.

Ritual Exchange of Sex Magical Energy

An Exercise in Energizing and as Preparation for Constructing a Magical Sentence of Desire

Both partners should be well rested and at the height of their energy. No food should have been consumed for several hours and you should not be under the influence of alcohol or other stimulants. The working room should be warm and the bed comfortable but not too soft, and both partners should be naked. All metal jewelery, apart from amulets or talismans, must be removed and the working performed in a protective circle.

One partner lies down on his or her back and relaxes to the gentle caresses of the other. Caress the entire body at first as described in the Depth Relaxation technique and then focus increasingly on the erogenic zones, *except the primary genitals.* The partner who is lying should be stimulated but not led to the brink of orgasm. With eyes closed and performing the Lesser Energy Orbit, he or she is abandoned to the touch of the other partner, but without losing sexual control. Once the partner is sufficiently excited and relaxed, a signal is given. Both partners now sit facing each other with closed eyes and become immersed in their own shared breathing rhythm. After a certain number of cycles, which have to be agreed upon beforehand, the partners switch roles while excitement of the first active partner is maintained (a male partner keeps an erection and a female partner remains close to orgasm). Once the second partner is also well stimulated, the partners couple in the sitting position and try to produce a synchronized breathing rhythm that is out of phase. Both partners continue with the Lesser Energy Orbit. Now the actual exchange of *magis* takes place: the partners kiss mouth to mouth and transmit their energy through mouth and genitals so that the energy which rises up the back of one partner is fed through the mouth into the orbit of the other one, who absorbs energy with his or her genitals and directs it up his or her spine. After a while, the direction of the flow is changed.

Once this has been achieved, both partners continue their intercourse gently but without allowing orgasm. This is important for two reasons: first, avoiding orgasm helps ensure a complete absorption of energy and, second, this practice is a good lead-in to a magical act of will, for which the orgasm should be reserved (for example, charging sigils or amulets). If the proper sensitization has been performed, the male fluid is perceived as hot and dry, whereas the female fluid is perceived as cold and damp. The sexual *magis* of each partner is "filtered" and sublimated by the other partner's *magis*. A Tao master would say "an excess of Yang is balanced by Yin" and vice versa. A distinctly higher polarizing or intensification can be observed, which frequently leads to a "valley" orgasm. But this too should be reserved for an actual magical working.

When only performing an exchange of energy—from which, by the way, both partners will benefit equally—the exercise will be ended without orgasm after a while. In this case you should have your next orgasm not earlier than four hours after the operation. You may as well experiment with this by, for example, lying down with your partner in this way for a week without having an orgasm and without bringing about orgasm in any other way in between. Eventually, after a week, the desired magical ritual is performed and climaxed *with* a genital orgasm by both partners.

You will notice that this exercise considerably intensifies your sex drive; it raises your energy level, increases health and vigor and multiplies your magical capacity. This is no empty promise. Trial will soon convince you that this is so!

Orgasm and Act of Will

If you have used the above heteroerotic practice as the introduction to a ritual act of will, you will now proceed as follows. If, for example, you are performing an invocation, you start by calling down the force and reciting the hymn while you work towards orgasm. It is not essential that both partners reach orgasm at the same time. If the operation is primarily for one partner, it is enough that the one should have the orgasm while the other partner provides a supply of energy. If the aim is a joint magical act of will, it would be an advantage if both partners were to have a synchronous orgasm, but this is still not absolutely essential. The superstition which arose in the '60s, through misguided sex education, that both partners should always "come together," has caused more harm than people admit. If you strive for this simultaneity, you find that it hardly ever happens, not to mention the fact that it leads to a new sort of inhibition because of the artificial obligation to succeed. Partners who harmonize well, and who have worked with each other for a long time, will have no problem in achieving it if they choose—but usually they too will decide to reserve synchronous orgasm for very special operations.

As already mentioned, Crowley insisted on consuming the "elixir," or mixture of the partners' sexual juices, after magical intercourse. He even read oracles from its taste and texture—with little success, as can be seen from his diaries. We have already suggested that behind this practice lies a naive belief in the primary importance of not wasting semen on any account. As Crowley almost never did this after autoerotic work, one wonders what was the point of it all. I won't give instructions on this practice; I only mention it for the sake of completeness. Of course, the secretion is often used to transfer sex *magis* onto a talisman, amulet, fetish or doll, but in that case it has an easily understood symbolic function that makes the procedure rather more meaningful.

Experience has proven time and again that magical operations performed in the above way lead to faster, more decisive results than others—even autoerotic ones. But you must gather your own experience for yourself.

Astral Sexuality

If your partner has mastered astral traveling, you can enjoy yourselves together on the astral level with no restriction to your imagination. It is a good method for overcoming physical separation, as it supports the magical independence of both partners as well as their magical activeness. It works particularly well *immediately after sexual intercourse*, both partners lying side by side in the death posture and astrally projecting themselves. There is also the possibility of physically coupling once again and leaving your bodies to continue your love play on the astral. Should this sound too fantastic, try it—the result will astound you! This is also a brilliant preliminary exercise for the ritual of the Chymical Hierogamy in the last chapter.

The moment after intercourse has taken place proves particularly good, because post-orgasmic exhaustion seems to loosen the ties of the astral body. A psychologist might point out that the tendency to "fly high" is particularly strong after orgasm. It is also possible to combine astral projection with orgasm by performing them at the same time.

After a valley or whole-body orgasm, astral projection is child's play. If you control your sexual *magis* properly, you will shoot out of your body like a rocket!

Intercourse with an Absent Partner

A popular method of overcoming geographical or temporal separation is by intercourse with an astral image of a partner. Technically speaking, this is an autoerotic practice, but, if the partners are imagined strongly enough, they can participate very intensely in such astral or mental intercourse! Many lovers experience this without any magical training. To them it is just an accidental encounter, whereas magicians try to achieve it by means of will.

Heteroerotic Work with Atavisms

If both partners are familiar with practical atavistic work, they can perform it together in a sex-magic ritual. The ritual is just the same as the one above, except that the partners project in animal form. The sexual position is immaterial and, in the course of the operation, you will probably thrash about anyway.[4] Each partner concentrates on his or her own atavism, so don't try to guess or see the atavism of the other partner. Once the operation has been performed on a high enough level, questions like this won't arise anyway.

Before you start working heteroerotically towards any definite aims, you should be thoroughly familiar with this form of atavism work. It may happen that the two *base atavisms* of the two partners do not match. A *base atavism* is, so to speak, the atavistic essence of a magician, a form of energy—usually an animal—which lies behind all others and which manifests itself only when the adept has reached a certain maturity. This base atavism is the primordial source of personal magical power. In African magic, they are called "clan animals."[5] In the Occident, we talk about the "Holy Guardian Angel" with which it is the highest task of magicians to seek contact. It is what is called the "higher self" in many occult teachings. Approaching it is the ultimate aim of all atavistic workings. Should such an incompatibility prove insurmountable, joint atavism work will have to be abandoned. One's own base atavism can nevertheless be trusted to seek for a suitable partner when the need arises.

If the partners' base atavisms match or complement each other well, there are no limits to their magical power. The Holy Guardian Angel is recognized as the highest level of magical initiation, but it does not mean that every magician who makes contact with the base atavism can live up to it immediately! This form of energy can be quite uncomfortable, because it tears us out of many cozy ideological, moral or social ruts!

A Partner as a Priest/Priestess—Working with Deities

Both partners do not necessarily have to be active in the same way. In the Satanic Black Mass, for example, a virgin serves as the altar and is penetrated by one or more male participants, thus playing a completely passive role. In similar pagan rites, she represents Earth, which has to be broken open and fertilized.

Less known are lunar-partner rituals, particularly of the new or dark moon, rituals of the Earth Mother or Hecate where a man is the passive, serving partner. The fact that his erection is necessary for the ritual does not alter anything; the function of erection is often wrongly interpreted as sign of pure activity. For example, it is a mistaken belief that a man cannot be raped by one or more women. If women handle it right and stimulate a man properly, there is no man who cannot be raped. No man with real experience of women, uncolored by his own inferiority feelings, will deny the immense active sexual power of women. Of course, women themselves know about it—and interestingly enough they also know more about passive aspects of male sexual power than men—because this is intuitive knowledge which men overlook for the sake of reason and logic that are of little help in real stress situations. It is no coincidence that most male adepts are real *moon magicians,* whereas female magicians often work better with the *solar principle.*

Being *priest or priestess* means being an agent or vehicle of a deity. If the woman plays priestess, she will lead through the ritual and her male partner will be her assistant—and vice versa if the man is the priest. Both partners act together as priests only when they conduct a group ritual such as the Great Rite in Wicca.

Working with deities includes invocation. Technically, we are talking about deliberately induced and directed obsession for a limited duration which is also directive; the form of energy which we call a "deity" takes over the adept's personality. For the duration of the invocation, one's own personality makes way for the deity in return for a measure of its power and abilities. The desired operation can be performed as if by *the deity itself* with considerably greater effect, while the noninvoking partner supports the operation. Technical support includes taking care of the incense, giving the necessary bell signals, reciting mantras and hymns in unison with the invoking partner and so on. Magical support includes helping to create the desired vibrations and intensifying the priest's vibrations with his or her own sexual *magis*. The exchange of energy between partners, described above, is also very helpful and effective. In some systems, for example in the Mass of Chaos, at the end of the ritual one partner exorcizes the partner who did the invocation, leading him or her out of trance and restoring normal awareness.

If a sex act is performed while a priest or priestess invokes a deity, the noninvoking partner can gain much of the deity's magical power through exchange of energy, and he or she can use this for his or her own magical acts. Any mixture of sex-magic forms may be used; for example, both partners may proceed heteroerotically as described above but without allowing orgasm and then finish the act by autoerotically charging talismans, activating sigils, influencing dolls and so on. There are no limits to the possibilities.

Sympatho-magically, a "binding" spell can be done by each partner identifying himself or herself with one of the persons to be brought together, performing the ritual so to speak as "living dolls." This of course needs a lot of imagination and also a thorough banishment at the end, but it is an immensely powerful operation!

On "Operation Moonchild" and the Homunculus

In his novel *Moonchild*, Aleister Crowley describes a magical operation for the creation of a human incarnation of the lunar principle. To achieve this, the mother is influenced by lunar operations and environmental conditions built up according to moon symbolism, and the act of procreation is also performed in a ritual way. Actually, we are talking about the creation of a homunculus, for which a secret IX° O.T.O. instruction of Crowley's existed (*De Homunculo Epistola)*, an excerpt of which is given below. For a better understanding, it should be pointed out that Crowley held the theory that a human soul enters the fetus for the first time at three months. Now follows his text:

I
Take a suitable woman willing to aid thee in this Work. Explain to her fully the precautions to be taken and the manner of life necessary. Let her horoscope be, if possible, suited to the nature of the homunculus proposed; as, to have an incarnate Spirit of Benevolence let Jupiter be rising in Pisces with good aspects of Sol, Venus and Luna; and with no notable contrary dispositions; or so far as may be possible.
II
Take now a man suitable; if convenient, thyself or some other Brother Initiate of the Gnosis; and so far as may be, let his horoscope also harmonize with the nature of the work.
III
Let the man and woman copulate continuously (but especially at times astrologically favourable to thy working) and that in a ceremonial manner in a prepared temple, whose particular arrangement and decoration is also suitable to thy work. And let them will ardently and constantly the success of thy work denying all other desires. Thus proceed until impregnation results.
IV
Now let the woman be withdrawn and carried away to a place prepared.
And this place should be a great desert; for in such do rarely wander any human souls seeking incarnation.
Further let a great circle be drawn and consecrated to the sphere of the work; and let banishing formulae of the Sephiroth, and especially of Kether, be done often, even unto five or seven times on every day. Outside which great circle let the woman never go. Let the mind of the woman be strengthened to resist all impression, except of the spirit desired. Let the incense of this spirit be burnt continually; let his colours, and his only, be displayed; and let his shapes, and his only, appear so far as may be in all things.

Further let him be most earnestly and continually invoked in a temple duly dedicated, the woman being placed in a great triangle, while thou from the circle dost perform daily the proper form of Evocation to Material Appearance. And let this be done twice every day, once while she is awake and once while she is asleep.

V

And let the quickening be a feast of the Reception of the Spirit. Henceforth ye may omit the Banishings.

VI

And during the rest of the Pregnancy let there be the Charge to the Spirit (so that the whole period of all this work is as it were an expansion in terms of life of the Art-formula of Evocation) in this manner.

Let the woman be constantly educated by words and by books and by pictures of a nature consonant, so that all causes may work together for the defence and sustenance of the Spirit, and for its true development.

VII

And let the delivery of the woman be retarded or advanced so far as possible to secure a rising sign proper to such a child.

VIII

The child being born must be dedicated, purified and consecrated, according to the formulae of the planet, element, or sign, of which it is the Incarnation.

IX

Now then thou hast a being of perfect human form, with all powers and privileges of humanity, but with the essence of a particular chosen force, and with all the knowledge and might of its sphere; and this being is thy creation and dependent; to it thou art Sole God and Lord, and it must serve thee.

Therefore the whole of all that part of Nature whereunto it belongs is thy dominion; and thou art Magister Octinomous.

X

Be wary, Brother Adept, and choose well thine object, and spare not pain and labour in the Beginning of thy Operation; for to have corn of so subtle a seed is a great thing once; to achieve it twice were the mark of a primal energy so marvellous, that We doubt whether there be one man born in ten times ten thousand years that hath such wonder-power.

XI

Now the Father of All prosper ye, my Brethren that dare lay hold upon the Phallus of the All-One, and call forth its streams to irrigate your fields.

And may the spirit of Prometheus hearken, and the Spirit of Alcides aid, your Work.[6]

That which is true in life is (usually) true in magic: Devising something and actually carrying it out are two entirely different things! This experiment was actually tried by two disciples in the year 1945 while the Master was still alive. One of the disciples was the scientist and rocket-fuel expert Jack Parsons, after whom a lunar crater was named; the second was Lafayette Ron Hubbard, who later founded scientology. When Parsons reported to Crowley, the Master was no longer so keen of the project. He answered in a letter, "I thought I had a most morbid imagination, as good as any man's, but it seems I have not. I cannot form the slightest idea what you can possibly mean." And to his American representative Saturnus, he wrote, "Apparently Parsons or Hubbard or somebody is producing a Moonchild. I get fairly frantic when I contemplate the idiocy of these louts."[7]

The only noticeable effect of this ritual was that Parsons and Hubbard fell out, and Hubbard ran away with Parsons' girl friend and yacht. Parsons thereupon conjured Bartzabel, which, according to his description, made the ship crash into a reef during a storm ...

Crowley's remark does not give the impression that he was really serious about his moonchild ritual. But was it then only a product of "morbid fantasy," as magical amateurs might suspect? Yes and no. Think of what we said about "mythical truth." In a mythic sense, the moonchild ritual has to be taken seriously, and it is even conceivable that it could become reality. The reason why we quoted this text was to show how easily magical reality and myth are combined and how quickly the borders become blurred. Devising such rituals is less for the purpose of actually practicing them than it is to expand one's own magical cosmos and extend beyond the limits of one's powers. This is the real reason that shamans and magicians often tell outrageous "cock-and-bull" stories—not deliberately to deceive, but because they live on a level where traditional bourgeois patterns of "right" and "wrong," of "true" and "untrue," no longer apply, and because illusion is often needed to create true facts. Every good stage illusionist knows how trickery can paralyze the psychic censor to such an extent that the most impossible things appear feasible—eventually the subconscious stirs and creates true magic among the audience.

Homoerotic Practices

That which we fear binds our energies, and it is the same with things we loath. It would be far more sensible to divert the energy we employ avoiding unpleasant feelings such as fear and loathing into solving these problems once and for all; then we would be many a step further on the path of self-knowledge.

Homosexuality has been outlawed, persecuted and punished for thousands of years, and this in the Occident where one might have assumed that we would have learned from the rich homoerotic culture of Greece! Even acknowledged occult authors such as Péladan and Papus decried homosexuality as "perverted." In this, they were entirely children of their time. A further sign of this disapproval of homoerotic sex magic is the fact that not a single work about sex magic known to me in German, English or French even mentions this form except in passing.

During its persecution, male homosexuality had to suffer more than female homosexuality—*because the latter was simply hushed up!* Although "sapphism" (named after the Hellenic poet Sappho, who ran a girls' school on the island Lesbos—hence the term "lesbianism") was known about, many saw it more as a sexual fantasy of men than a serious reality. Interestingly enough, the present stage of Sappho-studies raises considerable doubts about the actual sexual relationships of the poet to her pupils.

Anyway, lesbian sexuality did not become a criminal offence and was generally accepted as a forgivable gaffe of frustrated or inexperienced women—another attempt to belittle women as sexual entities and "defuse" their threat to male sexual supremacy.

Persecution has certainly not eradicated homosexuality; it has simply driven homosexuals to all sorts of stereotyped behavior which in turn becomes subject to proscription and mockery—e.g. so-called "poofy behavior." There is no such thing as total heterosexuality, as there is no such thing as total homosexuality, and therefore everything said here can only be incomplete.

The fact remains that homosexuality is, for many heterosexuals, the ultimate folly. Women seem to have slightly more interest in homoerotic experiments, but not significantly so. Men tend to react much more vehemently and intolerantly towards homosexuality than women. The problem is that everybody has a homosexual component in himself or herself to some extent which can emerge under stress (for example in prison or after long forced celibacy), when inhibitions disappear and homoerotic practices are permitted.

It is equally unreasonable to ask homosexuals to have heteroerotic intercourse. Let us be blunt: All imbalance is harmful for magic, whether heteroerotic or homoerotic. People who have an outspoken aversion against the other, opposite sexual practice tend to make an absolute dogma of their own preferences—as the history of the O.T.O. and its imitations has amply shown.

It is necessary to draw a distinction between two forms of homosexuality: homosexuality due to affection for one's own gender and homosexuality due to fear or dislike of the opposite gender. The first form is much less problematical than the latter, because its energy can be directed towards its own fulfilment, whereas homosexuality because of dislike binds strong energies into this dislike without freeing them to be directed towards self-realization. People who tend to homosexuality out of preference will find it easier to experiment with heteroerotic practices, because they have found their own sexual centers. Women-haters and men-despisers must also learn to work heteroerotically if they do not want to fail as magicians because of their one-sidedness.

The same applies to completely convinced homosexuals and fanatical lesbians, if they are unable to use any other but homoerotic sexuality because of their lust bondage.

Every magician should be able to perform *every* form of sexuality, so that real freedom from attachments and ingrained patterns is guaranteed. Such exchange of experience would also help to clear up many of the prejudices, aversions and misunderstandings between heterosexuals and homosexuals.

If you have not yet had homoerotic experiences, you should look for a partner who has already had such experience, paying more attention to sympathy and trust than to physical attractiveness. You should by now have reached a point where appearances are no longer important, at least not in sex magic. An experienced and understanding partner can initiate you into the technical subtleties of homosexuality and remove many inhibitory thresholds.

What are the advantages of homosexuality in sex magic? First, it reflects one's own sexuality, clearly showing one's own sexual limits and dependence. Men recognize their own animus, women their own anima.

Second, it increases one's understanding of one's own hetero-sexuality. Homoerotic practice on the one hand involves taking on the role of the opposite sex, and on the other hand maintaining one's own sexual role with a partner who has slipped into the opposite role. Men recognize their own anima, women their own animus.

Third, through recognizing one's own animus and anima, there is the possibility of attaining that highest level of being in which all opposites are transcended, in which male and female blend into a new unity, the *"androgyne,"* which has been worshipped since pri-meval times as the embodiment of oneness and control over the world of determinedness and material and spiritual attachment. This androgyny can be realized in its most harmonic physical form only by the heterosexual Chymical Marriage. Nevertheless for het-erosexuals homoeroticism, and for homosexuals heteroeroticism, usually precedes this final step of self-realization, because only the opposite sexuality holds the mystery of liberation from the deter-minedness of sexuality as a whole. This liberation does not necessar-ily lead towards asceticism and abstinence from sexuality, as is naively claimed by mystically oriented authors, but leads rather to-wards heightening of sexuality which not rarely culminates in con-sciously leaving one's body during the sexual act. Even experienced old boys in magic can be thrown off by such an encounter—which in itself says a lot for it!

Fourth, we should mention the entirely different energetic qual-ity of homoerotic sex magic, which can be compared to no other sex-magical practice. This, of course, is written for heterosexual readers; homosexual readers should think the same about heteroerotical sex magic!

Secondary Comment

One-hundred-percent bisexual people are very rare. Most bi-sexuals show a slight bias toward one or the other gender. In gen-eral, however, it can be said that bisexuals have a much looser and freer sexuality. In sex magic, this spares them many troubles that a non-bisexual has to go through if he or she wants to make progress. On the other hand, bisexuals often have to beware of ignoring sig-nificant differences out of intellectual laziness. Bisexual people fre-quently pay for their sexual carefreeness and liberty by being denied the sharpness of dispute with their own sexual fears. They have to "hype themselves up" more to evoke some of this tension that bestows a large part of the power of sex magic. Furthermore, adepts should beware confusing the inability to differentiate with the state of the Chymical Androgyne! Neither is every snooze a meditation!

Absorption and Harmonization of Yin Yang Energy for Homosexual Magicians

In principle, all exercises given under "heteroerotic sex magic" can be reworked for homoerotic practice. Though some Taoist masters recommend homosexual disciples to absorb female Yin energy that they partly lack (or with women, missing male Yang energy) by other nonsexual means, three sexual techniques will be described here, the first autoerotic, the second homoerotic and the third heteroerotic. The first case features the duality earth/female and fire/male; the second and third cases moon and sun.

Absorption of Yin Energy 1

An Autoerotic Method for Male Magicians

The magician looks for a place in the open countryside where it is possible to absorb earth energy in the nude. If possible, the ground should be soft and damp and should show uncovered soil. At a suitable time, the magician goes there, draws his protective circle, performs a magical banishing ritual and strips off all his clothes to face nature as a child in primeval innocence.

Now the magician lies on his stomach and snuggles into the earth, embracing and caressing it until he feels sexual excitement. Then he performs the Lesser Energy Orbit, feeding it with the earth energy through mouth and penis when inhaling, and letting it circulate through his entire body when exhaling. He continues until glutted on the female earth energy; then he rises and gives thanks to the earth energy as an end to the ritual.

Absorption of Yang Energy 1

An Autoerotic Method for Female Magicians

The female magician finds a place in the open countryside where it is possible to absorb fire energy in the nude. The ground should be hard and dry and should show uncovered soil. At a suitable time, she goes to this place, draws her protective circle, performs a banishing ritual and strips off all her clothes to face nature as a child in primeval innocence. She lights a fire within the circle and tends it with care.

Now she crouches down in front of the fire as closely as comfort permits. Once the fire seems friendly and no longer a burning force, she "caresses" its heat until she feels sexual excitement. Now she performs the Lesser Energy Orbit, feeding it with fire energy through mouth and vagina when inhaling and circulating it through her body when exhaling. She continues until she feels glutted with male fire energy; then she rises and gives thanks to the fire energy as an end to the ritual.

"Friendly fire" is largely a matter of how deep one's magical trance is. The burning and dangerous characteristics of fire can be toned down by extensive singing of mantras and other ecstasy techniques, so that one can encounter its naked energy.

Absorption of Yin Energy 2

A Heteroerotic Method for Male Magicians

The magician looks for a female partner who is prepared to support him in his Great Work. The partner should work sex magically with her female energy for at least one moon cycle; for example, by daily Moon and Venus rituals, by absorbing water and earth energy and moon rays, by visions, suitable elixirs and so on.

At a suitable time, both magicians retire to their temple, stand in the protective circle, call upon the Moon goddess and/or Great Mother and invoke Her into the female magician while the male partner serves the Moon Goddess/Great Mother and complies with all her wishes. Both adepts perform the Lesser Energy Orbit and exchange their energies. The male partner cherishes the female energy he receives and absorbs it into every cell of his body. The Goddess decides on the length of the operation, and the ritual is ended as usual.

Absorption of Yang Energy 2

A Heteroerotic Method for Female Magicians

The female magician looks for a male partner prepared to support her in her Great Work. The partner should work sex magically with his male energy for at least one solar month; for example, by daily Sun and Mars rituals, by absorbing fire and air energy, by martial arts, suitable elixirs and so on.

At a suitable time, both magicians retire to their temple, stand within the protective circle, call upon the Sun God and/or Great Allfather and invoke Him into the magician while the female partner serves the Sun God/Allfather and complies with all his wishes. Both adepts perform the Lesser Energy Orbit and exchange their energies. The female partner cherishes the male energy she receives and absorbs it into every cell of her body. The God decides on the length of the operation, and the ritual is ended as usual.

Absorption of Yin Energy 3

A Homoerotic Method for Male Magicians

The magician looks for a male partner prepared to support him in his Great Work. The partner should work sex magically with his female energy for at least one lunar month; for example, by daily Moon and Venus rituals, by absorbing water and earth energy and moon rays, by visions, suitable elixirs and so on.

At a suitable time, both magicians retire to their temple, stand within the protective circle, call upon the Moon Goddess and/or Great Mother and invoke Her into the partner, while the magician serves the Moon Goddess/Great Mother and complies with all her wishes. Both adepts perform the Lesser Energy Orbit and exchange their energies. The magician cherishes the female energy which he receives and absorbs it into every cell of his body. The Goddess decides on the length of the operation, and the ritual is ended as usual.

Absorption of Yang Energy 3

A Homoerotic Method for Female Magicians

The female magician looks for a female partner prepared to support her in her Great Work. The partner should work sex magically with her male energy for at least one solar month; for example, by daily Sun and Mars rituals, by absorbing fire and air energy and sun rays, by martial arts, suitable elixirs and so on.

At a suitable time, both magicians retire to their temple, stand within the protective circle, call upon the Sun God and/or Allfather and invoke Him into the partner, while the magician serves the Sun God/Allfather and complies with all his wishes. Both adepts perform the Lesser Energy Orbit and exchange their energies. The magician cherishes the male energy which she receives and absorbs it into every cell of her body. The God decides on the length of the operation, and the ritual is ended as usual.

Once you have performed these three rituals—if possible one shortly after the other—you will soon discover what the different sex-magic energy qualities are like! Of course, you may vary these rituals and adjust them according to your needs. Male magicians may also, for example, support heteroerotic Yin absorption during the preparatory phase by working with the same energies and in the same way as their female partners, or they may deliberately deal with the male energies in order to experience the contrast with Yin energy even more strongly. Female magicians may similarly adjust these rituals according to their needs.

Do not forget: the goal is to give you the ingredients of magic so that you can experiment to your heart's content however you wish!

What was said concerning homosexual magicians also applies to heterosexual magicians when they work on homoerotic sex magic. Feel free to experiment with the Yin and Yang aspects of your own personality and those of your homoerotic partner. The basics have been supplied to you here; you must vary these according to your own needs.

In general, homoerotic sex magic is used for mystical attainment and for such destructive work as harming spells, cursing and combat magic. Of course, this also applies to heterosexuals who use homoerotic practices as the exception. Here anal intercourse is said to be best for destructive operations, though this is also claimed for heterosexual anal sex. One cannot help but suspect that this opinion reflects an aversion for so-called "perverted" anal intercourse, which has long been seen as bestial and punished with hypocritical moral indignation by church and society. Only the fact that anal intercourse denies any form of reproduction is a symbolic argument in favor of that idea. As a matter of fact, anal intercourse is employed as a means of contraception in many countries of the Middle and Far East. But the symbolic argument applies equally to oral intercourse, masturbation and numerous other nonreproductive forms of sexuality. Such "teachings" have to be taken with a pinch of salt, because often they reflect no more than the prejudices of their founders.

Should you have similar experiences, however, you may of course stick to them.

For homosexual magicians, the same instructions apply as for heteroerotic sex magic, with one important difference: most homosexuals have some heterosexual experience, whereas most heterosexuals have no homosexual experience. So the threshold to contrary sexuality can be different.

It is typical that, in Crowley's O.T.O., there were no written instructions for XI° work, the homoerotic grade. There are several mundane reasons for this, such as the social unacceptability and illegality of homosexual activities, but there are also some good magical reasons. Most members in the order were, as far as we know, neither homosexual nor bisexual. They only got into such practices through knowing the Master Therion, who hardly did it in a squeamish manner. For this reason, if not for any other, homoerotic sex magic had an extraordinarily explosive force, which was furthered by keeping silent about it.

Finally, I want to describe a very instructive magical experience that reveals the different energetic qualities of homoerotic and heteroerotic sex magic. To my knowledge this subject is not dealt with in any work on applied sex magic, but it is nevertheless of crucial importance to success.

About five years ago, a client whom I had not previously known asked me to produce a talisman for the purpose of intensifying love, harmony and sexual contacts. After a short discussion, we decided to charge a Venus talisman. I calculated the birth chart of my client and also determined a suitable date for the ritual charging of the talisman. The client received the talisman from me by mail, together with detailed instructions as to how he should activate a sympathetic-magic contact to this talisman and how he should look after it.

Two weeks later, my client called me and complained that the talisman gave him the creeps—after he had received it, some unpleasant events had occurred in his professional and personal life. When questioned more precisely, I found that he had not stuck to my instructions. For example, he had not waited to start wearing the talisman on the prescribed day. Anyway, he did not want to give in, so I gave him further advice as how to treat the talisman. That seemed to be that, and I did not hear from him for a long while.

About three years later, I had another call asking me to do something about his Venus talisman—perhaps by discharging it—so we arranged a meeting. Only now did I learn that this man was a homosexual living in a permanent relationship with a partner. The "personal problems" that the talisman had given him were quite informative. He had felt his relationship becoming too close, but he was psychologically unable to form sexual contacts with other partners. The talisman should have helped him to do this, but meanwhile the relationship to his original partner became more and more intense; their love increased until there was no longer any question of him "playing away"! Instead, my client had nightmares of naked women from which he would wake up bathed in sweat! This was significant insofar as he was not one of those homosexuals with an aversion to females, nor was he bisexual. When we talked about the nature of the Venus principle, which had obviously not been clear to him three years before, he admitted that the talisman had indeed worked in the way I had originally intended. He should have told me about his homosexuality, and it was my mistake not to have asked him. I did not see any indication in his horoscope, either.

This anecdote is quite informative because it also provides evidence against the placebo or suggestion theory of magic common among amateur psychologists. My client had contravened my "instructions," but believed he was getting the effect he had in mind when he commissioned it from me. In reality, the talisman had a completely different effect, in exact correspondence to the Venus principle with which it had been charged, so suggestion or the placebo effect was out of the question.

This story also illustrates the need to be familiar with the deeper meaning of magical symbols. If my client had described his true situation, I would have recommended a Mercury talisman, because the Mercury principle works for both bisexuality and homosexuality. Uranus, as the higher octave of Mercury, is a sort of "patron saint" of homosexuals—at the turn of the century they were called "Uranians." Since traditional planetary magic works only with the seven classical planets, Uranus does not come into it, and so Mercury and the Sun principle are assigned to such operations.

Secondary Comment

None of these comments affect the actual technique of sex magic. Although one has to adapt the symbolism, the basic principles remain the same. The reason this is underlined here for the third time is that most beginners and even some experienced magicians do not accept the fact and put it into practice, as needed for successful work. This book is not directed at homosexuals, nor does it exclusively consider heterosexuals. It sets out to show sex magic as a discipline *for all:* beginners and advanced, heterosexuals and homosexuals. The superstition that there must be a separate formula for each magical problem has led to a host of cumbersome "recipe books" instead of small, precisely formulated reference books that would be far more useful in practice. It is like the ABCs and basic arithmetical operations: once you master the basics, the rest of arithmetic follows and leads on to algebra, and geometry and trigonometry become meaningful. Most magical authors seem to enjoy offering a result for any imaginable calculation. To stick to our image, this would be like a calculation book listing all conceivable calculating operations together with their complete answers. For example: "3 x 9 = 27," "3 x 543 = 1629," "5783.48 / 14 = 413.10571," "87 + 78 = 165," "1234 − 987 = 247." Numerous magical books proceed similarly, providing recipes such as "spells to bewitch the neighbor's cattle," "spells to bewitch the neighbor's crop," "spells to bewitch the neighbor's servants" etc. In the end, they look like the Chinese restaurant menu: "duck with almonds," "duck with water chestnuts," "duck with pineapples" etc.

It is obvious that such attempts are not only of a doubtful value, but they can even be harmful. On one hand, they foster belief in an unattainable completeness; on the other hand, they confuse readers and, because of so many individual instructions, successfully prevent readers from ever perceiving the basic rules of magic in order to develop relevant rituals themselves. This "old guard occultism" demands less from the intellect, but it also offers nothing but off-the-peg clothing which has to fit the prospective adepts whether they like it or not. Of course, this may seem easier than going through the trouble of learning tailoring, but it is less complete and prevents real mastery through exact knowledge of the subject. All this helps the few "in the know," who abuse their positions in artificial hierarchies to profit from the stupidity of their followers. The history of magical orders is full of such examples. It has little to do with magical freedom and should therefore be opposed.

Ritual Group Sexuality

The Black Mass

Hardly any area of sex magic, a subject already controversial enough, has suffered such bizarre fantasies, insinuations and prejudices as has ritual group work. Of course, magicians themselves are not without blame. They have often enjoyed flaunting their pose as "bogey of the middle classes" with emotive sexual claims. Also, trendy occultism with its armchair Satanists has contributed its part to the ruin of the reputation of *all* sex magicians.

An amateur hearing the phrase "group sex magic" will primarily think of the infamous black mass. By this, he will usually understand a Satanic sex orgy wherein the Catholic mass is parodied and mixed with blasphemous elements (urinating into the communion cup, smearing the cross with excrement etc.). We cannot deny that doings such as these occasionally occur. The term "black mass" has become a synonym for all sorts of bizarre sexual practices. In most cases, the people involved do not understand the first thing about sex magic; they are just living out their sexual fantasies! There is nothing to be said against this, but all it really has in common with a black mass is the name.

Unfortunately, this is equally true of "real" Satanists. When you look at the black mass as supposedly celebrated in Satanic circles, it appears at first to be simply ridiculous. A defrocked Catholic priest (because no one else has the necessary apostolic succession) must deflower a virgin on the altar (the virgin herself often represents the altar) while the Lord's Prayer is recited backwards—or even the entire Mass is celebrated in an inverted manner, the cross hanging upside down. The host, properly consecrated by the priest and therefore "flesh of Christ," is desecrated and tromped on. Instead of Christ, the goat Satan is evoked. The whole spectacle amounts to a total inversion of the Catholic Mass and thus is a purposeful blasphemy. The details of this ritual may vary occasionally. Since apostate priests are as rare as willing virgins these days, most Satanists will have to put up with substitutes.

It is plausible that such a Black Mass can only work for rebellious Catholics. *Hate* for something is a form of energy similar to *love* for the same thing. People to whom the Catholic Mass does not mean anything—either because they were raised within a different religious system (just imagine how odd and downright bizarre a black mass must seem to a Muslim or a Buddhist!), or because they have emancipated themselves inwardly from Catholicism—would consider a black mass as a silly masquerade and would raise no power by it.

But it would be dismissing the subject too lightly if we left it at that. Here again, one must not make the mistake of mixing the outer form with the content, taking exception to detail without knowing the structure behind it. Basically, the black mass is the Christian counterpart to the already mentioned ritual of *Pancha makara*, which equally offends against all the taboos of Hinduism and Buddhism— against the ban of eating meat, drinking alcohol, consuming fish and sexual taboos including—in some Kaula sects—homo-eroticism. Among formerly strict Catholic adepts who are still Catholic-minded, the black mass may have the odd liberating effect. And if one thinks of its gruesome variants, one of them being child slaughter (which by the way, was probably rightly claimed for Gilles de Rais), as was proven in the Montespan affair in France during the time of the Sun King, it seems probable that the black mass will still have its "effect" in a thousand years. But we do not have to dive into the sinister area of cannibalism to get to a more practicable and above all more effective form of a modern black mass.

Let us take ourselves back into the situation of a doubting Catholic at the turn of the century, that era which was called "decadent." His faith is shaken by science (for example, Darwin) and philosophy (for example, Nietzsche). Rationalist "Life of Jesus" research and the reactionary cultural war harass the old values without, however, actually creating new ones. Repression by institutionalized religion is revealed day by day, but still society will not and does not throw it off. Industrialization has fortified a new social class, the bourgeoisie. The economy is booming; expansion has its heyday. New foreign colonies are conquered, and there are new chances for social ascension. Bohemian artists set the example, and "freedom" seems only a stone's throw away. Now a Satanist approaches our doubting Catholic to tell him about this new independence, bringing up that most sensitive of all points, namely sexuality, and promising undreamt of sweet ecstasy with sex and drugs (the laws against opium and other narcotics are still far away in the future). Above all, the Satanist promises him the final divorce from the great Moloch Church, which condemns every physical lust, which devours its children and—shortly before the turn of the century—feeds them the dogma of papal infallibility and the Immaculate Conception. What could seem more enthralling than smashing everything restrictive and enforcing his intellectual, sexual and existential liberty with a wild, desperate gesture? Did not Nietzsche demonstrate it? Had not artists been preaching it all the time? Therefore, turn to the black mass and a reversal of all values. The scepticism of the doubting mind is allowed to change into a pure but well-ordered nihilism, and is allowed to defile, blaspheme and whore within the strict frame of the ritual. Religiously hyped up, our Christian is suddenly permitted to do what he would never dare to do of his own accord without the safeguard of a new ideology.

Denial and destruction of everything which restricts, inhibits and limits you—*that* is the true formula of the black mass! This is the rule of calculation and structure from which we can develop everything for ourselves.

Therefore a black mass at the close of the 20th century, an age marked by technology and scientific thinking, an age of information and threats of environmental catastrophe, of urban brutalization, might employ the following elements: smashing and "defiling" an expensive computer; burning scientific magazines on the altar; destroying the image of an atom bomb; sexual asceticism as a protest against the degradation of sexuality by the so-called "sexual revolution," with its pornography industry, peepshows and sex clubs; reciting stock market reports, calorie tables and job center statistics backwards, and so on. This list does not necessarily reflect my personal dislikes, and you might disagree with some of the above points, but you will have realized by now that what actually counts is our context. To finish this subject, here is another quote from Peter J. Carroll and the legendary *Liber Null:*

> There is no limit to the inconceivable experiences into which the intrepid psychonaut may wish to plunge himself. Here are some ideas for constructing a latter day black mass as a blasphemy against the gods of logic and rationality. The Great Mad Goddess Chaos, a lower aspect of the ultimate ground of existence in anthropomorphic form, can be invoked for Her ecstasy and inspiration.
>
> Drumming, leaping, and whirling in free form movement are

accompanied by idiotic incantations. Forced deep breathing is used to provoke hysterical laughter. Mild hallucinogens and disinhibitory agents (such as alcohol) are taken together with sporadic gasps of nitrous oxide gas. Dice are thrown to determine what unusual behavior and sexual irregularities will take place. Discordant music is played and flashing lights splash onto billowing clouds of incense smoke. A whole malestrom of ingredients is used to overcome the senses. On the altar a great work of philosophy, preferably by Russell, lies open, its pages fiercely burning.[8]

You can recognize the basic structure of a black mass even in its modern form. What matters is to take on today's current taboos instead of assaulting the dead gods of the past.

How to Handle Group Energies in Sex Magic Rituals

Ritually produced group-sex-magic energy needs to be dealt with separately. It is also a matter of concern whether a group consists of three or 30 magicians. Some magicians refuse to work with more than two or three colleagues at a time, whereas others, particularly those in shamanic traditions, like to have dozens or even hundreds of participants. Group sex energy also depends on the individual development of the group's members. It is not always an advantage to have only experienced magicians, because sometimes beginners bring in fresh energy and a certain innocence which make possible things that otherwise would require much more effort. On the other hand, beginners may disturb the operation by their unfocused reactions. All this should indicate that there can be no precise advice for sex-magical group work, and the following explanations can only be a rule of thumb to be varied in individual cases.

There are basically two possibilities for the handling of ritual group energy working: with a ritual leader and without one. Both ways are complicated and demand much experience.

Group Rituals with a Leader

The ritual leader is usually appointed before the ritual; occasionally, the office is given spontaneously during a ritual. The leader should have a great deal of private and group ritual experience, and experience in the particular field of sex magic is indispensable. Furthermore, the ritual leader must be able to perceive group energies and direct them toward the desired goal.

The choice of group members is of the utmost importance. Since the sexual *magis* raised in groups is extraordinarily strong, it must be ensured that each participant can really handle such energy. It is not necessary that all participants have the same level of sex magic experience, but *everybody* should at least have some autoerotic sex-magic experience. This will also depend upon whether the ritual leader decides the structure of the group, which may be hierarchical as in the teacher-disciple relationship of a brotherhood. It is not desirable that all members of the group already know one another; on the contrary, a certain amount of non-familiarity lowers the threshold of inhibition and allows energy to flow more freely. At least for the first few operations, it often seems most sensible if partners have met only briefly before. This of course depends on circumstances.

The question whether "singles" are admitted is also a matter of personal taste. One cannot cover oneself against all odds, but it should be obvious that sex-magic group ritual requires a great amount of mutual trust and cannot tolerate any jealousy. The first joint work will frequently concentrate on how to lower the threshold of inhibition, and only during following meetings can work go on into more depth. The ritual leader should nevertheless take care that his group does not waste too much time on psychological exercises, sensitivity practices and "spiritual sexuality." Such "spiritualization" is in most cases little else but idealized fear of the "grossness of the flesh," whereas sex magic takes place on *all* levels simultaneously. Nothing is intended here against true spirituality, which builds on fleshly experience and has lived through the heaven and hell of sensuality.

The ritual leader is responsible for the administration and orderly course of the ritual, and is often its creator, unless the group has developed it together. In most cases the leader will also perform the office of high priest or priestess. *During the ritual, the word of the leader is law*—not only for reasons of discipline, but also to create an authority for the orientation of group members. This may prevent one's ego from taking control, with its legion of fears and attachments, its prejudices and petty protests.

Traditional rituals use the leader mainly as an absorber of group energies and for performing the magical act as a representative of the whole group. This may be a sex-magic act such as the Great Rite in Wicca, which we will deal with later, or it may be another magical operation such as invocation, conjuration, charging amulets or healing. In these cases, the priest serves as a channel and, during this time, a representative will stand in as group leader.

Another form of ritual may build up the desired magical energy under supervision of its leader, after which the energy is used by all participants for their own magical purposes independently. In this case, the ritual leader gives the signal at the crucial moment, as is done anyway between each ritual phase.

Another very important task of the leader is to check the level of energy of every single participant at regular intervals and to use relevant means to clear possible blockages; for example, by giving magnetic passes, giving instructions for correct breathing or providing treatment with mantras, cymbals, bells, magical weapons or fetishes. It should be understood that it is the overall harmony that comes first, and intervention takes place only when it is essential.

If the group works heteroerotically, the number of female and male participants should be balanced. Although there are several variants where only one or two representatives of the other sex are present, as in the traditional black mass, people frequently also work in groups of three, which has an entirely different quality than work with four or more participants.

Much more could be said on the subject, but these clues should be sufficient because they cover the essential points. If you stick to them, nothing can hinder your successful sex magic.

Group Rituals Without a Leader

This type of ritual is generally said to be the most difficult. If the group consists entirely of experienced magicians who are used to one another, there should be no problems. But it is different if this is not the case, and even more so in *spontaneous ritual*. Spontaneous rituals can be divided into two main groups: those rituals which develop on the spur of the moment without any planning, when sex magicians are gathered together, and those rituals that have been planned before but are allowed to develop by themselves. Occasionally, temporary ritual leaders may emerge to direct the ritual for a while.

Spontaneous rituals have the advantage of adjusting to the group's makeup and the quality of the moment, but they also demand a maximum amount of inner centerdness and maturity from all participants, because only rarely are precautions taken in case one or more participants experiences a crisis in between. The modern form of black mass described above is such a spontaneous ritual, where "bloody beginners" can be a disturbing influence and where the degree of familiarity between participants needs to be higher than it is with structured rituals.

Because of its spontaneity, this form of ritual should have a set *purpose* and should not be performed solely for its own sake. If there is no purpose, the sex *magis* aroused might not find an outlet through which it can constructively discharge itself.

Secondary Comment

One problem to be guarded against in sex magic is that of *energy vampirism*. There are numerous variations, beginning with an immediate loss of energy to another partner who, in return, will come out of the ritual with a corresponding gain of energy, and leading up to a clearly noticeable loss of libido suffered by females and males alike. It is not true, as claimed in older books, that only women suck out energy and that men have to guard themselves against it! This opinion is an excessive extrapolation from the equations: "female = receiving = absorbing" and "male = active = giving = ejecting." We see from this example how analogies have to be applied with reason and moderation.

This energy robbery mostly happens subconsciously, and it is nearly inevitable if the absorbing partner has a lower level of energy than the victim. The "sacrifice" should not be pitied, however, because vampirism can only occur through carelessness, overestimation of one's abilities and insufficient magical protection. If you remain in your Hara, activate your protective symbol and keep up your Lesser Energy Orbit, none of this should happen to you. Tell this to the energy robber in the nicest possible manner and suggest other ways that they can acquire their needed energy. Above all, do not fall into the paranoia of smelling enemies everywhere, all of them after your precious *magis!* Do not start by assuming that other people are deliberately abusing you as a source of energy. Should this actually be the case, cut off all magical contact with the robber— particularly, of course, sex-magic contacts. In this case, you may decide to counterattack, but you will have to be a born combat magician to cope with the nervous tension involved. Even then, magical war is to be avoided. It is a highly uneconomical venture which frequently ends in insanity, illness and death...

The Great Rite

The Great Rite is the ritual of the so-called "third grade" in Wicca, which is the neo-pagan witch cult. This cult is very diverse, and some of its groups do not have a grade system, but the Great Rite is generally known as its highest level. It is first celebrated within the group, but, after necessary energies have been built up, its members usually retreat so that priest and priestess can perform the act in undisturbed togetherness. There are also variants where the Great Rite is performed by all participants as a sacred orgy. In the Middle Ages, it was occasionally practiced in fields by large groups of country folk to increase fertility and ensure good harvests.

Here again, we want to introduce a quote, this time from Wicca literature, which describes the Great Rite. It is from J l rg Wichmann's work, *Wicca—Die magische Kunst der Hexen* (*Wicca—The Magical Art of Witches*):

> The Great Rite is the union of god and goddess, of heaven and earth, the fusion of polarities. The Horned One and the Earth unite in ecstasy and rapture. The Great Rite is performed by priest and priestess who have identified themselves with the deities. It may be performed physically or symbolically.
>
> Symbolically performed it is done by wand and cup, the priestess holding the filled cup, the priest thrusting the wand. The priestess approaches from West, the priest from East, and they unite silently in the center of the circle.
>
> Both symbolic and physical performance of the Great Rite are obvious in their magical and sacred meaning. It needs no verbal accompaniment if performed with clarity and intensity. It is important that priest and priestess keep their magical consciousness even during physical ecstasy. Take care to direct the energy raised into earth or towards a certain aim, if the magical couple does not need it for itself.
>
> The Great Rite may also be performed at annual feasts (especially Walpurgis). The frame of the Great Rite is the usual basic ritual. It is the climax of magical art, ecstasy and meditation; it is the

most sacred ritual.

Do not forget: the *gods* shall unite in this ritual.[9]

The Great Rite may be performed by a couple on their own without a group. It has great structural similarity to the Chymical Marriage, which we will introduce in the last chapter.

Symbolical performance of the Great Rite already crosses the border into *sex mysticism*. Note that whereas the black mass is by its intention a *negation* of fetters, the Great Rite is an *approval* of life. This is only a gross analysis, because true black masses also subscribe to sensuality and approve it, but it nevertheless serves as a general illustration. For readers who are not into Wicca, there now follow two other rituals, the first of which strongly activates the male, the second one the female sexual *magis*. Like all our recommendations, they are only a framework which you should adjust according to your needs.

The Night of Pan

This ritual may be performed in any season but is best when the weather is warm, although it may also be done at the beginning of spring. At a suitable place in the wild, where there is no possibility of being disturbed, the male and female magicians gather in the late afternoon before sunset, and each brings his or her offering of food which is sacred to Pan and which should therefore be as ample and fresh as possible. Suitable foods include white bread, goat's cheese, olives, onions, lemons and resinous wines. The offerings are laid out on an altar decorated with flowers, together with any objects one might wish to charge such as magical weapons, talismans, amulets or fetishes. A large campfire should be prepared, but a number of outdoor flares or large torches would do—so long as there is enough fuel to last for several hours. Musical instruments such as flutes, panpipes, drums, rattles and percussion sticks are also excellent additions.

The participants should have spent at least one week in preparation by meditating about the principle of Pan and its mythological contents, or by daily invocations of Pan while reciting a hymn to Pan or by stimulating themselves sexually while avoiding orgasm, which is saved for the ritual itself.

At sunset the introductory meditation begins. Afterwards, the circle is consecrated and ritually protected. Then follows another

The Night of Pan

short meditation, music and the recitation of hymns and texts appropriate to Pan. The hymns should ideally be written by the magicians themselves using rhymes and rhythmical language to support the recitation. Should you not be confident enough to write your own hymns, you had best use invocations from the Orphic tradition. Also suitable are two texts of the old master Aleister Crowley: first, the *Liber A'ash vel Capricorni Pneumatici*[10] is recited, and then the *Hymn to Pan*,[11] the latter as often as possible, until the desired energy is built up. While the music is performed, the participants dance and summon the Great God Pan. One invocation formula often used is:

> IO PAN! IO PAN!
> IO PAN PAN! PAN!
> IO PANGENITOR! IO PANPHAGE!
> IO PAN! IO PAN!
> IO PAN PAN! PAN!

This ritual may be performed with or without a leader. If there is a leader, the group summons the Pan energy to indwell the leader. The leader will know beyond all doubt when Pan has come and must then transmit his energy to all other participants by dancing and laying on of hands. If the group works without a leader, each must summon Pan into himself or herself.

Making rules for the next phase of the ritual would be absurd, for Pan is the All-principle which tolerates no fetters! Pan Himself will decide what happens next. Participants give themselves to the orgiastic ("panic") energy of Pan and perform the sacred act while affirming their magical will. After a certain point, such rituals appear on the surface to be nothing more than a group sex orgy, but everyone involved knows that in fact it is quite different, being suffused with enormously high-level energy which gives immense magic powers—quite the opposite of "dissipation."

After the climax of the ritual has passed, a further meditation follows in which the participants quietly feel their pulsating body energy. Then all the offerings are consumed. Pan likes to laugh, so jokes (including dirty ones!) are entirely appropriate. Grim determination and doleful expressions are no way to invoke Pan!

Finally, depending on the level of energy, the orgiastic Pan principle may be activated again for further sex magic or else the ritual ends with a short thanksgiving, a banishing ritual and a formula of dismissal.

If the leader notices any participants having difficulty entering their gnostic trances, then they should be helped along, provided they are willing to accept such help—this must be discussed *before* the ritual! Apart from that, everybody will experience this ritual in a different way—although numerous coincidences and synchronicities will crop up in discussion after the ritual.

The ritual may be performed either heteroerotically or homoerotically. It can even be performed on one's own, but group work is better because of its far greater energy.[12]

The Night of Hecate

This ritual is about contact with the principle of Hecate, the primeval dark mother, the ruler of the underworld who commands death and reincarnation. She is responsible for the darker aspects of magic, because she symbolizes the shadow side of the female principle. This ritual should also be performed in the wild and is best at New Moon when the darker energies prevail. Winter and autumn are particularly suited for this ritual, but this may cause problems in colder climates, so ideally an underground cave should be chosen as the ritual place.

This ritual is similar in framework to the previous one; I will therefore only mention the differences.

Offerings may be corn products, agricultural crops, poppy seeds, figs, pomegranates, water, John Barleycorn with mint, beer, pork, ham, pumpkin etc. The altar may be decorated with corn flowers, garlands of corn, mistletoe and similar items, but also with poisons, because Hecate is also the goddess of the mixing of poisons and destructive magic. The music used should be somehow melancholy and gloomy, although it may have a sort of somber serenity after the Hecate principle has been activated.

Participants prepare themselves for the ritual by traveling in their spirit bodies into the underworld and by sexual asceticism and fasting. You should also meditate on the mythological aspects of this deity.

The ritual's procedure is identical to the program in the Pan ritual. Again, you should write hymns yourself, but, to give you an idea, I want to show you here one example of mine which you are free to change and "exploit":

The Night of Hecate

Hymn to Hecate

Black Moon, Lilith, sister darkest,
Whose hands form the hellish mire,
At my weakest, at my strongest
Molding me as clay from fire.

Secrets sinister of my psyche—
Shadow woman revealed by you—
In my self-tormenting torture
You feast upon my bitter dew.

You who bleed in starlit forest,
Quickened by your womb's own sheen,
Die in the Lord of Shining Pastures—
God ever agéd, ever green.

Your death unveils the naked mirror,
Stained dully in the Woods of When . . .
Oh, the sun lets blaze its ardor,
Grabs attention, grasps . . . and then?

Black Moon, Lilith, Mare of Night,
You cast your litter to the ground
That earth might live, that earth might sound
To the thunder as hooves pound,
Fodder for the Gods' delight.

Moon Lady, Dead One, hear me.
Moon Lady, Dark One, embrace me.
Moon Lady, Sinister One, strangle me.
Moon Lady, Dourest One, cast me down.

Hurl me to your very deepest
Shades that beckon, shades that tempt,
Whose siren spell has drawn my reins
Tempting from the birth of Time.
Beneath the irons of your kisses
Sand is trickling through my veins . . .
. . . and the land be barren-fruitful!
. . . and the land be barren-fruitful!

(Translation by Ramsey Dukes and Frater U∴.D∴.)

A general formula used in Wicca to summon the Great Goddess, as well as in nearly all rituals which call on female deities, goes like this:

ISIS ASTARTE DIANA
HECATE DEMETER KALI INANNA

While their ecstasy mounts, all participants prepare inwardly for an inner descent to the underworld where the goddess dwells. In this underworld-trance, the sex-magical work begins as described.

Don't misunderstand the gloomy undertone of the Hecate principle. It has surprising orgiastic potential. After a successful invocation, the heteroerotic act will usually be performed with the men lying down and being ridden by the women—but this should not be a rigid rule!

This ritual, too, may be performed heteroeotically or homoerotically. Autoerotic work is also possible, but, here again, group work is far better.

If you prefer to work with the "lighter" aspects of the feminine principle, you may, of course, construct your own appropriate ritual along similar lines to the Night of Hecate. To help you with this, here is a hymn to Artemis, goddess of the Moon, of love and beauty and—in her form of *Diana Artemis*—of hunting. Here we have the more pristine aspect of the virgin sister expressed.

Artemis, my sibyl sibling,
huntress of the earthy skies,
wayfaress in silver rippling—
in your hands my power lies...

lies my dream and all my making
muted might in liquid pose,
lies my giving and my taking,
caressing friends and smiting foes

in your light and metal sheen,
waxing, waning, touched, unseen,
ever-moving curvéd bow
ever-whirring arrow's flow
to the core of mine own heart

hitting mark, a gentle dart
strikes my body, strikes my soul,
fondles part and fondles whole
towards my ever-pulsing spell:
give me heaven, give me hell
take from me what makes me sink
with your sleight of hand and wink—
Goddess of the nightly sweep,
through the starlit mires seep,
never solemn, yet possessed,
by your mastery expressed,

all your vision's harvest keeps...
all your vision's harvest keeps...

The Astral Sabbath

We have already described sex magic on the astral plane. The astral Sabbath works on the same principle, but with a whole group of magicians. Participants will have to have plenty of experience with astral projection to ensure success. It is not absolutely necessary for the ritual itself that all participants are in the same physical location, but in the beginning this is easier to handle. Also, it is advisable to perform the astral Sabbath immediately after some physical ritual as, for example, at the Pan ritual described above, after the feast when the sexual *magis* stirs again. It can also be practiced for experimental reasons, to test or strengthen the astral-projection ability of all participants.

Apart from that, the astral Sabbath has no fixed content and any group ritual can be performed in this manner. Arrangements must of course be discussed in advance, and the ritual itself then goes ahead in exactly the same way as it would on the material level—astral offerings are tendered, astral incense is burned, and so on.

It need hardly be pointed out that the astral Sabbath is only suitable for very experienced magicians. It demands the highest standards of self-control and magical ability. The quality of the energy it raises, however, is incomparable. Most magicians will experience such an astral Sabbath only rarely in their lives, although there are some witch groups experimenting with it more frequently. So-called "witches' ointments" or "flying ointments" are meant to be helpful, but they are not only illegal but also harmful. The highly poisonous nightshade in these ointments demands extremely careful dosage. This, by the way, is said to be how the "Witches' Sabbath" in the Middle Ages was performed.

Secondary Comment

Most literature about sex magic is restrained when it comes to homoerotic practice, but is completely silent beyond this variety of sexuality. This is astonishing, since we know a host of examples from history in which other forms of sex played their part in magical cults.

It is certainly not bad tactics to leave disciples to their own fantasy, encouraging them to take a peek *behind* the veil of mystery to find out that behind the veil is nothing but a mirror, revealing one's own countenance and the truth that seeking is more important than finding. This gives adepts the feeling that everything was acquired by their *own* efforts, which is eternally true even when we do not want to admit it.

Yet it is unwise to not move with the times. Modern humanity has moved on to different areas, adopted different forms and developed different needs. It is no longer meaningful to follow overtrodden paths while new tasks arise in magic.

It is not our intention to boast that "at last and for the first and only time in the whole of history, all mysteries are to be ruthlessly unveiled," as numerous other magicians have done before, and not always so clumsily! True mysteries always protect themselves. We never entirely fathom them, and each epoch approaches them in its own way. Who knows, maybe they do not need humanity at all and created us only to serve their own pleasure. Anyway, the times are past when it was enough to go peddling vague hints about pearls of wisdom too sacred to reveal. Today's magicians have the task of continuing what their predecessors began a hundred years ago—examining magic and its relation to humanity as a psychological entity in the age of technocracy. The task is to free magic from all the junk and cobwebs which it has accumulated over the millennia. The overpowering influence of the Middle Ages—a great epoch of magic but not its greatest—must be thrown off before we can liberate ourselves from the Judaeo-Christian perversion which still sticks to magic like a poisonous miasma. It is one thing to sneer at magicians of the Middle Ages who hid their cursing formulas and death spells behind Christian phrases and endless prayers to their grotesque slave god and his smugly pious successors, but it is quite another matter to recognize the real reasons for this coverup and to learn to find its echoes in our supposedly liberal age. Thus we might realize that our predecessors did not so much seek the favors of the omnipresent and all-powerful Church but rather that they knew that it is important for magicians at all times to live in harmony with their environment and avoid unnecessary friction. A banal cognition, maybe, but it has to be repeated over and over. This example is only one of many ways one can win new wisdom from old facts by new ways of looking at them afresh. Ultimately, magicians should be wise and not just men and women of action. We all are far from ultimate wisdom—but on our path we gather experience, and occasionally we go round in circles. But only thus may we become one with the gods.

Let us therefore pull the wool from our eyes and question ourselves continuously. Let us strip away every new mask until eventually it is revealed "what holds the world together"—namely ourselves. *Homo est deus*—Man is God, albeit a sleeping one. That which obstructs our vision is called "cultural trance," "blinkers," "historical determinedness" and "chains of idleness." It helps us to lessen and ease the constraints of the outer world and the universe in which we survive against all probability, even though we jeopardize this same survival again and again. On the other hand, it prevents us from seeing the horizon and enlarging our field of view and perception as far as is possible.

All this will probably sound really nice and maybe even inspiring—so long as it does not touch our innermost being! Being earnest along these lines, however, means changing one's entire life and entering a new universe—a universe strange and threatening on the one hand, but so attractive on the other that only few who know it will ever seek to return. The sacrifices it demands are the most difficult of all; namely, habits of thinking and feeling, of faith and knowledge, of desire and refusal, habits which lead us to believe in freedom of will while subtly tightening the bonds.

Such philosophical considerations are occasionally necessary to keep magic in perspective. It is as dangerous to overestimate magic as it is to underestimate it. The crux of the matter is humanity. For this reason, it is vitally important for magicians to *know themselves*, as was written as an admonition over the entrance to the oracle of Delphi. Sex magic cannot totally answer the three Gnostic questions: "Who am I?" "Where do I come from?" and "Where am I go-ing?" but it does point the way so that everybody may get a personal answer by his or her own means.

Other, So-Called "Deviant," Practices

Some sex contact advertisements are worded along these lines: "I'll join in anything, except perversions." What on earth, one might ask, does the advertiser mean by the term "perverse"? Originally, the word meant "twisted, " but in the course of time its meaning has shifted considerably. Today it basically designates "to differ from the general norm"—which is a long way from meaning "pathologi-cally different" as is often assumed.

Modern sexology therefore has opted for the more neutral word "deviant," which also means "diverging." This is not just a quibble; on the contrary, the above-quoted advertisement shows the thoughtless way in which we deal with the language of sex. It is only a matter of convention and personal attitude as to what may *still* be called "normal" or is *already* "deviant." There are cranks who would brand a book like this one as completely "perverted. " Others may ask why homoerotic practices are not classified under "deviations, " whereas yet again others will find it strange that something so "nor-mal" as fetishism is placed in this section. By using this division, we keep to the present norm without taking it as an absolute—hence our use of the phrase "so-called" deviations.

You may think that you have already gone beyond the limits of what is acceptable with the exercises and practices already de-scribed; but, on the other hand, maybe you feel that we have missed some of your personal preferences.

Now, sex is so manifold that it is impossible to list all its varie-ties, let alone deal with them from a magical point of view. I can only compromise and list some of the more "way-out" practices with re-gard to their sex-magic potential, but without going into much de-tail.

Legal problems may also be encountered here. Some sexual deviations are generally outlawed; for example, sodomy and necro-philia. Therefore, recommendations cannot be made that would in-cite readers to break the law. But neither should this be necessary; serious magicians do not allow limitations to be forced upon them anyway. They know how to read between the lines and draw their own conclusions. Many of the things which we now describe may be of purely theoretical interest because of the light cast on the spiritual and technical potential of sex magic.

The Holy Fetish: A Reservoir of Power

It should have become clear by now that a fetish is here considered to be a magical tool and not, as is common in sexology, an object for the exclusive transmission (or, rather, projection) of lust. The subject is not "pathological" or morbid fetishism, where all sexuality and lust is pinned entirely on a fetish. Also, the meaning of the term is strictly limited to outer, physical, "inanimate" objects and does not include parts of the body, certain viewpoints or erotic situations.

The sex-magical charging of fetishes in connection with talismans and amulets has already been discussed in detail. Fetishes were called magical accumulators of energy, and it was described how power can be transmitted to them in a sex-magic way. Having a reservoir of energy is only sensible if the energy can be taken out again when needed. Just as the fetish is charged, so the *magis* can be withdrawn again by sex-magical means. This happens by intercourse and absorption of power, as with the heteroerotic exchange of energy between two partners, but an important qualification must be added: When dealing with a fetish, it is not so much a complete sexual act that counts as it is an erotic act released and reinforced by the fetish. The *erotic* way of dealing with a fetish is more important than the *sexual!* Occasionally, a fetish may stand in for a partner who charges it with energy that one can withdraw later as needed. Or the magician can, for example, charge a healing fetish and instruct a patient how to withdraw healing energy from it. For many magicians, particularly for beginners, this is easier than a purely astral transmission of power.

Occasionally, several different energies are bound one after another into a single fetish. Later, the magician reabsorbs this new "energy alloy" resulting from the mix. A sex-magic absorption of energy has the advantage of being quick and effective, replacing time-consuming meditations, preparatory exercises and difficult sympathetic magical adaptations of energy.

Occasionally it can happen that an outside spirit or some etheric energy takes possession of a fetish and forces the magician to perform repeated sexual acts with it. This is a very dangerous situation. On the one hand, it could be an initiation to the highest grade, because things like this happen only when a magician is in a highly polarized state. On the other hand, it may be an attempt by a demonic entity or another sorcerer to take possession of the magician's body. Should you experience something like this, approach it with the utmost care and make sure you maintain a genuine *magical* trance. Do not slip into will-lessness or unconsciousness.

The Ritual of the Goat of Mendes

This ritual was performed in ancient Egypt, and it achieved somewhat dubious notoriety through association with Aleister Crowley.

The cult center of Mendes in Lower Egypt was the capital of the 16th Lower-Egyptian district. It reached its cultural peak in latter times when the nameless Ram-God was worshipped, whom the Greeks later equated with Pan. Mummies of the worshipped animal were found there and elsewhere. The ram was the master of fertility and was celebrated as "copulator in Anep and inseminator in the district of Mendes," where women were blessed with children. Women therefore exposed themselves in front of the cult image, and both Pindar and Herodotus report that they even used to perform ritual intercourse with it. In this ritual, a goat was frequently used instead of a ram.

Crowley performed a similar ritual in his Sicilian Abbey of Thelema, during which his Scarlet Woman was to be mounted by a goat which would be beheaded during the climax. Unfortunately, the goat did not want to perform the sexual act. Therefore, as he pleasurably reported, the Master himself had to make up the loss afterwards.

It is interesting that ritual bestiality is nearly always restricted to intercourse between a male animal and one or more women, whereas purely sexual bestiality happens between men and animals. The meaning of such operations is also to work with animal atavisms and absorb their primordial powers. If necessary, the acts may be performed on an astral level. Be aware, however, that sodomy is regarded as an offense in most countries.

Sado-Masochism, Bondage and Sex Magic

Sado-masochism has a boundary-breaking function in sex magic. Some highly masochistically shaped practices are handed down from Crowley in the XI° workings, but without comment and without giving them any independent theoretical status. The same applies to anal intercourse, which he, unlike Kenneth Grant, did not mystically superelevate.

Sado-masochistic orgies frequently take the form of a black mass, but this has more to do with the sexual fantasies of their participants than with any real correlations to "applied blasphemy." In the interest of "trimming" or even destroying one's false ego, sado-masochistic operations are occasionally performed wherein magicians submit completely to a partner who has previously invoked some magical force or entity. This may include the use of bondage techniques, whips, canes and leather gear.

This, however, is generally an act of absolute devotion which equates only superficially with masochism. The invoking partner embodies the deity called down and acts according to it—and not according to *any* false ego. This again *may* or may not result in sadistic actions. Not much more can be said about such operations because they tend to follow their own rules. Generally, it may be said that using pain to induce gnostic trance can only be recommended *in extremis* and only under expert instruction; this weapon becomes quickly dulled, and the level of pain has to be increased more and more. As in all sex-magic practices, the same rule particularly applies here; namely, that any dependence on certain forms of stimulus has to be avoided! Apart from that, sadism/masochism is a very specialized sexual discipline which requires some training.

In fact, the S&M scene worldwide has its own mores, rites and lingo to which a newcomer has to be thoroughly introduced. There are a lot of rather rigid rules in "classical" sado-masochism, so that it is permissible to speak of a real "cult" of sorts. However, like all cults, organized S&M tends to become a somewhat sterile affair devoid of truly creative elements. What new practices and peaks of sadistic lust could ever be invented after the sexual—and philosophical—fantasies of the "Divine" Marquis de Sade, or after Sacher-Masoch's *Venus in Furs?* The highly stylized code of behavior between masochists and sadists goes to prove that the primary aim of these practices is not actually sexual but rather the pursuit of power, violence and its ecstasies.

Thus it is not surprising that sadomasochistic practices proper have a strong ritual element to them which can indeed be exploited within the wider context of sex magic, should the magician(s) so desire. (In a similar vein, a visit to a gambling casino could actually be exercised as a ritual in the "Temple of Fortuna, " and indeed this has been done on a fairly regular basis by some of my pupils and myself in the last few years.)

The ritual use of pain and agony as an access mode to trance and magical power does have its limits, though. For one thing, physical pain tends to dull the senses in the long run, so that stimuli have to be increased incessantly. This may quite easily lead to grave bodily harm, not to mention the fact that it can become downright addictive and lead to a kindled frenzy not very easily mastered. Furthermore, such practices usually involve a great deal of paraphernalia, precise dramatizing and plenty of physical and psychogical energy that might be employed more efficiently in other realms of sex magic. On the other hand, there is certainly something to be said for the raw and earthy Martian and Plutonian energies to be evoked by this approach. While they cannot exactly be termed "charming," they do tend to facilitate experiences not so easily gained from more conservative sex-magical activities.

Coprophagia and Its Varieties

Coprophagia, which means consumption of excrement, here also includes consumption of other secretions such as urine and sweat. It was ritually practiced from early times on the sympathetic-magic principle that the secretions of any entity contain part of its *magis*. Crowley, for example, occasionally offered his disciples in Cefalu the excrement of a goat. This frequently met with no small disapproval!

Sexology recognizes coprophagia and its variants as a pathological phenomenon among schizophrenics, but it also plays a certain part in sado-masochism and forms an independent sexual discipline in its own right. This gives us clues for its use in sex magic. It may be used as a threshold experience because, with many people, it will lead to a trance of loathing. On the other hand, it represents extreme carnal devotion to somebody else. But here again, no special instructions are necessary.

Ritual Necrophilia

Necrophilia, or intercourse with corpses, is also an ancient practice mentioned in Egyptian pyramid texts and other papyri. For example, Isis mounts the dead Osiris to conceive from him and let his soul enter into her body to be reborn as Horus. This is a variant of the Red Rite described by Peter J. Carroll in *Liber Null,* only in this case it is performed by a female partner. Inasmuch as such reports can frequently be found in Egyptian religious literature, we can be sure that these rites were more than isolated phenomena. Whether this act was meant to be physical, symbolic or merely etheric is arguable.

Another aspect of necrophilia is found in Indian/Tibetan Kaula Tantra. Here, it has the prime function of an initiation by terror; for example, when an adept copulates with a Yogini on top of a corpse, which is itself not usually included in the act but serves to create horror. Of course, it also serves to remind us of the transcience of all being and the unity of sex and death.

Again, we have to point out that necrophilia is a criminal offense and thus cannot be recommended here.

This list of possible forms of sex magic could be spun out *ad infinitum,* but there is no real need for this. Given the basic principles, you can weave any form of sex into your sex magic. Studying the history of morals in different cultures shows that there is nothing new under the sun. Sex and magic have always shaped our lives, and any attempt to suppress them has merely served to re-emphasize their enormous importance and power. Your own magic depends entirely on you, which paths you want to follow and how able you think you are. Nobody but *yourself* can dictate the tempo and direction!

Before concentrating on *sex mysticism,* it is time to summarize the perils of sex magic in a special chapter as promised. By now, you will have the necessary background to understand my viewpoint on this subject.

Notes

[1]Michael D. Eschner, *Die geheimen sexualmagischen Unterweisungen des Tieres 666,* Berlin: Stein der Weisen, 1985, p. 93. He incorrectly names Marcello Motta as head of the Californian O.T.O. (p.92) and confuses the magazine *Saturn-Gnosis,* produced by the Fraternitas Saturni, with the order itself. Despite his criticism, he largely stuck to Grant's system in his own, now defunct, order: "A∴A∴ Thelema."

[2]Compare my essay, "Wie schächte ich mein Alter Ego? Anmerkungen zur Dämonenmagie," *Unicorn* 13 (1985).

[3]For handling shamanic practices—in particular power animals—compare the excellent book by Michael Harner, *The Way of the Shaman*, New York: Harper and Row, 1980.

[4]Do not make the still quite common mistake (as can be found in one of the offprints by the Fraternitas Saturni mentioned earlier) of using "polarization tables" of certain sex positions and following a "scoring system" when having sex! Such practices show that the great sex-magic wisdom claimed by their authors is erroneous, and are rather an indication of an intellectualization and hostility towards the flesh—both equally harmful for magic—which can get you into a great deal of trouble when dealing with the *magis*. These techniques, like many other magical systems, work well in accordance with the placebo principle. The universe in its generosity will concord with anything you want, if only you believe in your claims strongly enough. This argument is equally valid for our own comments, because in the end you will have to check everything for yourself and either confirm or refute it. But then of course, you will have to respect the conclusions of others, even entirely contradictory ones. This is the fascination of magic—it is individual and versatile, with magicians still able to meet at some point for successful work together. To make this possible, magicians have to come either from the same tradition with the same magical training and development, or they need to have sufficient knowledge about the basic structures of magic to be able to work with any system without being finicky about details. In the era of dogmatic magic, magicians held on to the former position, but even this proved no guarantee of success. The latter stance has only been available to the West since the advent of modern magic, which came to terms pragmatically with the different natures of alternate systems and knew best how to effectively use them and learn from them all without claiming any system to be the one and only.

[5]More information about those clan totems can be found in Johanna Wagner's excellent book, *Die, die so aussehen wie jemand, aber möglicherweise etwas ganz anderes sind. Aus der Praxis afrikanischer Medizinmänner*, Berlin: Verlag Clemens Zerling, 1985 (English title: *Be Stronger than Bad Magic*. See bibliography).

[6]Francis King (ed.), *The Secret Rituals of the O.T.O.*, London: C.W. Daniel, 1973, pp. 236–238.

[7]John Symonds, *The Great Beast. Life and Magick of Aleister Crowley*, London: McDonald, 1971, pp. 394.

[8]Peter J. Carroll, *Liber Null & Psychonaut*, York Beach, ME: Samuel Weiser, 1987, p. 44.

[9]Jörg Wichmann, *Wicca: Die magische Kunst der Hexen. Geschichte, Mythen, Rituale,* with a foreword by Hans Biedermann, Berlin: Edition Magus, 1984. Also includes an appendix, "Buch der Schatten" (not paginated).

[10]Aleister Crowley, *Magick,* York Beach, ME: Samuel Weiser, 1974, pp. 496-498

[11]*Ibid.,* pp. 125-127

[12]For Pan rituals, compare, for example, my "Versuch über Pan" in *Thelema: Magazin für Magie und Tantra* 7 (1984), pp. 4–9. Due to an unfortunate printing error, two footnotes at the end of this article have been mixed up. Two Pan texts, two mistakes—an outstanding example of Pan's roguery!

Perils

The real dangers of sex magic are no different from the perils of magic and sex in general. Since sex magic is so effective, you may have to take greater pains to avoid or at least be properly prepared for danger. As already said, magic is no more dangerous than driving a car, but it would be stupid to neglect simple precautions; this could lead to catastrophic results.

This short chapter has been written to remove any remaining doubts you may have about sex magic, as well as to give additional advice for dealing with possible difficulties and dangers.

Fear

Fear is a magician's worst enemy if it takes control and cannot be exploited as a means to trance—as, for example, in initiation through terror. Exact knowledge of one's own magical and sexual fears and their causes is a basic requirement for any successful sex magic or mysticism. This is easier said than done. On the one hand, many fears remain latent and only become active in exceptional situations. On the other hand, the causes of fear can be so complex that we may never discover them all. The greatest teachers often maneuver their disciples into horrible situations in order to goad their fear into revealing itself.

The point is not to declare all fears equally harmful and try to forcibly eliminate them. First, this would be of dubious value because some fears are indispensable for our biological survival. Second, fears can be a tremendous source of power because of their psychological potential to heighten tension. There are frequent reports of people who, in their moment of greatest mortal agony, became capable of superhuman feats. "Fear is a great motivator"—this is valid in magic, too. The point is rather to recognize one's fears and grow clearer about one's strengths and weaknesses. And fear must never be allowed to take control; your magical consciousness must always keep the upper hand. This happens to some extent when one faces one's fears by deliberately courting situations where one is terrified—and by surviving them. *Absolute honesty* with yourself is the highest law! Do not put it off with cunning excuses. The range of reasons for avoiding fear begins with hypochondria, continues with the old defense of "not enough time!," and ends up with an overestimation of one's own "capabilities" ("I no longer need to do this; I'm too advanced!"). Such patterns are harmful and can actually paralyze you in moments of real danger. The best protection against fear is magical trance and the magician's "poise."

Megalomania

The converse of fear is megalomania, a phenomenon which unfortunately is the rule rather than the exception among magicians. Occasionally, megalomania can be employed in rituals where the purpose is to gain power by self-assertion. Like a real braggart, the magician boasts of his or her successes and trophies. But the real danger of megalomania is an arrogance towards other people and other teachings. Magic, particularly in its "lower" levels, hardly encourages the magician to be humble, and yet total overestimation of self is the most frequent cause for magical catastrophes. As fear paralyzes people and reduces their judgment, megalomania makes magicians become careless so that they take risks that they are not yet prepared to handle. Losing your energy to other people is very often caused by carelessness and a "nothing can happen to me" attitude. Just as failure can lead to depression and feelings of inferiority, success can spur on boisterousness and subconscious self-punishment patterns until the prospective adept gets his or her well-deserved punch on the nose.

The best defense against megalomania is to keep thorough control over your success and never lose sight of your own weaknesses and failings, while looking out for people and teachings which can expand your horizon. Of course, there is nothing wrong with hearty self-confidence; it prevents one from being overwhelmed by fear, and it centers one's sexual *magis*.

A very subtle type of megalomania is to feel that one is a victim pursued by the whole world. Such paranoia assumes the mask of the underdog while inflating one's image by assuming that one is the specially elected (and thus, most important) target of a mighty "conspiracy."

Self-Deception

What has been said about megalomania is equally true of self-deception. It is covered separately here only because it is such a serious danger in the highly subjective world of sex magic. Self-deception and megalomania combine to give a recipe for disaster! Magic should be tempered with a sound scepticism. By this we do not mean the exaggerated scepticism of fanatical materialists, which normally consists of little else but a welter of prejudices that they try to enforce by "experiment," but rather that scepticism which dissects all magical action and seeks absolute clarity before it judges. Its criteria for judgment do not have to be strictly materialistic, for there are *also* magical means of achieving things. The idea is not to play off "scientific" parapsychologists against "unscientific" magicians!

A very good example of the exacting magical attitude is Aleister Crowley's testing of *The Book of the Law,* which was "revealed" to him. When he received it in Cairo in 1904, he did not immediately recognize its true value. Only years of further discoveries about inner correlations within the text and most thorough cabalistic calculations could convince him in the end that he had found his own True Will and destiny in this book. His diaries give plenty of information about how magicians should deal with such matters. They also provide many examples of quite the opposite attitude, so every reader interested in master magicians and their psychology is strongly recommended to study Crowley thoroughly.

Paranoia

Magical paranoia is a two-edged sword. Magicians need it to test success in magical operations; for example, to look for meaning in every event, even the seemingly most "coincidental" ones. A touch of paranoia is always useful. It is a divine gift because it places humanity at the center of the universe, and that increases magical power. However, paranoia can overwhelm any sound judgment. There are no tidy rules for avoiding this danger because we are here moving on such subjective ground. Perhaps the matter can be clarified with an example which illustrates the dangers—not a far-fetched example, really, but one rather typical of magical development gone wrong.

A magician receives a "revelation" that he has been chosen to save the world from cosmic catastrophe because he is a flawless being who is destined to receive the "just" reward for his efforts (megalomania plus self-deception).

Of course, this heady message is tempered with humility ("I am only a tool," "It is not I who am important, but the work at hand"; i.e., fear of responsibility plus self-deception). From the fact that all traffic lights always switch to "green" as soon as he approaches, he concludes that the universe is on his side (paranoia). This makes him identify more and more with his role as world savior (fanaticism). He preaches his message of salvation to his friends and acquaintances and tries to convert them. When they mockingly turn away, he will at first see himself as a "misunderstood prophet." With increasing failure, however, this feeling grows little by little into deep depression. Eventually our magician feels that he is being victimized by forces of evil throughout the entire world (how peculiar that traffic lights are now always red!), and he develops the "martyr" syndrome (that is, fear of pursuit plus self-punishment plus self-underesteem).

You may object that the above story could equally describe a typical religious fanatic. This is true, and it always happens when magic turns into religion. Space does not permit a digression here to show you the numerous magical elements in all world religions, in support of the old thesis that religion is basically a watered-down form of magic for the masses even when it originally starts as a minority movement. Just as magic and mysticism join together constructively and lead towards transcendence, so do magic and religion join together destructively to become fanatical yet barren ideology.

This phenomenon is particularly bad in sex magic because honesty in sexual matters is so very rare. There has been a host of magical and pseudo-magical sex cults in history which seem to have been founded simply to provide religious justification for the sexual fantasies of their founders. Therefore, you have to be very careful if you come into contact with such influences. In magic, there are many wolves in sheep's clothing—but also many a sheep in wolves' clothing!

Fanaticism

Fanaticism is often the result of a fusion of the formerly described perils of sex magic, and it is equally difficult to spot. On the one hand, every magician has a duty not to be taken in by this, but, on the other hand, there are definite phases of magical development in every magician's life that involve missionary zeal. If one's own magic is unsuccessful, this is less likely to happen. If there are real or imagined successes, however, it is a completely different ballgame. Fanaticism is always an evil thing because it is fed by the unadmitted fear of maybe being in the wrong after all. A surfeit of intentions of "peace and happiness" always carries considerable destructive drives in its shadow aspects—as every crusade and "holy" war will show us.

Should you meet fanaticism in other people, I can only advise you to stay away from them. In my experience, discussion with fanatics leads nowhere and may bring a great deal of heartache and even outright war. Fanaticism often promotes unconscious energy vampirism. Leaders frequently live off their followers' power, which is one of the reasons why it is so difficult to influence leading politicians by magical means. If the politicians also have sexual charisma, it becomes almost entirely impossible to affect them; they are raiding the most powerful primordial energies of their followers.

All fanaticism is one-sided, and that is exactly why sex magicians have to protect themselves from it. They cannot afford to see the highly explosive energies they are working with from one perspective only. To do so would misjudge their true, all-embracing nature.

Projections of Blame

If we magicians have one reason to be grateful for Aleister Crowley's Law of Thelema, it is that it made us see that everything we encounter in life stems from our own decisions—and that we must not assign the blame for our suffering to anybody but ourselves.

One of the reasons why every knowledgable magician warns against starting a magical war is that it may lead to paranoia. Nerves become overstrained through permanent tension—magical wars continue round the clock with no agreed breaks—and a lot of wrong responses can occur. The principle of blaming others for our failures is very old. The "scapegoat" of the ancient Hebrews was one very graphic way of handling this. Never make the mistake in sex magic of blaming others if an operation should fail! To do so would be to weaken your own power by showing in a subtle manner that you doubt your own capability and correctness of decisions. Should somebody else really have done you harm, then think first before you hit back about why you allowed this situation to arise.

Many magicians confuse the legitimate *search for faults* after failed operations with an *assignment of blame.* This, however, binds energy into the wrong channels. Then you will be concentrating on patterns of hate and accusation rather than starting to solve your real problem. "Look for the slave within yourself!"

Slips in Ritual

Mistakes in ritual play an important part, particularly in the dogmatic tradition of magic. Since rituals are often laid down to the smallest detail and even the slightest departure from these rules is said to have dire results, there is plenty of scope for errors—and ensuing blame!

I think that the basic idea behind this is correct; it has only been interpreted wrongly. It is not really vital whether the full moon ritual starts at the exact minute or the Venus candles are just the right shade of green, but the quality of the magical trance you attain is important. If you force yourself into a corset of rules, don't be surprised if the slightest mistake blows up into a catastrophe—you asked for it!

On the other hand, nowhere is careless work more dangerous than in sex magic! It is only that the real dangers lie not in tiny lapses from a supposedly "correct" pronunciation of a Hebrew god-name and so on, but the manner in which magicians deal with the energies awakened is important. Lack of concentration and low energy can show disastrous results, especially if there is no inner-centerdness. A real magician can do magic in a public toilet or in an underground carpark if need be—nor are the regalia and ritual equipment truly essential. What one cannot do without is the magical trance, will and imagination—and the thorough training of these three. This is the right idea of which dogmatic magic is also basically aware and which is taught within traditionalist systems. However, the mistake is often made of either denying this wisdom—"after all, equipment is nothing but a crutch"—or simply ignoring it. Sometimes this statement is even spoken out quite openly, but among dogmatic magicians, it nearly always has the character of mere lip-service.

Mistakes in a ritual can only be prevented by great attention, concentration, experience and careful inner preparation. Equally careful and regular documenting of the work and its success also contribute to improving the quality of ritual. And practice counts as well; if you perform one or two rituals per year at the most, you will normally lack the experience and confidence demanded for this type of work. In the beginning, this means jumping in at the deep end—but this is not only valid in sex magic!

The Error of Spiritualization

Of course, sex magic has its purely spiritual aspects, but it is a great mistake to let sex magic happen only on a "spiritual" level. In nine out of ten cases, this "spiritualization" turns out to be mere intellectualization caused by inhibition rather than enlightenment! This "flight into spirituality," frequently observed among occultists of all schools, is rightly denounced by materialists. Behind it lies a pure fear of the power of polarities and their demands, in particular the fear of one's own sensual drives.

So-called "spiritualization" of sex magic and sexuality is frequently a mere excuse for living out one's deepest desires and drives. Such magicians may try to make contact with a sexual partner in the following way:

"I am an emissary of a secret lodge with ancient knowledge which must be revealed only to a few worthy initiates [the classic introduction!]. Now we who have been scrutinizing you have noted that you have an exceptional talent for the secret arts . . ." [occasional variants: "Now your aura/vibration/horoscope has told us . . ."] "I have been assigned, in the name of our lodge, to address a few chosen people and discuss with them the possibility of being taken on by our group. We have access to the most secret knowledge of the Holy Grail [or an equally popular subject, which is often decorated with suitable stories about the persecution of the Knights Templar and the terrible curse of Jacques de Molay on the stake]. However, it is first necessary for us two to enter into a 'spiritual marriage.' No, fear not. This is not what you might think it is, but ..."

It seems too absurd to be real, but this example is actually taken from life! Of course, later on it becomes clear that it was *exactly* what one guessed it would be in the first place! The really fatal thing about it is that these "magicians" are in most cases so unaware that they themselves believe what they tell people—which is one of the reasons why they can sound so convincing. Such an approach naturally works best with people to whom "spirit" is so much more important than physical matters.

As said before, there is nothing against true spiritualization, but when it becomes a cowardly evasion of the responsibility for one's own flesh, it only causes harm and exacerbates existing weakness, imbalance and fear.

The opposite extreme to be avoided with equal diligence is to deny sex magic any spiritual component. This would be just as dangerous. It reduces our discipline to a mere sexual tickling of the palate and has as little to do with magic as the "black masses" of the average sex club have to do with true Satanism.

Loss of Energy

One very real problem of sex magic is the loss of energy which sometimes occurs, whether in autoerotic work or with partners of either gender. The fact that it can happen in autoerotic work indicates that the cause is not necessarily subconscious vampirism by one's partner, as is commonly stated.

If you feel completely empty after a sex-magical act—and this feeling can last for days or even weeks—then you have made a mistake. Certain sex-magical rituals can be strenuous and therefore demand that you allow yourself a recuperative break afterwards. If performed in the right way, however, the overall effect should be stimulating or at least catapult the magician into a state of hyperlucidity.

Loss of energy is best avoided by paying attention to one's own centerdness. If you maintain your Lesser Energy Orbit, stay in your Hara and possibly keep your protective symbol about you, no loss of energy should occur. Additionally, of course, you must remain within the limits of your physical powers. These obviously vary widely among individuals, so no precise rule can be given. And if you should lose energy, above all do not panic. Just make sure that you pay more attention to your energy "credit balance" from then on and see to it that you charge yourself with additional energy before any sex-magical operation.

As already said, the real fault is usually not a vampirizing partner but rather a *leak* in your own flow of energy. Delicate areas for such leaks are the genitals, for both sexes, so you should always control your flow of energy in this area and harmonize it by mental suggestions. Should you still suffer from loss of energy during sex magic, it is advisable to avoid genital orgasm for a longer period. Instead you should welcome and fully enjoy a whole-body orgasm; this is always energy giving. For heteroerotic and homoerotic operations, it might be sensible to manage some time without vaginal or anal penetration.

The Magical Ricochet

Finally, one more magical phenomenon for which there is no remedy: the so-called "magical ricochet." It occurs mainly with operations of combat magic, attack spells, destructive spells and death spells, and it can happen in either direction. To give you two examples: you attack an enemy, but, instead of his being hurt, his wife, his child or somebody else very near to him gets hit and even killed. Or you yourself experience the attack, and if you are well protected, it is your environment that bears the full brunt of the onslaught.

At our present level of knowledge, steps can only be taken with any certainty to exclude the second case; for example, by using a deflection doll or by initiating people close to you into protective magic, or by you yourself protecting them.

The first case is more problematical. Unfortunately, as far as its ability to satisfy today's demands for precision, our present magical technology is still very much in the Stone Age. Hitting the bull's eye does happen now and again, but it is an exception; as a rule you still hit wide off the mark. This is partly because the blurred nature of symbols does not allow extreme precision. If this theory is correct, magic will hardly ever meet the accuracy and reproducibility of science, even though it is more powerful than science within its own sphere.

For magical attacks, you will have to calculate this risk before you start out. Diligent training and careful work will certainly help prevent mishaps, but even the most experienced magician occasionally has to face such "slips," particularly with sex-magic operations performed with partners. Therefore, in my opinion, assaulting or cursing rituals should be performed on one's own, autoerotically, if at all; the risk of working with a partner is in my experience only justified in exceptionally difficult situations.

Being Dependent on Sex Magic and Sex Mysticism

Everybody who has worked with magic successfully for some time will agree that it can be addictive. This is particularly true for sex magic because of its strong stimulation and its high rate of success. Now, no form of dependence is acceptable. Full-blooded magicians may never want to give up magic (why should they, anyway?), but they should be on guard against too great a bias for or against certain magical disciplines. Magical masters occasionally forbid their disciples any magical activity for a long period of time. It is well known that the greatest temptations occur during these phases, but on the other hand an acolyte may learn more about the high art of magic in such periods than even in the best times of intensive teaching.

Therefore, if you notice that you can no longer survive without sex magic, you should alternate periods of concentrated sex magic with occasional phases of total abstinence from it.

There is a magical oath whereby the adept vows to interpret everything in life as a direct personal message, which means to understand even the smallest detail of everyday life as being "loaded with meaning." In Crowley's A∴ A∴, for example, every Neophyte who took this oath could immediately receive the highest grade! However, taking this oath was and still is considered very dangerous, because, from a psychological point of view, it amounts to opting for permanent paranoia. If you have taken such an oath, other laws are applicable to you, and you will know how to weigh our warnings. If not, you should make sure that your non-magical sexuality does not become entirely taken in by your sex magic. Do not judge your rituals purely according to their sensual delight: to do so is to risk not only slipping into dependence, but also losing a large part of your magical powers!

These are the main dangers of sex magic as I see them, but most of them apply equally to magic in general. People who feel unsure of themselves should begin by practicing protective magic before venturing into sex magic. This book should have made it clear by now that sex magic is not for the weak of heart—for, above all, nothing ventured, nothing gained!

The Chymical Hierogamy

The Spiritual Androgyne and Practical Sex Mysticism

The term "Chymical Hierogamy" or (holy) "Marriage" has been borrowed from alchemy, and particularly from the classic text, *The Chymical Marriage of Christian Rosencreutz—Anno 1459*, probably by Johann Valentin Andreae. This document was published in 1616 and caused an outburst of Rosicrucian mania across the whole of Europe.[1]

The Chymical Marriage has become the embodiment of Western sex mysticism, although in Andreae's script we find no more than allegorical allusion to the subject. Instead of long introductions, two possible rituals will be described to show how the Chymical Marriage may be performed within the framework of sex mysticism.

Please note that these rituals are nothing but *outlines* that you should adapt according to your own needs. First is a partner ritual; it is followed by an autoerotic ceremony.

The Chymical Marriage for Couples
Casting

One partner embodies the male principle. Here, he is called "The God." The other partner embodies the female principle and is called "The Goddess."

Preparation

For one calendar month, the God meditates on the male principle; for example, by invoking the Sun, by wearing golden jewelery and yellow clothing, by consuming food attributed to the sun and by generally employing himself with "solar" activities. He also charges his ritual dagger.

The Goddess meditates on the female principle for one lunar month; for example, by invoking the Moon, by wearing silver jewelery and white clothing, by consuming food attributed to the moon and by generally employing herself with "lunar" activities. She also charges her ritual cup.

During this preparatory phase, both partners should abstain from sexual activity. All sexual energy should be sublimated and fed into the Lesser Energy Orbit.

The Protective Circle

The ritual is performed within the usual protective circle. This should be large enough to allow ample room to both partners and a comfortable bed, which may, for example, be made of cushions.

The Altar

On the altar in the East are arranged solar and lunar symbols in harmonic equilibrium. These include six golden and nine silver candles, all coloured right through to the wick. Also there should be one candle of pure beeswax to symbolize the Great Work. Additionally, there should be the dagger and cup plus two incense bowls. In the bowl to the right, solar incense is burned; in the bowl on the left, lunar incense. The temple is otherwise decorated according to the means of both magicians.

The Ritual

Both partners enter the temple and close it after thorough ritual washings and unctions.

After a short meditation, both perform an introductory protective ritual such as the Lesser Banishing Ritual of the Pentagram to secure the circle.

Now both partners together invoke the lunar energy into the Goddess. This may be by meditation, invocations or hymns. During this phase only solar incense is burned, and no lunar incense.

The Chymical Marriage

Instead of a rather asymmetric joint invocation of the lunar or solar energy, both partners may independently invoke their individual energies. In this case, the two incense mixtures are not burned until after the invocation, because the mixture of the two fragrances might be irritating during the phase of invocation.

Now the Goddess consecrates the cup with lunar energy and performs the Lesser Energy Orbit with silver energy.

The God consecrates the dagger with solar energy and performs the Lesser Energy Orbit with golden energy.

Once cup and dagger have been consecrated, both partners place themselves in front of the altar, the Goddess on the left and the God on the right. They raise their magical weapons towards heaven and turn to each other with raised arms. After a short period of meditation, the Goddess kneels down in front of the God and raises her cup toward him. The God places his dagger with its point downward. Both close their eyes and concentrate on the following symbolic magical act.

(From now on, the ritual may be performed in silence. No more hymns or chants are necessary, although magicians who value spoken texts are free to integrate such into the ritual. Most important is an etheric perception of the activated energies.)

The God points his dagger into the cup until the tip touches the bottom. The Goddess concentrates on flooding the dagger with her lunar energy. The God concentrates on injecting the cup with his solar energy. At this stage, no conscious absorption of the partner's energy takes place!

Once their magical weapons have been charged with the opposite polarities, the God removes his dagger from the cup and raises it again. The Goddess stands up and raises her cup again.

Now the Goddess walks around the altar deosil (clockwise), the God widdershins (counterclockwise). The Goddess takes her place on the right side of the altar (in front of the solar incense bowl), while the God takes his at the left side (in front of the lunar incense bowl). The Goddess lays her cup down on the solar side, the God his dagger on the lunar side of the altar. Both raise their arms with closed eyes again and meditate on the Great Work which they are about to perform.

God and Goddess face each other. The God concentrates on perceiving the etheric lunar energy of his partner, whereas the Goddess concentrates on perceiving his etheric solar energies.

Both partners embrace each other and couple in a sitting position. They synchronize their breathing, and each concentrates on his or her own Energy Orbit. The God breathes for a while into the left nostril of the Goddess, who draws in breath at the same time. Then they switch roles, and the Goddess breathes into the right nostril of the God, who draws in this breath. Eventually, their mouths join in a kiss, and an exchange of energy takes place. (Further tips on this can be found in the chapter on heteroerotic sex magic.)

God and Goddess continuously heighten their ecstasy, but do not seek to achieve peak orgasm. The God recognizes his inner female aspect in the Goddess; the Goddess recognizes her inner male aspect in the God. If a sexual climax occurs, it should increase their ecstasy to a point where consciousness is entirely occluded and nothing but pure energy flows.

Should you experience a valley or whole-body orgasm, on no account try to carry it into peak or genital orgasm! Give yourself entirely to this whole-body orgasm. This applies to both partners. In most cases, both partners' valley orgasms will start together, but this is not essential. It may also happen that one partner experiences a genital orgasm and the other a whole-body orgasm; in this case, the first partner may go on to experience a whole-body orgasm because of the higher energy level of the other. In any case, if orgasm occurs, it should be allowed to happen naturally and spontaneously and not be forced deliberately. Remember, it is perfectly all right to do entirely without orgasm.

After ecstasy has faded, both partners conclude the ritual together: thanksgiving, banishing and dismissal.

Please note that the Chymical Marriage involves no obvious magical act of will. No sigils are activated and no talismans or amulets are charged. It is the aim of this mystical ritual to attain a transcendent experience beyond the polarity of genders and to give birth within oneself to a mental or spiritual androgyne. One single ritual is not usually enough, and it is advisable to perform a sex-mystical exercise for several days during which this ritual takes place a number of times.

This ritual may in fact be performed either heteroerotically or homoerotically. If it is a homoerotic work, both partners should have performed the Chymical Marriage with a heteroerotic partner before so that they can experience and differentiate the energy quality of their partner more accurately.

The Chymical Marriage of Occidental tradition is equivalent in its intent to the "unification of Heaven and Earth" in the Inner Alchemy of Taoism. Its highest level is perceived when working autoerotically, when both sexual poles are united in harmony within oneself *with no outward projection* onto a partner. Only then does one achieve true detachment from the conditions and dependencies of material existence. This ideal is equivalent to the the concept of *individuation*, or becoming Self-aware in the depth psychology of C. G. Jung.

Occidentals, because of the traditional contempt for the flesh in their culture and religion, frequently make the mistake of confusing the quest for transcendence with a flight from this world. But exactly the opposite is meant: only in transcendence does the material level find its full satisfaction, and vice versa. Transcendence needs a material basis; without this, it is nothing but an escapist fantasy. It is significant that most great mystics—and equally most magicians and shamans—were far from being mere ecstatic visionaries. They were also conscientious in looking after their worldly tasks.

Autoerotic sex mysticism bears the particular danger that it can deprive subconscious fears and neuroses, through "spiritualization," from the risk of manifestation on the level of material reality. If somebody seems to achieve the goal too rapidly, it is a matter of concern that he or she is entirely independent from all superficiality. In most cases, a downright sham existence is hidden behind it! This is why the Chymical Marriage in its autoerotic manifestation has been left until the end of this book, and is only presented in an abbreviated form. We believe that it should only be undertaken when all other types of sex magic and mysticism have been thoroughly practiced. Anything less would be to risk self-deception!

Here follows the framework for a Chymical Marriage adapted to autoerotic use and suitable for magicians of either sex.

The Magician's Inner Chymical Marriage

The magician prepares for 69 days (six = Sun, nine = Moon) for the Chymical Marriage by exploring and exercising daily the Sun and Moon aspects of his or her personality.

Altar, protective circle and temple furnishings are the same as for the previous ritual. In general, the solo Chymical Marriage matches the Chymical Marriage of a couple in nearly every detail except that the magician performs both roles. Female magicians start with an invocation of the lunar energy, whereas male magicians start with the solar energy. Dagger and cup are handled as described before.

The magician should at one and the same time feel the countersexual energies to be both outer, objective entities and inner, subjective qualities—a paradoxical state which cannot be described any better by language. Only experience with the practices recommended earlier will ensure that this ritual can be performed correctly.

The magician feels more and more like an embodiment of both male *and* female energy, a recognition which will induce ecstasy. As this ecstasy reaches its climax, the autoerotic act follows, and, at its climax, the solar and lunar energies merge in an explosion. No language can express the state that follows. In every other respect, the magician proceeds as described in the Chymical Marriage for couples.

Thus the circle of sexuality is closed. We began with autoerotic practice and continued with sex magic performed with a partner; now we return to autoerotic practice. But it is an autoeroticism where the outer world in all its fullness has been integrated, so that the magician has become a self-complete entity which no longer needs the outer world. The magician has become an entity which lives *within* this world, but which is not *of* this world. As shown on the Tarot card of that name, The Magician knows how to juggle with the elements—in short, he is a God.

This handbook intends to be both an introduction and a practical textbook, but in many respects it had to remain incomplete. It is my opinion that *material*, fleshly experience should always be preferred to purely mystical speculations. Only when this has been mastered will sex mysticism make any sense, and only then can the symbols become alive and images turn into reality. Still, there will always be new questions and new beginnings and paths to explore. The life of a magician is one of continuous learning, and any earlier development is worth no more than the power it gives to the present—and how far it can point to the future.

Notes

[1]The best German edition at present is probably Joh. Valentin Andrea*e*, *Fama Fraternitatis (1614); Confessio Fraternitatis (1615); Chymische Hochzeit: Christiani Rosencreutz. Anno 1459 (1616)*, edited and with a foreword by Richard van Dülmen. [Quellen und Forschungen zur württembergischen Kirchengeschichte 6] (Stuttgart, Calwer, 1973).

Select Bibliography

It is hardly possible to list all relevant literature on this subject, as this alone would fill several volumes. Covering only subjects such as "Tantra" and "Magic" would already imply naming several thousand titles. We have therefore made an admittedly very personal selection to enable the reader personal access to the various pertinent fields of study.

Andreae, Joh. Valentin, *Fama Fraternitatis (1614); Confessio Fraternitatis (1615); Chymische Hochzeit: Christian Rosencreutz. Anno 1459 (1616)*, ed. and introduced by Richard van Dülmen. (Quellen d. Forschung zur württbg. Kirchengeschichte 6) Stuttgart: 1973.

Bardon, Franz, *The Practice of Magical Evocation: Instructions for Invoking Spirits from the Spheres Surrounding Us*, Wuppertal: Rüggeberg, 1975.

—*The Key to the True Quabbalah: The Quabbalist as a Sovereign in the Micro- and the Macrocosm*, Wuppertal: Rüggeberg, 1971.

—*Initiation into Hermetics: A Course of Instruction of Magic. Theory and Practice*, Wuppertal: Rüggeberg, 1971.

Carroll, Peter, *Liber Null & Psychonaut*, York Beach, ME: Weiser, 1987.

Crowley Aleister, *Gems from the Equinox: Instructions by Aleister Crowley for his Own Magical Order*, ed. Israel Regardie, St. Paul, MN: Llewellyn, 1974.

—*Liber A'ash vel Capricorni Pneumatici sub figura CCCLXX*, comm. and tr. J.S. 209 and Frater V∴D∴, *Thelema* 10 (1985), pp. 23-28.

—*The Qabalah of Aleister Crowley*, New York: Weiser, 1973.

—*The Magical Diaries of Aleister Crowley*, ed. Stephen Skinner, York Beach, ME: Weiser, 1979.

—*The Magical Record of the Beast 666*, ed. and annotated John Symonds and Kenneth Grant, London: Duckworth, 1972.

—(Gregorius), *Aleister Crowleys magische Rituale*, Berlin: 1980.

Culling, Louis, *The Complete Magick Curriculum of the Secret Order G..B..G..*, St. Paul, MN: Llewellyn, 1971.

219

—*A Manual of Sex Magic*, St. Paul. MN: Llewellyn, 1971.

Dadaji, *Sinistroversus*, privately printed, London: 1981.

—*The Yoni Tantra*, privately printed, n.d.

David-Neel, Alexandra, *Iniation and Initiates in Tibet*, London: Rider, 1932.

Devi, Kamala, *The Eastern Way of Love: Tantrik Sex and Erotic Mysticism*, New York: Simon & Schuster, 1977.

Douval, H.E., *Eros und Magie*, Büdingen-Gettenbach, 1959.

Eliade, Mircea, *Shamanism: Archaic Techniques of Ecstasy*, tr. W. W. Trask (Bollingen Series 76), Princeton: Princeton University Press, 1972.

Ellert, Peter, and Wichmann, Jörg, "'Der kleine Gott. In jedem Quark begräbt er seine Nase.' Ein Komplementaritätsmodell von Magie und Naturwissenschaft," *Unicorn* 13 (1985), pp.100-105.

Evola, Julius, *The Metaphysics of Sex*, New York: Inner Traditions, 1983.

Fischman, Walter I. and Warren, Frank Z., *Chinas Geheimnis der Liebeskraft. Die 5000 Jahre alte Methode zur Bewahrung und Belebung der Liebeskraft durch Akupunktur und Akupressur*, Munich: 1981.

Flowers, Stephen Edred, *Fire & Ice: Magical Teachings of Germany's Greatest Secret Occult Order*, St. Paul, MN: Llewellyn, 1990.

Foral, Susanna, *Die Orgie: Vom Kult des Altertums zum Gruppensex der Gegenwart*, Munich: 1981.

Frater U.'.D.'., "Ausländischer Schweinekram? Sexualmagie zwischen Mystik und Verklemmung," *Unicorn* 9 (1984), pp. 84-88.

—"Geldmagie, oder mit Dreck fängt man keine Mäuse," *Anubis* 1 (1985), pp.13-21.

—"Mythen in Tüten—Vom magischen Umgang mit Analogien," *Unicorn* 11 (1984), pp.221-229.

—*Practial Sigil Magic*, St. Paul, MN: Llewellyn, 1990.

—*Sigillenmagie in der Praxis*, Berlin: Edition Magus, 1985.

—"Spaltungsmagie: Der Doppelgänger als magisches Faktotum," *Unicorn* 2 (1982), pp.79-81.

—"Versuch über Pan," *Thelema* 7 (1984), pp.4-9.

—"Wie schächte ich mein Alter Ego? Anmerkungen zur Dämonen-magie," *Unicorn* 13 (1985), pp.64-69, note p.119.

—"Zufall natürlich! Das Problem der magischen Erfolgskontrolle," *Unicorn* 7 (1983), pp. 225-229.

Frick, Karl R.H., *Die Erleuchteten*, Graz: Akademische Druck und Verlags-Anstalt, 1973.

—*Licht und Finsternis*, Graz: Akademische Druck und Verlags-Anstalt, 1975.

—*Licht und Finsternis II* (Die Erleuchteten II/2), Graz: Akademische Druck und Verlags-Anstalt, 1978.

—*Satan und die Satanisten I*, Graz: Akademische Druck und Verlags-Anstalt, 1982.

—*Satan und die Satanisten II*, Graz: Akademische Druck und Verlags-Anstalt, 1985.

Grant, Kenneth, *Aleister Crowley and the Hidden God*, London: Muller, 1973.

—*Cults of the Shadow*, London: Muller, 1975.

—*Images and Oracles of Austin Osman Spare*, New York: Weiser, 1975.

—*The Magical Revival*, New York: Weiser, 1972.

—*Nightside of Eden*, London: Muller, 1977.

—*Outside the Circles of Time*, London: Muller, 1980.

Gregorius, Gregor A., *Exorial. Der Roman eines dämonischen Wesens*, Berlin: 1960.

—*Magische Briefe*, Berlin: Schikowski, 1980.

—*Die magische Erweckung der Chakra im Ätherkörper des Menschen*, Berlin: Schikowski, 1978.

Harner, Michael, *The Way of the Shaman: A Guide to Power and Healing*, New York: Bantam, 1982.

Hirschfeld, Magnus, *Geschlechtsverirrungen: Ein Studienbuch für Ärzte, Juristen, Seelsorger und Pädagogen*, exec. and arr. by his pupils, Constance: n.d.

Ivanovas, Georg, "Räucherwerk—Nahrung der Götter," *Unicorn* 5 (1983), pp. 80-84.

King, Francis, *The Magical World of Aleister Crowley*, London: Weidenfeld and Nicolson, 1977.

—(ed.) *The Secret Rituals of the O.T.O.*, New York: Weiser, 1973.

—*Sexuality, Magic and Perversion*, London: Spearman, 1971.

Klingsor, Dr., *Experimental-Magie*, Berlin: Schikowski, 1976.

Miller, Richard Alan, *The Magical and Ritual Use of Herbs: A Magickal Text on Legal Highs*, Seattle, WA: n.d.

Möller, Helmut, and Howe, Ellic, *Jahrhundertfeier: Vom Untergrund des Abendlandes*, Göttingen: 1975.

—*Merlin Peregrinus: Vom Untergrund des Abendlandes*, Würzburg: 1986.

Mumford, Jonn, *Ecstasy Through Tantra*, St. Paul, MN: Llewellyn, 1990.

Randolph, Paschal Beverley, *Sexual Magic*, New York: Magickal Childe, 1990.

Rawson, Philip, *Tantra: The Indian Cult of Ecstasy*, London: Thames & Hudson, 1984.

Rosenberg, Alfons, *Praktiken des Satanismus*, Nuremberg: 1965.

Saraswati, Swami Janakananda, *Yoga, Tantra and Meditation in Everyday Life*, London et al.: 1978.

Sayjan, Lus de, *Magie des Sexus oder Pan-Amrita-Yoga*, Freiburg i.Br.: 1966.

Seller, Terence, *The Correct Sadist*. London: Temple Press, 1990.

Serrano, Miguel, *El/Ella: Book of Magic Love*, tr. F. MacShane, London: Routledge and Kegan Paul, 1973.

Spare, Austin Osman, *The Collected Works*, ed. Christopher Bray and Pete
   Carroll, Leeds: 1982.

Gerald Suster, *Hitler: The Occult Messiah*, New York: St. Martin's Press,
   1981.

—*The Legacy of the Beast: The Life, Work and Influence of Aleister Crowley*,
   York Beach, ME: Weiser, 1989.

Symonds, John, *The Great Beast: The Life and Magick of Aleister Crowley*,
   London: Macdonald, 1971.

—*The King of the Shadow Realm. Aleister Crowley: His Life and Magic*,
   London: Duckworth, 1989.

Tegtmeier, Ralph, *Aleister Crowley: Die tausend Masken des Meisters*,
   Munich: Knaur, 1989.

—*Der heilende Regenbogen: Sinnvolle Spiele, Experimente und Meditationen
   zum kreativen Umgang mit den geheimnisvollen Energien von Klang, Farbe
   und Licht*, Haldenwang: 1985.

—*Musikführer für die Reise nach Innen: Kosmische Klänge zum Entspannen
   und Meditieren*, Haldenwang: 1985.

—*Okkultismus und Erotik in der Literatur des Fin de Siècle*, foreword by Dr.
   Hans Biedermann, Königswinter: 1983.

Thirleby, Ashley, *Das Tantra der Liebe: Eine Einführung in die altindische
   Liebeskunst—der Schlüssel zu sexueller Freude und seelischer Kraft*,
   Munich: 1979.

—*Tantra-Reigen der vollkommenen Lust: Die Geheimnisse der Vielfalt und der
   höchsten Steigerungsform altindischer Liebeskunst*, Munich: 1983.

Thompson, Charles Fairfax, *The Forbidden Book of Knowledge*, Los Angeles:
   privately published, 1981.

Volin, Michael, and Phelan, Nancy, *Sexuelle Leistungsfähigkeit*, Munich: n.d.

Wagner, Johanna, *Be Stronger Than Bad Magic: A Collection of Traditional
   African Methods Against Witchcraft and Sorcery*, Göttingen, 1983.

Waldemar, Charles, *Lock. Potenz bis ins hohe Alter. Yoga und Sexualität.
   Erotische Energiekunst*, Zürich et al.: n.d.

—*Magie der Geschlechter. Jungwärts durch Sexual-Magie*, Munich: 1958.

Wichmann, Jörg, *Wicca: Die magische Kunst der Hexen. Geschichte, Mythen,
   Rituale*, Berlin: Edition Magus, 1984.

Williams, Strephon Kaplan, *Jungian-Senoi Dreamwork Manual*. Berkeley,
   CA: Journey Press, 1980.

The Magical Diary—"Mirror of the Soul" (pages 21-22)

Shamanism Uses Dance to Bring the Organism to Its Limits. (page 29)

Magic Circle (pages 37-38)

Bellows Breath (page 46)

The Dynamic Dance (pages 55-56)

Opposite Emotions (page 76)

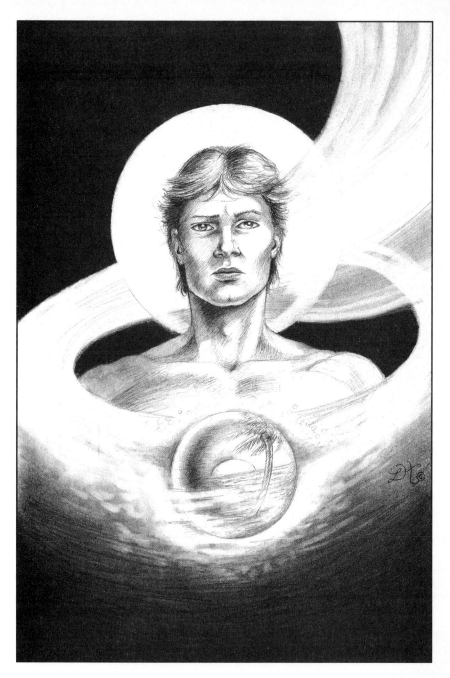

The Use of the Crystal Ball Gaze (page 87)

Sex-Magic Invocation I (pages 105-106)

Astral Projection (page 117)

Orgasm is the Moment. (page 131)

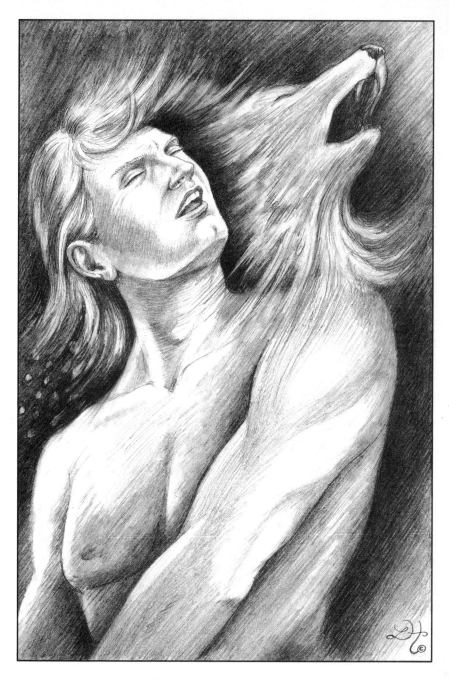

Autoerotic Workings with Atarisms (pages 147-148)

Heteroerotic Work with Atarisms (page 156)

The Androgyne (page 164)

The Night of Pan (page 182)

Ritual Necrophilia—Isis and Osiris (page 195)

The Chymical Marriage (page 215)

INDEX

Llewellyn publishes hundreds of books
on your favorite subjects.

LOOK FOR THE CRESCENT MOON

to find the one you've been searching for!

MULTICULTURAL MAGICK

To find the book you've been searching for, just call or write for a FREE copy of our full-color catalog, *New Worlds of Mind & Spirit*. *New Worlds* is brimming with books and other resources to help you develop your magical and spiritual potential to the fullest! Explore over 80 exciting pages that include:

- **Exclusive interviews, articles and "how-tos" by Llewellyn's expert authors**

- **Features on classic Llewellyn books**

- **Tasty previews of Llewellyn's latest books on astrology, Tarot, Wicca, shamanism, magick, the paranormal, spirituality, mythology, alternative health and healing, and more**

- **Monthly horoscopes by Gloria Star**

- **Plus special offers available only to *New Worlds* readers**

To get your free *New Worlds* catalog, call 1-800-THE MOON

or send your name and address to

Llewellyn, P.O. Box 64383, St. Paul, MN 55164–0383

Many bookstores carry *New Worlds*— ask for it! Visit our web site at www.llewellyn.com.

LLEWELLYN
New Worlds of Mind and Spirit